PEPPERMAN'S PROMISE

PEPPERMAN'S PROMISE

PREQUEL TO THE PEPPERMAN MYSTERY SERIES

BILL BRISCOE

Editor: Lori Freeland
Cover Design: Fiona Jayde, Fiona Jayde Media
Formatting: Tamara Cribley, The Deliberate Page

eBook ISBN: 978-0-9986425-0-5
Paperback ISBN: 978-0-9986425-1-2

www.billbriscoe.com

This book is dedicated to Liz, my best friend and loving wife.

Thanks for all your support.

CHAPTER 1

Spring 1966
Odessa, Texas

I SLAMMED THE DOOR TO MY PICKUP AND HAMMERED MY FIST into the steering wheel. Today, I was grateful for my 6' 3", 220 pound linebacker frame. After Coach blew the whistle, Joe head-butted me under the chin. A cheap shot. He was a good guy, but at times, a little too aggressive. We'd both made the All-State team and been keys to Odessa Permian's first high school football state championship last season, and ever since, he wanted to be captain of the team. Joe busting my chops could be his way of getting the coach's attention.

I checked my chin in the rear view mirror. Peeling off the blood-soaked gauze exposed a nasty gash, but I wouldn't miss the Black and White spring scrimmage tomorrow night.

The traffic on 42nd Street was jammed when I left the parking lot to head home. A maroon pickup with a white Uzzo Oil Company logo passed me two blocks from our house. It looked like Dad's boss, Mr. Gurley.

I pulled in the driveway, and my appetite spiked like it could smell Mom's cooking. I pushed through the back door. The kitchen was dark and quiet. And didn't smell like dinner. Something was wrong. "Mom, what's for supper? I'm starving."

No answer.

I checked the fridge. One piece of cherry pie left on the top shelf. Dad's favorite. I grabbed the plate and a fork, shoveling a huge bite of the pie into my mouth. Dad wouldn't mind. Mom would make him another one when he got home.

Like the kitchen, the living room was dark, except for the small lamp on the end table. Mom sat rocking in her chair. A thin line of black makeup eased down colorless cheeks and strands of brown hair draped over her left eye. Her hands were shaking.

"What's wrong?" I swallowed hard and set my fork onto the plate. "Where are Blythe and Brook?"

"Your sisters are next door with Rita." She pointed to the sofa. "Jim, please sit."

I didn't sit. I couldn't sit. Something was very, very strange. "Mom, what is it? Tell me."

"Your daddy . . ." She cleared her voice. "Mark Gurley said your daddy had an accident at the rig."

The pounding of my heart came so hard the pulse in my neck beat a rhythm I couldn't control. The fork slid from the plate and tumbled end over end until it hit the hardwood and spun out of control. The plate followed and shattered. Dad's cherry pie splattered in every direction. "Where is he? Why aren't you with him?"

But somewhere deep inside I already knew the answer.

"There's no other way to tell you." Tears dripped onto her collar. "He's gone . . . your daddy's dead."

Dead. Dead. Dead.

The word echoed in my head. The noise grew as big as the Grand Canyon, tightening into a chokehold, a chokehold that wouldn't let go. I stumbled back to the sofa and went down hard.

Everything had changed. Nothing would be the same. Dad was dead.

CHAPTER 2

MOM MADE BREAKFAST ON SATURDAY MORNING—DAD'S favorite—pancakes and bacon. She set a plate for him between Blythe and Brook. She didn't have to say the meal was a tribute, but I knew it was. She wasn't about to break our Saturday family tradition that started years ago.

I stared at his empty chair. The thought of him never sitting there again ripped me apart. I'd taken Dad for granted, and in the last two days since his death, his absence crushed all the joy out of my tired body. How could I handle the funeral? Tomorrow? The day after?

Mom's quiet strength made me feel secure, but how would she raise three kids alone? My sister Blythe, five years younger than me, was twelve, and Brook was only four.

At seventeen, I had to man-up and take responsibility. But how could I replace Dad?

Leaving the kitchen, I pulled back the living room curtains to a damp, cloudy day. The newspaper rested on the front porch. The concrete was slick as I bent to pick up the paper. I shook the dew from the wet pages and returned to the sofa. If I read Dad's obituary—maybe then I would believe he was really gone.

PATRICK PEPPERMAN

ODESSA — Patrick Pepperman, 39, died on Thursday, April 28, 1966, in Odessa, TX. Services will be held in Odessa on Monday, May 2 at 10:00 a.m. at St. Joseph's Catholic Church with Father Mario Aguilera officiating. Graveside services are scheduled for Wednesday, May 4 in North Arlington, New Jersey at Holy Cross Cemetery. Officiating will be Father Michael Ashdon.

Pat was born on November 4, 1926 to Dana and Wilhelm Pepperman in Belleville, New Jersey.

Survivors include his wife of eighteen years, Elizabeth, a son Jim, and two daughters Blythe and Brook.

There was one thing that bothered me. Dad had been a driller on an oil rig for twenty years. On the day of his death, the steel cable that hoisted the pipe to the top of the derrick parted, then snapped. The falling pipe crushed him.

Dad should have noticed the drilling line was frayed and replaced it.

That was careless. Dad wasn't careless. Ever.

CHAPTER 3

THE FLIGHT TO NEW JERSEY FOR DAD'S BURIAL WOULD MAKE a long day. Before take-off I looked out the window at the flat, barren land surrounding the Midland-Odessa airport. I hated Odessa when we moved here. I loved it now.

I eased back in my seat, closed my eyes, and saw visions of Dad. His death still gripped me like a hellish nightmare. My best friend was gone.

Brook and Mom settled across the aisle. Blythe sat by the window, an empty seat between us. She was silent. Her red swollen eyes needed no explanation.

I touched her shoulder. "You want to hear a funny story?"

Without looking, she nodded.

"I remember the day ten years ago when Dad broke the news we needed to move to Texas. I wanted no part of it. Belleville, New Jersey was the only home I'd ever known. At seven, Dad's dumb job didn't matter as much as my little league baseball team and a good lemon ice."

Her head was down, but the corners of her mouth turned up.

"The day before we moved I dragged my travel bag out from under the bed and slammed it on the mattress. I yanked open the top flap, not caring that the hole at the end of the zipper tore even wider than before. My catcher's mitt and mask went in first. Next, the New York Giants sweatshirt. Couldn't leave that behind. Then my underwear and my black-and-white checked good luck socks. The tote wouldn't zip even after I sat on it. Too full. I reached in and tossed my underwear. After that, it closed just fine."

Blythe turned her head toward me and gave me a grin I hadn't seen in days. "Really? You took out your underwear?"

"Of course. Had to make room for the important things."

She gave a soft, happy chuckle.

"I dragged the bag behind me and plodded down the stairs determined to move in with Nanny. Dad met me at the bottom. He tilted his head to one side, glanced down at the bag, then back at me. 'Son, where you going?' My chin dipped toward my chest. 'To live with Nanny.' He hung his arm over my shoulder and asked if I'd sit on the porch with him. 'Why would you want to move in with your grandmother?'

"I stepped away from his almost hug. Too old for that. Then asked why he needed that stupid new job anyway? Dad squinted. 'Well, son, sometimes parents have to make hard choices. There's a great job working in the oil fields in the Lone Star State. With a good job I can buy you and your sister extra ice cream. Sounds good, doesn't it?'

"Ice cream sounded good, but I'd give it up to stay in New Jersey. Told Dad I didn't like Texas. He asked, 'Why? What's wrong with Texas?'

"Didn't want to say. The scary stuff made me feel like a baby, but I knew Dad would wait until he got an answer. I reached over and gripped his leg. Might be too old for hugs, but sometimes something strong to hold on to was okay. I told him there were cows with horns as big as swords that could stick you. Rattlesnakes as long as garden hoses. But the spiders were the worst. They're bigger than your hand. Texas was just no good.

"Dad paused, biting his lower lip and asked how I knew that. I stood and placed my hands on his shoulders and said, 'I saw it on cartoons. *Tom and Jerry*.'

"He stroked his chin. 'You make a good point. If you saw all that on *Tom and Jerry*, it must be true. I'm going to miss you. So will Blythe and Mom'. Dad turned his palms up and shook his head. 'Your little sister will have to protect herself from those big spiders. With no big brother to watch after her, what will she do?'

"Dad put his hands over his eyes and brought up Mom. Who would help her take out the trash and rake leaves? Who would he get to help him work on the car? No one could hand him a wrench better than me. He said he'd understand if I stayed there. A man's got to do what he thinks is best. Said he'd get the car and drive me to Nanny's. Dad looked sad when he got his handkerchief, blew his nose, and walked in the house.

"I sat alone on the top step. I rested my elbows on my knees and thought about our conversation. Dad returned, ruffled my hair and asked if I was ready to go?'

"'No, sir.' I straightened, puffed out my chest, and clutched my bag. Couldn't let Mom and Dad down. And you? I'd feel terrible if one of those big spiders bit you because I wasn't there with my baseball bat. I loosened the grip on my bag and let it plunk onto the porch. Pushing back my shoulders, I gave him a man-to-man look. 'I'm just too important to this family to stay behind.'

"Dad shook my hand and said, 'Thanks, son, I know it will be hard with all those scary things down there, but we can survive if you're with us. How about I get us some ice cream from the kitchen?'

"I nodded and lay back on the porch, hands clasped behind my head and thought . . . what would my family do without me?"

"You were stupid at age seven," Blythe said with a smile that exposed her braces.

I nodded. "Couldn't agree with you more."

The pilot's voice came over the speaker warning us of choppy weather ahead. I checked Blythe's seatbelt like Dad used to check mine.

I was lucky. I'd had a great father. He understood me even when I didn't understand myself. Instead of yelling and grounding like other guys' dads, he taught me to brainstorm solutions when faced with a problem.

Blythe leaned her head back against the seat. "Why did God take Daddy?" Her voice was quiet. Tears pooled in her eyes. She hadn't talked about Dad's death until now. I guessed her emotions had been tucked away in a secret place. "I miss him," she said. "I liked it when he let me interview him on my tape recorder."

I touched her head. "I don't know. Dad wouldn't want us to cry forever. If he knew you were sad, it would make him sad."

She grabbed my forearm. "I don't want Daddy to be sad."

"Why don't we talk about the fun times? That would make him happy."

Blythe said, "Like when we moved to Odessa. Tell me again."

I remembered everything about the move. "It didn't take long to make friends. At noon, we ate on the playground and traded lunches. I always wanted a beef and bean burrito."

Blythe traced her lips with the tip of her tongue. She liked them too. "What if you got something yucky?"

I shrugged. "I'd trade with someone else. And everyone talked funny. Every other word was *y'all* this or *y'all* that. I had no idea what it meant."

She grinned because she grew up saying *y'all*.

"Then there was *jeet yet*. Rickey walked up, dropped his arm over my shoulder, and asked, 'Jim, *jeet yet*?'"

"That didn't sound anything like 'Jim, did you eat yet?'"

Blythe giggled. "I like Rickey. He talks so-o-o slow."

The plane hit an air pocket and dropped. A collective bunch of oh's echoed through the cabin.

"You probably don't remember Gerald from a few streets over, but he had yellow teeth with brown spots. And dog breath."

She held her nose. "I don't remember him. Guess I was too little."

"My friends and I were playing Kick the Can one day and Gerald showed up. Yellow Teeth grabbed Sam around the neck and told us to give him candy or he'd make Sam eat a bug. Another day he took Pete by the arm and swung him around three times, then let go. He hit the ground so hard it busted his nose. I ran in the house . . . my heart sputtering like a model airplane engine."

"What happened?" Blythe turned toward me in her seat.

"Dad saw me sitting on the couch and said, 'Son is there a problem with some of your playmates?' When I shook my head, he said, 'Are you sure?'"

Blythe focused on every word.

"Dad knew if I wasn't telling the truth. 'There's a mean kid that scares me.' He asked how he scared me. I told him he pushed me around and breathed in my face and he stunk. Then he asked why the kid didn't like me. I said, 'Don't know. I haven't done anything to him.'

"Dad said, 'Well, maybe he just needs a friend. Have you asked him if he wanted to play with you and your buddies?' I moved to the edge of the couch, arms crossed. 'Yes, plenty of times. He said he didn't want to play with a bunch of sissies.'

"Dad scratched his head. 'Well, it seems you have two choices. Find a way to get along or stand up for yourself.' He left it up to me to solve my own problems. The way I saw it . . . I had to back down or face my fears."

Blythe placed both hands on her cheeks, resting her elbows on the arms of the seat. "What did you do?"

"The next afternoon I waited for Gerald." I could still feel the tension from that day. Facing him had been hard. "I tried to be brave when I told him I wanted to be his friend, but inside, my gut wrenched and my legs went limp like lukewarm spaghetti. It didn't help when he coughed up a loogie, then spit."

Blythe wrinkled her face. "Yuck."

"Then Gerald said, 'What do you want, Yankee boy?' and my buddies shouted my name. I looked at Yellow Teeth and said, 'I'm not afraid of you.' He popped his knuckles. 'Are you going to fight like a man or kick and bite like a girl?'"

My sister giggled, opened a bag of M & M's, and slipped several in her mouth.

"I remembered watching fights on TV with Dad. The boxers jabbed with their left hand, then punched with their right. We circled each other. I tried to look tough, but my confidence ran back to the house and hid. I felt like throwing up. Gerald was so big. And mean. His hands hung loose around his belly." I showed Blythe what I meant.

Her hands fisted.

"Dad taught me to keep my hands near my face."

Blythe copied what I said, then smiled.

"I was getting ready to punch him, the whole time wondering if I could do it. I sucked in air through clenched teeth and lunged forward. My straight right fist struck him on the nose. His head snapped back, and he went down like a sawed off tree. My friends cheered. I took a deep breath and pushed out my chest. It swelled like a circus balloon."

She softly clapped and whispered, "Way to go Jim."

I slouched back in the seat. "Gerald yelled at the crowd to shut up, then ran home holding his nose. Everyone danced around, shouting, pumping their fists.

Sticking up for myself made me proud. But, if Gerald had decided it was better to be a friend, I would have been just as glad. The day after the fight, Dad and I were changing the oil on our 1954 Chevy Station Wagon."

Blythe tugged my arm. "I remember that car. It was blue and white."

I smiled and nodded. "Dad was underneath the car removing the oil plug when Gerald and a man walked up. He was an older version of Yellow Teeth. He looked tough, broad shouldered with a reddish complexion, and a scruffy face. I didn't know what would happen, but it couldn't be good."

Blythe rolled her lips waiting for my response.

"The guy kicked the bottom of Dad's size fifteen shoes. 'Is Jim your son?' Dad didn't answer so he kicked his shoe again. 'Your kid and two other boys beat up my son, and I'm gonna even the score, so get out from under the car.'"

Blythe swiped her curtain of hair aside, squinted, and asked, "What did Dad do?"

"Well." I turned to face her. "Dad took his time getting out from under the car."

"Daddy wasn't scared, right? He was a big man."

I nodded.

"Dad was all calm and cool. He said, 'First of all, let's get the facts straight. There weren't two other boys, just my son.' Gerald's dad puffed up. 'You calling my boy a liar?'"

Blythe pounded her fist into her palm. Her voice was crystal clear, and I knew the direction she was going. "I bet Dad punched him, didn't he?"

I chuckled to myself, loving her spunk.

"No, Dad removed the tobacco stub, spit, and said, 'Let's just say he got his facts wrong. Now you do what you have to do, but not here in front of our sons. We'll go out on a dirt road to work things out, and I'll decide when the fight is over.' Dad leaned in so close to Gerald's dad, I almost didn't hear him say 'I will break every bone in your face.'"

"Then Dad punched him out?" Blythe asked.

"Nope, Gerald's dad started breathing weird. I had never seen a grown man so shaken. He apologized and walked off. Yellow Teeth never came back."

"Do you think Dad would've hurt him?" she asked.

"Well, Dad told me, 'Jimbo, that guy was tough looking. I'm glad I got my bluff in.' Then he put the cigar stub back in his mouth. You know how he never lit the thing, just chewed on it. Then he rubbed my head and crawled back under our car. But, I think Dad would have done it if he had to."

That incident with Yellow Teeth started my fondness for fighting. I never initiated a scuffle, but always stepped in to help the underdog. My buddies dubbed me 'Bully Basher.' Kids came to me if they had a problem. Dad called me *Captain America*. His way of poking fun. To keep me from fighting so much, he turned my attention to football.

The flight attendant pushed her cart down the aisle and asked if we wanted something to drink. It was two more hours to New Jersey so I'd have plenty of time to continue the story if Blythe wanted. Her relaxed shoulders, the dimples in her cheeks, and her smiling eyes, told me she was enjoying the family history.

We ate peanuts and drank Coke, then Blythe asked me to tell her what happened next."

"Dad said he would take all of us to a football game. The morning of the game I snatched his bathroom chronicles off the grass and sprinted back in the house."

Her mouth squared and she wrinkled her nose. "Whoa, what are bathroom chronicles?"

"That's what Dad called the newspaper." I winked. "Because he only ever read it in the bathroom."

Blythe shook her head. "Gross."

I shrugged. A guy thing. "I pulled out the middle portion and flopped down on the couch. A headline of the sports page of the *Odessa American* read: Texas Tech Red Raiders Host Seventeenth Ranked TCU at Jones Stadium in Lubbock. Excitement bubbled out of me."

Blythe's eyes ignited. She loved football.

"You'll get a kick out of this. Mom was in the kitchen frying bacon and making pancakes. She was pretty in her chenille bathrobe and pink bunny rabbit house shoes. Then she yelled, 'Pat, how many pancakes and strips of bacon do you want?' Dad cleared his throat and answered in a deep, funny voice. You know how silly he could be. 'Eight pancakes and twelve slices of bacon.'

"Mom shot back. 'Gee whiz, that would feed half the Russian army, and we don't have that much bacon anyway.'

"Dad looked over the top of the paper and gave me a funny, straight-lined grin, then crossed his eyes. Mom never seemed to know when Pops was teasing.

"After gulping down breakfast, I started to my room and told Dad I was getting ready for the game. He laughed at me because it was only 7 a.m. and the game didn't start until 2 p.m. I told him I didn't want to miss the kickoff. He tousled my already messy hair. 'Okay, go get your Mackinaw coat, gloves, and your stocking cap. It's going to be cold and windy today.'"

Blythe said, "I was too little to remember the game, but the horse. I remember the horse."

"It took me ten minutes to get my stuff, but no one else was ready. Mom wanted to give you a bath. You had syrup in your hair, and I didn't get it . . . why were you and Mom going anyway? Football was a man's game."

Blythe looked at me as she blew a loose hair from her face. "That's not nice."

"At 9:00 we piled into the station wagon. You and Mom sat in the back, and I was co-pilot. When we got to Jones Stadium in Lubbock people were running around like ants. I couldn't count them. Dad bought us cocoa and a hot dog. We sat on the first row, in line with the goal post. The band played and the fans shouted, 'Go Red Raiders. Beat TCU.' You cupped your chubby little hands over your ears to block the noise."

"Did not." Her eyebrows furrowed.

"A huge black horse came out of the stadium tunnel, just a few yards from our seats. On his back was a man dressed in black, wearing a red cape and a mask, sort of like the Lone Ranger. The horse reared up on its hind legs and pawed the air with its front ones, then galloped onto the field."

Blythe tapped my shoulder. Her voice excited and pitched. "See I told you I remembered that horse."

"I shouted and jumped up and down like everyone else in the crowd. The horse circled the field then stopped right in front of us. So close, I could see its flared nostrils and white puffs of smoke on that cold winter day. The masked rider looked at me and shouted, 'Go Red Raiders.'"

From that day forward football was an integral part of me. I could no more extract it from my chemical make-up than remove my heart and expect to live.

CHAPTER 4

I COULDN'T WRAP MY HEAD AROUND THE IDEA DAD WAS gone. He wouldn't be there to watch me win championships. He wouldn't be there to see Blythe graduate from college. He wouldn't be there to walk Brook down the aisle.

After the graveside service, we went to my Grandmother Brownlee's house in Belleville. The day was hot and muggy following a brief shower.

Mom took me outside, and we sat on the porch steps. She put one hand over her mouth as though she wanted to muffle her words. "Jim," her tone soft and aching, "when summer comes, we're moving back to New Jersey."

"What?" I was stunned. My plans for a football scholarship and making Dad proud—none of that would happen if we moved.

Mom closed her eyes and looked away. She tried to suffocate her crying. "We have to Jim. I'm sorry."

I felt like someone pulled the plug on my life support. "It's my senior year. I think Coach Fulton from the University of Texas might offer me a football scholarship."

She interlocked her hands and touched her lips.

"Please, don't do this to me." I lowered my voice to a whisper.

"We can't make it in Odessa without your dad. I need the emotional and financial support of my family." She raised her head and looked at me.

"We can make it work. I'll get a job, do whatever you ask. Please."

She covered her pale face with her shaking hands and sobbed. "I'm sorry. My mind is made up."

"Just let me stay in Odessa until football is over. Then I'll come."

Mom clenched her fist. "No. I won't separate our family."

"It's not fair." I stood up and slammed my knuckles into the front porch pillar. "You're ruining my life. You're wrecking everything for me . . . just like Dad."

It ripped my heart out thinking about what was going to happen. I would have to tell Coach Stephens. Disappoint a man I admired.

Over the next few weeks I realized Mom was right. She needed the support of her family. She cried a lot, couldn't make decisions, and seemed lost. Although Belleville was her home, it wasn't mine, would never be mine. Thinking about living there devastated me. Blythe and I finished the last days of school, and Mom sold the house, the cars and most everything we owned.

The afternoon before we left Texas, a red Ford Mustang stopped in front of the house. The doors opened and out stepped the guys I called *Dos Amigos*— Don Billips and Harry Greenlee.

They went to Odessa High, our rival. Don had the reputation of being a tough guy. He enjoyed fighting but wasn't a bully. Kids from both schools had wanted a match between Don and me and encouraged a battle to determine the toughest guy in Odessa. Our fight was inevitable.

We'd met one night in the parking lot of Barrett Field, the high school football stadium. The struggle lasted a good eight minutes. We pulverized each other and the fight was considered a draw. People asked when the rematch would take place. It never did, thank goodness. One tussle with a human pit bull was enough for me.

Conflict could drive people apart or bring them together. Fortunately for me, Don and I became good friends. I'd learned a valuable lesson from Dad. He said everyone had good qualities, and it was my job to find them.

Don, Harry and I sat on my porch and talked about our friendship until raindrops began to splatter onto the sidewalk. Don looked up and pointed to the southwest. "Guess we'd better be going, Harry. That front's moving in pretty fast."

Harry nodded, then turned to me. "You're flight's leaving at 12:30 tomorrow — right ?"

"Yeah." I was beginning to feel a little depressed. Harry was buying my 1957 black Chevy pick-up. The paint was chipped and the windshield had a crack that wormed its way across the top. The tailgate was missing — two big Permian linemen had sat on it and snapped the sucker. But, the truck was mine. A gift from Dad and I loved it.

Harry adjusted his glasses. "I'll be here at 8:30 in the morning to get the pick-up." He paused, looked down, then up at me. "I know how much your wheels mean to you. I'll take care of it."

Don jumped off the porch as the rain increased. "You know the old saying about West Texas. We get fifteen inches of rain a year and you should be here the day it happens." His tough guy grin came with a guttural laugh.

I watched them run to Don's car. I'd gained two friends because of a fight, and it stirred memories that made me feel as though I was leaving more than just my home. I'd miss Don and Harry and, most likely, never see them again.

I gave each of them a smile of respect. As they drove away I wondered how their lives would turn out. I wished the best for them.

The darkening sky rumbled. Rain or no rain, there was one more thing I had to do.

CHAPTER 5

I PICKED UP THE TRUCK KEYS FROM MY DRESSER AND HEADED to the front door needing to do the one more thing. I couldn't leave Odessa without visiting the place Dad died. It was time for me to man-up.

"There's a flashflood warning in effect." Mom stopped me by the door and grabbed my hand. "Please don't go." She squeezed until her arm shook. "It's too dangerous."

"I have to go to the drilling site." I gave her a gentle hug. "It's important to me."

Mom wiped a single tear from her cheek, then nodded.

Halfway there, the rain intensified and so did the wind. The windshield wipers almost couldn't keep up with the slashing downpour. My pickup weaved from side to side on the dirt road like a ship in an ocean squall.

I pulled up to the rig and a bolt of lightning snaked its way behind the cold, metal drilling tower. I stepped out of the truck into the slick, chalky soil, grasped the neck of my jacket, and yanked my baseball cap down on my head. In seconds, the rain soaked my shaking body. I labored, feet caked with heavy mud, toward the spot where Dad fell six weeks earlier.

Sam Bass, the tool pusher, came out of his trailer, held a raincoat over his head. "Jim, you can't come on the drill site," he shouted over a clap of thunder.

I kept walking. The caustic odor of diesel fuel nauseated me. My throat tightened. I swallowed over and over. The oilfield stench reminded me of Dad's work clothes, and sadness overwhelmed me. My heart tightened into a hard mass.

The rain came so fast it cut trenches in the caliche dirt. Shaking, I dropped to my knees and pounded my fist on my thigh.

"Dad, why did you have to die?" I struggled to get the words out. "Why did you do this to me? Why didn't you notice the frayed cable?" My voice quivered. "Everything's changed. My life is shriveling up from the inside out. I'm scared . . . really scared."

Another burst of thunder ricocheted through the dark, grey clouds, startling me. I looked up at the tower where the pipe broke loose and shivered in the cold rain. God help me to honor my father.

"I promise to take care of Mom, Blythe, and Brook. No matter what." I stood. "Dad, do you hear me? I promise."

CHAPTER 6

MY THOUGHTS WERE SOMBER AS WE LEFT ODESSA. I FINALLY understood the old cliché "You don't know what you have until it's gone."

Uncle Avin, Mom's brother, and Aunt Ora Mae met us at the airport in Newark, New Jersey. The musty air caught my attention. The short drive up Highway 21 to Belleville took about twenty minutes. Although it was early June, the temperature felt cool, and I already missed West Texas.

Blythe and Brook were young enough to adjust to the move, but me — I wasn't sure. Moving before my senior year was difficult. At least I had all summer before meeting my new classmates. I'd take whatever I could get.

The buildings in Belleville were old — maybe built during the 20's and 30's. The businesses showed a mix of cultures. Through the open car window, the smell of the meat and vegetable pies from Pesci's Pizzeria made me hungry. Cassity's Bar and Grill was an Irish pub. Zeka's Meat Market was a throwback to the old days before supermarkets. Fresh sausages stacked tightly together like Lincoln Logs in the window. This was a blue collar town like Odessa, but that's where the similarities ended.

We turned on to Passaic Avenue and the high school caught my attention as did the light poles of the football stadium. My gut twisted into pretzel knots. Reality touched me again. I wouldn't be playing for Permian in the fall. Everything I'd worked for, sacrificed for, had been swept away in an instant. The world was against me, and I didn't like it.

We spent the night at my aunt and uncle's house. The next morning we loaded in their station wagon to look for our own home. My aunt and uncle had already checked out a few places in the neighborhood so we went to those first. The realtor had planned a full day.

House hunting bored me. The female chit-chat drove me crazy. All I heard was the color of this was wrong, the kitchen was too small, or, for gosh sakes, there's not enough closet space.

We wasted the entire day looking at homes all over town, and then Mom ended up making an offer on a two-story frame house on Albert Street—the first one we'd seen.

CHAPTER 7

ADJUSTING TO MY NEW ENVIRONMENT WAS TOUGH. I SPENT much of my time walking the neighborhood or going to the stores downtown. Back in Odessa the boys wore t-shirts, blue jeans and cowboy boots, but not in Belleville. The guys wore cream colored jeans, plaid shirts, and wimpy penny loafer shoes. My boots definitely stood out.

One Saturday the family piled into Uncle Avin's car. We drove past Gloria's Diner, and I noticed a sign in the window — *MAINTENANCE MAN WANTED*.

"Hey, Mom, can I check out this job?" The summer was dragging. I needed something to do.

"Oh, Jim," she said, her voice apprehensive. "I don't know."

I ran my hand over the top of my head. "It's the second week of summer and Blythe and Brook are already getting on my nerves."

She puckered her lips. "Maybe you do need something to do."

Uncle Avin agreed and pulled up to the diner to let me out.

"How can I help you today? Cheeseburger baskets are on special. How about one?" The tall, big-boned black lady behind the counter spoke in a surprisingly soft, slow southern drawl.

"Ma'am, I'd like to apply for the job." I offered her my hand. "Jim Pepperman."

Her strength was evident when she shook it. "Honey, I'm Glynna Helmsly, the manager. I'd love to talk with you." We walked around the cash register into the back office.

"The main things I need help with are keeping the windows clean, cutting the grass in the front, and hosing down the pavement at closing time. Oh, and, anything else I ask you to do." She chuckled, her body shaking like a tree in a spring windstorm.

I didn't blink. Her respectful tone made me feel good. "If you'll have me, I want the job."

"Hold on, Sugar." Glynna put up her hand as if to caution me not to agree too soon. "I haven't told you how much the pay is."

"Don't care. I have two little sisters at home all summer." My jaw tightened. "I'd almost work for nothing."

"I have a son about your age." Her voice was sympathetic. "He has younger brothers and sisters too. I catch your drift. When can you start?"

"How about tomorrow?"

Glynna angled her head and stared at my feet. "Are you planning on wearing those boots to work?"

I hesitated, not sure how to answer. "Yes, ma'am?"

"I hope you can take the teasing." Her smile warmed and turned into a smile my mom often gave me. "You gonna stick out like a rose in a thistle patch."

Glynna Helmsly was one of those people you instantly liked. And I couldn't wait to start work.

My first day on the job, I mowed the little strip of grass in front of the diner using a push mower. The rusty blades were duller than a two dollar pocket knife. A major challenge.

Around 3:00 p.m. a carload of high school boys pulled up to the diner. The driver pounded his open hand on the side of the black Camaro. "Hey, look, John Wayne's over there mowing the grass."

I couldn't help a quick glance at my cowboy boots.

"You taking that grass home to feed your horse?" he asked in a sarcastic voice.

An outburst of laughter erupted from the group.

His taunts lit a torch under my skin.

Glynna popped out of the diner, her hand on one hip and motioned me inside. "Big Boy, don't pay those fools no mind."

Big Boy. I liked the nickname and followed her in. "Who are those guys?"

She wiped her hands on a towel in an angry way. "They're football players. The one driving the black car, he's the captain. His name is Phil Anderson. Rumor has it everyone in town is afraid of him."

This was going to be an interesting summer. Newcomers weren't welcomed in Belleville.

Mom picked me up at closing in the 1963 white Ford station wagon she'd just bought. I walked out to the parking lot and the guy in the Camaro returned. I'd managed to put the knucklehead out of my mind and now he had to show up — like a bad dream.

I walked toward Mom's car. The guy pointed at me as he hung his head out the window. "John Wayne, your mommy came to take you home. How sweet."

His buddy laughed and slapped the dashboard.

Mom stiffened. "What's going on, Jim?"

I slipped onto the seat and slammed the door. "I don't know." My voice and pitch dropped into a fighting mode.

She grabbed my shoulder, her face was stone cold. "No fighting. You promised."

"Okay, I said I wouldn't." I moved away from her touch. "You don't have to remind me." It was a promise I regretted.

The following evening a group of girls came to the diner. The first girl through the door was a knockout. The way she carried herself caught my attention. Her body was straight and well proportioned. Each step exuded confidence. She was taller than the other girls, and her long curly brown hair fell over her shoulders. Her friends were cute, but nothing close to her beauty. They sat at the back corner table sipping on frosted sodas.

Busing tables would have to wait. I slipped around the counter toward Glynna. "Do you know the girl with the long brown hair?"

"Sure, Big Boy, that's Laura Pomroy." Glynna laughed like she knew exactly where this was going. "Pretty, isn't she? Want to meet her?"

"No . . . I don't." My palms were sweaty. "I wouldn't know what to say." My voice cracked.

"Big Boy, she's just a girl. Get over there and introduce yourself." Glynna gave me a not-so-gentle nudge around the counter.

"I've got work to do." I walked away as fast as I could, not looking at Laura.

All I could think about the rest of the evening was Laura Pomroy. Odessa had pretty girls, but none that made my heart stutter and my words die. Besides, even if I did try to talk to her, she probably wouldn't even give me a courtesy smile.

At closing time, just after 11:30, an electrical storm moved into the area. I flipped off the OPEN sign and locked the door. The rain came down so hard I couldn't see across the street. Peels of thunder rumbled like rapid cannon fire. Brilliant flashes of lightning seared the pitch black evening.

I was sweeping the floor when a bolt of lightning struck the transformer in front of the diner. Balls of fire exploded from it like Roman candle fireworks. We lost power. The transformer was still spewing red and white projectiles when another lightning flash illuminated a man standing outside the locked door.

Another flash filled in the picture of a huge person in a hooded raincoat. He had to be 6' 5". I stepped back. My heart pounded against my ribcage. I didn't know how fast a person's heart beat before it made an emergency exit from a body, but mine was close.

I whispered for Glynna who'd gone to the freezer at the back.

The man pounded on the glass. "Momma, are you in there? It's Tony."

I could hear Glynna's feet sliding across the linoleum as she turned on the flashlight. She went to the door and unlocked it, then pointed to me. "Baby, you scared the pee waddin' out Big Boy. Why are you here?" She put one hand on her hip and waved the flashlight in his face.

"I didn't want you to come home by yourself in this storm."

"What about your brothers and sisters?" Her eyes narrowed.

"They're fine. I took them to the neighbor's. Our lights went out too."

Glynna grabbed Tony's cheek and gave it a gentle tug. "Son, you are a true blessing."

She flashed the light in my direction. "Tony ... meet Jim Pepperman."

"Jim, this is my son Tony."

Tony pulled back the hood of his raincoat and extended his wet hand. His palm engulfed mine and when he squeezed I heard my bones crack. I'd never forget that rock solid grip.

Our eyes locked in mutual respect. The way I felt after meeting Glynna for the first time was exactly how I felt about Tony. I didn't have to ask if he was an athlete. His build told me that. I hoped we would be friends. I needed one.

CHAPTER 8

One day at work Glynna asked, "Big Boy, would you and your family like to come over for Sunday lunch?"

Blacks and whites seldom socialized, but I didn't see Glynna as black. All I saw was a good person my family would like. Her husband Ed had died two years earlier in an auto accident. The Helmsly family mirrored our tragedy. It might help Mom and the girls to be around people who understood.

"Let me check with Mom." I knew the answer. I'd told Mom about Glynna and she looked forward to meeting her.

A few days later Mom, the girls, and I piled into our station wagon and headed to the Helmsly's house.

The moment we stepped out of the car, two little boys ran up to greet us. They were Glynna's three-year-old twins, Burl and Earl. They weren't bashful. Burl latched on to my right ankle, Earl the other. Neither one would turn loose as I stiffed-legged toward the house.

The rest of the family waited for us on the porch. Tony laughed. "If you plan on coming over here, this is what you can expect. Meet my sisters, Belinda, eleven and Mary Nelle, seven."

Glynna greeted each of us with a bear hug, Mom first, then Blythe, Brook, and me. "Tony, it'll be about an hour before lunch. Why don't you and Big Boy do something until then? Mary Nelle, you and Belinda go play with Blythe and Brook and watch after the twins. Liz and I are going to get acquainted."

When Glynna turned her back, Tony grinned and gave her a military salute. This family loved and respected each other, but they could also poke fun.

The Helmsly's accepted us wholeheartedly. Was God watching out for us?

"Let me help with lunch," Mom offered.

"Come on. I never turn down help." Glynna fast-stepped to the kitchen, motioning Mom to follow.

I waited in the dining room while Tony went to get a basketball. I could see into the kitchen and watched Glynna hand Mom an apron. "Jim told me why you moved to Belleville. I am so sorry about your husband. It's not easy dealing with life right now, is it?"

"I'm still in shock," Mom admitted. "I wake up at night wondering how we're going to make it. Pat had some life insurance, but it isn't going to be enough. I'm frightened. I worry about my children, and I really miss Pat. It's hard to think about facing the rest of my life without him."

"I know how you feel, honey. When Ed passed away the twins were a year old. I had a job, but money was tight."

"How did you get through it?"

"Prayer, lots of prayer. First year after Ed's death was a blur. I had friends who supported me, and honey, I'll help you. . . . You can count on it."

I saw Mom struggling to hold back her emotions.

"Go ahead, Sugar. Let it all out." Glynna locked her arms around Mom until the tears stopped. "Liz, tell me about Pat."

"He was a big man physically, but a gentle person . . . up to a point. Pat was sensitive to the needs of all of us, especially the children. There were times he would go to events for each of the kids all in the same day. When Brook's Singing School had a program, Blythe would have a volleyball match followed by Jim's football game."

Mom snickered, leaned against the wall, and put her hand over her mouth. "One thing about Pat that you could count on was the cigar stub in his mouth. He never lit the thing. It was so commonplace, half the time he didn't remember having it between his lips. Once he bent to kiss me on the forehead and that nasty cigar poked me in the eye. That was funny to him, but not to me." Mom grinned, and her eyes were smiling too as she relived that day.

It appeared a friendship was developing. I thought this relationship would be good for Mom.

Glynna belly-laughed as she tied an apron around her waist. "How did you and Pat meet?"

"We met at Saint Peter Catholic Church here in Belleville."

"Tell me about it."

I smiled because I always liked this story.

"Pat attended mass regularly. I had my eye on him for sure. After services one Sunday, he approached me. We talked every week after that. Finally he asked me out. Our first date was a New Year's Eve dance at the Knights of Columbus. Oh, what a night. . . . I'm sure you are aware of Germans and their fondness for beer. Most everyone in our parish was German so . . . let's just say . . . a few beers were consumed that night. One guy came over to our table and asked me to dance. Of course, I refused. He did this about three or four times. Each time I politely said, 'No thank you.' The last time he came over, he whispered in my ear. Well, Pat didn't like that. He never said a word as he stood up, and with one swing of his big right fist caught the guy square on the jaw. It knocked him over a table, and he was out cold."

"Sounds like a man who had his priorities in order, but don't get on his bad side, right?" Glynna questioned.

"Exactly, and Jim is just like him."

I rolled my eyes when I heard that.

"What did that man say to you when he whispered in your ear?" Glynna asked in a warm, lighthearted tone.

Mom shook her head. "I won't repeat it."

While Mom and Glynna were preparing lunch, Tony and I went to the park to shoot hoops. I didn't play basketball, but we needed to kill time and it gave us a chance to get to know each other.

Once we reached the basketball courts, Tony needed a pit stop. This left me alone in the predominately black neighborhood. I was sitting on a bench waiting for Tony's return when three guys approached me. I could sense trouble so I stood to face them.

The leader had an Afro with a big comb stuck in the side. "What you doing here, white boy? You looking for trouble?"

Tony walked toward us behind them.

The tough guy doing the talking saw Tony. "Hey, T. H., look what we have here. This cracker thinks he can come down and use our park."

"Who you calling a cracker, you fool?" Tony snapped at him. "Can't you tell he's my brother?"

"Oh . . . oh . . . now I see the likeness," Ol' comb-head stuttered. "You guys is brothers. My mistake, T. H."

"Get out of here, chumps, before I start cracking heads." Tony grabbed him by the collar and lifted him off the ground. The three did what he told them to do. Who in the heck wouldn't? He was big and scary looking. Tony could make Frankenstein back up.

Tony pitched me the ball. "Take a shot."

I let it fly, and the ball went over the backboard, touching nothing.

The expression on Tony's face said — you have got to be kidding me. "Jim, you've got brick hands. No touch on the ball." His words were harsh, but his tone was kidding.

We hadn't been friends long, but I thought he felt comfortable making a joke.

He looked at his watch. "Well, it's been forty-five minutes and lunch should be ready by the time we get home. I know round ball isn't your sport so do you play football?"

"Yeah, middle linebacker."

"I play offensive and defensive tackle." Tony dribbled the ball on the uneven concrete sidewalk as we walked back to his house.

"Do you want to play college ball, Tony?"

"Sure. That's the only way I can get an education. My dad told all of us we had to get a college degree."

"Same thing from my dad." I looked at Tony. His hands were so big it looked like he carried an orange instead of a basketball. "Where do you want to play?"

"Don't really care. I've been getting letters from Notre Dame, Rutgers, Michigan, and Virginia. How about you?"

"I want to play for the University of Texas. Leon Fulton, the linebackers coach at UT, contacted me my junior year. I sent him a letter explaining why we moved, but I don't expect to hear from him."

Tony played at Central High in Newark, a non-integrated school. I didn't have to ask if he was good. The recruiting letters answered that question.

When we reached the gates to Tony's yard, Burl and Earl greeted us. I ended up dragging them back to the porch once again. A special relationship was developing between those two little guys and me.

"You boys get in here, wash up, and get to the table." Glynna barked at the twins like an impatient drill sergeant.

"Momma, we don't need to." Burl ran up and tugged on his mom's dress. "We took a bath last night, and we ain't dirty."

Glynna gave the little tike a love tap on the behind and said, "Tony, take them in the bathroom and clean them up good."

After the bathroom detail, Glynna asked us to take a seat at the large dining table. Tony started to sit next to me when Earl pushed him aside. "No, Bubba. Burl and me want to sit by Big Boy."

Burl joined in, "Yeah, Bubba, you go sit by Sister."

Tony gave me a you-are-special grin and rubbed the heads of his two brothers.

Glynna adjusted her chair. "Would you say the prayer, Tony?"

"Momma, it's my turn to pray," Earl interrupted as he picked up a fork and tapped his plate.

"Well, okay, Mr. Earl, go right ahead." Glynna lowered her head as she winked at her son.

He closed his eyes and placed his little hands together. "Dear Jesus . . . thank you for Momma . . . Bubba . . . Belinda . . . Mary Nelle . . . Burl . . . Big Boy's Momma." Then he stopped and whispered. "Big Boy, what's your sisters' names?"

I leaned toward him. "Blythe and Brook."

Earl continued, "Thank you Jesus for BLICE and BWOOK . . . and the food. Amen." Then he surprised me. "Momma, Belinda had her eyes open when I was praying."

"How do you know she had her eyes open?" Glynna asked.

"I saw her."

"Well, shouldn't you have had your eyes closed while you were praying?"

You could tell Earl's little mind was going as fast as a gerbil on a treadmill. It was evident he had no answer. "Momma, can I have some mashed taters?" Everyone at the table burst out laughing.

Glynna served meatloaf, mashed potatoes, green beans and hot rolls. She set down a plate of meatloaf in front of me, and I took a small portion and started to pass it around. I noticed the Helmslys were all staring at me.

"Honey, don't you like meatloaf?" Glynna asked with a hint of sadness in her voice.

"Yes, ma'am, it's one of my favorites."

"Well, that whole plate is yours. There's one just like it for Tony. Now eat up."

Glynna treated me like one of her family. I felt as much at home there as I did in my own house. Driving home that night, I wondered how many other surprises awaited me in my new home town.

CHAPTER 9

GOING TO WORK EVERY DAY HAD ITS UP AND DOWNS. PHIL Anderson made a daily appearance at the diner, but his annoying remarks took a vacation. Maybe he didn't appreciate his sarcastic insults being ignored.

Laura came by most nights. I wanted to talk with her but, I was too dang shy. When she looked at me, I'd cut my eyes to the floor.

One Monday night Big Mamma'd had enough. She grabbed me by the neck and forced me to Laura's table. "Laura, I want you to meet Jim. He's a little quiet, but he's a good guy." She gave me an athletic slap to the backside, then strutted to the register.

I was petrified.

Laura looked up. Those brown eyes made me feel like silly putty. "Did you just move to Belleville?"

"Yes." Wow. That one-word answer was guaranteed to impress.

"What's your last name?" Her sympathetic tone hinted she might understand how hard it was to be the new kid.

"Pepperman." My stupid voice cracked on the last syllable, making me sound like a seventh grader. I quickly sucked in a breath. "I . . . ah . . . have to go back to work." What a total screwed up conversation on my part. But at least I'd talked to Laura Pomroy. A skyscraper hurdle for me.

That night I sat next to Mom in the living room and asked what I could say to Laura the next time I saw her.

"Just be yourself," she said. "Talk about the first thing that pops into your mind."

"Differential calculus popped in my mind. Come on, Mom. Are you kidding?"

Blythe and Brook stuck their heads around the corner. "Jim has a girlfriend. Jim has a girlfriend." They ran down the hall, their chant echoing after them.

I got up from my chair and started toward the two. They ran into their room and slammed the door. Great. Those little pests would tell everyone. Geez, why did they have to listen to every conversation I had with Mom?

The following evening I was outside the diner picking up empty paper cups. Phil Anderson pulled up to the diner about 7:00. He banged his hand on the side of his car and yelled, "Hey, Cowboy, you missed some trash over there. Pick it up, you pathetic hick."

Phil's words rattled in my head like a bad dream. I wanted to pull him out of the car and smack him.

The passenger side window was rolled down. Laura sat in the seat next to Phil. No, not her. Why would she be with him? I had no right to be jealous of Anderson, but I had a sad feeling deep inside, and I knew that feeling was because of Laura.

At closing time I was hosing down the parking lot when Laura pulled up in her car and motioned me over. I ignored her.

She got out of her car and approached me, arms folded, staring at the ground. "What Phil said to you, the way he treats you, is wrong. I apologize."

"Why are you apologizing for him?" I turned off the water and disconnected the hose. "Is Phil your boyfriend?"

She brushed her long hair to one side. "Absolutely not. He's been asking me out all summer, and I've refused. Tonight I agreed to get a soda, but told him I had to be home in an hour. I won't be going out with him again."

We looked at each other and I realized I wanted Laura Pomroy to be more than a friend. My heart was pounding so hard I could hear it. I began to shake inside. I forced my words. "Laura, if I ask you out, will you go with me?"

Laura angled her head and smiled a pleasant, calming smile. "Yes, of course I will."

The rest of the summer proved uneventful as far as Phil Anderson was concerned. However, Laura and I were a different story.

She came by the diner most nights, and Glynna cut me some slack and allowed us to visit when business slowed. The juke box played a lot of Frankie Valli and the Four Seasons. Every time I heard one of their songs, it reminded me of her.

On one of my days off, Laura came by the house and we sat in her car. Our conversation centered around life after high school. She was smart. I could tell by the way she talked. I adjusted myself in the seat so I could look at her. "What do you want to study in college?"

She paused, then looked at me. "I've thought about the medical field. Nursing appeals to me." Her pitch was confident, and I sensed she had more than a passing interest in nursing.

I shifted my body against the door trying not to stare at her stunning face. "Have you checked with anyone about nursing school?"

"Not yet, but I'll visit with Mrs. Wrenn, the guidance counselor, when school starts." Laura cocked her head and gave me that cute grin that turned me into slush. "What about you, Jim?"

I shrugged. "I'm pretty good at math, but we don't have extra money for college." I looked out the window, not wanting her to see my disappointment.

"You used to play football, right?" Her voice changed, more excited.

"Yeah, back in Texas," I answered wondering where she was going with the question.

"What about a football scholarship?" She touched my hand.

"I'm not going to play this fall . . . not interested." I avoided eye contact, ashamed to tell her I had no time for football anymore. Not when I was trying to help support my family.

"Why wouldn't you play?" Laura turned facing me. Her tone softened.

"I need to work." My jaw tightened. Saying the words felt like someone ripped open my chest. Football meant everything to me. Mom had said I could play, but I didn't see how. Every day I thought about my promise to Dad. I had to take care of Mom and the girls.

Phil Anderson pulled up in front of Laura's car. He got out and approached me.

I stepped out to meet him.

"Laura is my girlfriend. You stay away from her." Phil spit on the sidewalk in an obvious challenge. His red lips parted in an ugly snarl.

Laura rushed out of the car and stepped between us. "Stop it, Phil. I'm not your girlfriend." Her voice trembled and her body shook. "And Jim and I are just friends."

Phil stuck his finger in my face. "You going to let a girl protect you? I knew you were a coward." He pushed me, then walked back to his car. "This isn't over, Pepperman."

Laura grabbed my arm. Phil revved his engine and peeled out.

She covered her mouth and tears leaked onto her cheeks.

"Hey, everything's all right. Nothing happened. He's a hot head. I've dealt with people like him before. Don't give the jerk a second thought."

We walked back to her car. I opened the door. "You okay?"

She said, "Yes," but her pale skin and drawn cheeks indicated something else. She pulled her car away from the curb and headed home.

I stared after her. Phil pushed me too far this time. I had to find a way to get even. Football. I'd go out for football and make him pay. I popped open the front door and found Mom in the kitchen. "I want to play football. You said I could. Do you still mean it?"

"Yes, I do. Son, I saw what just happened." Her eyes were dark and focused. "There comes a time when you have to stand up for yourself. That's what your Dad would want."

"I know I need to work, but I can do that after practice and on weekends."

She closed her eyes, took a deep breath, then exhaled. "Jim, don't worry. I told you we'd manage."

"You're the greatest mom. I won't let you down. You'll see. I promise I'll be there for you and the girls.

It's payback time, Anderson. You have no idea what's about to happen.

CHAPTER 10

FALL FOOTBALL PRACTICE BEGAN THE FOLLOWING MONDAY. I walked across the parking lot to the field house, full of anticipation for the upcoming season. Hopeful for a championship year. The fresh cut grass brought back memories of every season I'd ever played. I loved this game.

The diner didn't have the coffee chat about the upcoming season. What if the players here didn't see football the way they did in Odessa? My excitement shrank like a distant memory.

Belleville Buccaneers was spelled out in gold on the faded blue metal door leading to the locker room. I hesitated, my hand on the knob, not sure what to expect. I'd give anything to be back in Odessa. But life was what it was. And if I wanted to play football, I'd have to play here.

Pushing through the door, I stopped the first person I saw. "Who's the head coach?"

"Ronnie Mancuso," the slightly built guy pointed behind me. "His office is over there."

I knocked on the partially opened door.

Coach Mancuso glanced up. He ran a hand through his short, blonde crew cut and looked at me with penetrating blue eyes. He gave the impression he was a no nonsense coach, the kind of coach I liked.

"How can I help you, son?" There was a Marine Corps rasp to his voice.

"I'm Jim Pepperman. I'd like to try out for the team."

He motioned me to sit and stuck a pencil behind his ear. "We have guys try out all the time. They find out real quick it takes more than size to play this game. Football in New Jersey is rough." Scratching his head, he spit his brown saliva into an empty Coke bottle. Tobacco stains caked the corners of his lips. "Really rough."

There's no way it's rougher than West Texas ball — not a chance — no way.

He leaned back in his chair and eye-balled me like a fresh cut rib-eye steak. "I'll tell you what, if you make it through the first practice, I'll think about letting you play." He retrieved his pencil and started writing, "Go find Coach Keener in the equipment room around the corner of this office." He didn't even bother to look up. "He'll get your equipment."

I got my gear and picked out a locker.

Phil Anderson was across the room talking to his teammates when he noticed me. A look of disdain stretched across his broad Spartan face as he approached me. "What the heck are you doing here, Cowboy? You get lost looking for the YWCA?"

The others heard Phil's remarks and circled in. I felt like chum at a shark feeding. I turned back to my locker and put on my shoulder pads. Adrenalin pumped through me like a high pressure water hose. The pulse in my neck throbbed so hard I thought it was going to rupture.

The other players hee-hawed in a way that made me feel nothing less than mocked.

Phil walked back to his locker, mumbling, "I'm going to hurt this Texas puppy."

Coach Mancuso had us lap the field twice to warm up. The rest of the morning we did conditioning drills. I was in much better shape than I thought. I knew one thing—New Jersey football conditioning had nothing on Texas.

Toward the end of the practice, Coach rubbed his palms and told us to gather around. His eyes were as big as Dixie cups. I couldn't stop staring at his thick rubbery lips and his yellow stained teeth. "Okay, men it's time for the Buccaneer Challenge."

Everyone on the team jumped up and down, shouting, "Chall-enge, chall-enge," and pumped their fists into the air.

I had no idea what was about to happen. My heart rate picked up the chant.

"Coach Keener, get me two blocking pads." Coach Mancuso barked the order like a drill sergeant.

Coach Keener laid the pads three yards apart. Then I knew we were going to do a toughness drill. At Permian High we called it Between the Dummies. The drill consisted of a running back, an offensive lineman, and one defensive player. The running back got the ball behind his offensive blocker. On the coach's whistle, the back attempted to run between the dummies. The defensive player tried to defeat the blocker and tackle the ball carrier.

I loved this drill because it determined who was the toughest. Man on man, bone on bone. And I wasn't going to let that ball carrier and offensive lineman win this challenge. I was pumped like a race horse on steroids.

Coach Mancuso gathered the team around the dummies. He placed his gnarled fingers on his hips. "Who wants to challenge first?"

Phil Anderson pushed forward from the back. "I'll be the running back."

All the offensive players bellowed a guttural sound, "An-der-son . . . An-der-son."

"Let me be the first blocker." A big offensive lineman stepped up.

The guy next to me whispered that it was Delmar Boldin, an All-State tackle the previous year. He looked mean as a junk-yard dog, had a thick neck, and his legs resembled fifty-five gallon barrels. He gave the impression he could rip off your head and spit down your throat.

"Defense," Coach yelled, "who wants to go against these two?"

It was so quiet you could hear traffic two streets over.

"Coach, let me go." I stepped to the front.

Mancuso removed his cap and wiped the sweat from his forehead "Son, you don't know what you're getting in to." He looked to his left, then right "Who else wants to go?"

No one had the courage to challenge Boldin and Anderson.

I eased the helmet over my head and fastened the chin strap. "Coach, give me a chance."

He looked at me and placed both hands on his knees. "Get in there. Let's see what you've got." He said this like a fly in a spider's web had a better chance than I did.

Boldin got down in a four-point stance and snorted like a bull in a rodeo. Snot dripped off his face mask, and I did a double-take as steam seemed to come out of the ear holes of his headgear.

Anderson got the ball and lined up three yards behind him.

As a linebacker, I positioned myself three yards in front of Boldin. I sucked air through my teeth. The mood was tense. I waited for the impact.

All the chatter died down until you could hear a blue jay pass gas.

I glanced at Coach Mancuso, who stood by himself opposite the team, arms folded, legs apart, eyes fixed on us. He blew the whistle.

Boldin came at me in a low position with his head up. His face, framed in a cold gray face mask, was blood red. He targeted the center of my chest.

I stepped up to meet his charge—my shoulder pads and body lower than his. Bam! The collision sounded like a shot gun blast. Boldin's momentum stopped and I threw him aside.

Anderson headed toward me.

I maintained my low body position and met him squarely between the two blocking bags. My helmet made contact in the middle of his chest and I drove him to the ground. I leaned over him, sweat from my cheeks dripped onto his face.

His eyes were the size of Mason jar lids. I offered my hand to help him up, but he pushed it aside.

I looked at Coach Mancuso. His face was frozen in disbelief and the whistle dangled from his lower lip.

After getting over the initial shock, Phil stood. "Coach, let's do it again." His tone was pure determination.

We lined up like before.

Coach blew the whistle.

Same result—except this time Phil had a large cut caused by my helmet. Blood flowed down his chin and onto his white jersey.

Revenge felt great. I wanted this piece of trash to try again, but he waved me off. He's smarter than he looked.

The Buccaneer Challenge ended the morning practice, and Coach Mancuso approached me. "Son, where are you from?" Now he seemed eager to talk to me.

"Texas"

"What town?"

"Odessa," I said.

"Where in the heck is Odessa?"

"In West Texas. About halfway between Dallas and El Paso."

"Was your team any good last year?" His voice had a tinge of hopefulness.

"Yes, sir. We won the 5A State Championship."

"What does 5A mean?"

"It's the largest school classification."

"Well, you keep your pads. I think we can find a place for you." He patted my shoulder and strutted away.

The players were bunched up when Phil approached me in his blood-soaked jersey. "Okay, Cowboy, you and me. Meet me at the park as soon as you get dressed. I'm gonna make you pay." Everyone heard the throw down.

I'd been in plenty of fights and tough talk didn't faze me. "A fist fight won't accomplish anything."

"Don't show up if you don't want to. Everyone knows you'll get whipped anyway." Phil pushed me and volleyed a series of cuss words.

I grabbed his face mask. "You don't want to do this."

He slapped my hand away. "Are you going to chicken out like you did when Laura protected you?"

I took a deep breath. "Fine . . . let's do it."

Everyone showered and dressed as quickly as they could and headed to the park.

Boldin approached me in the locker room. "Do you know where the park is?"

"No."

"How about a ride?" Boldin told me about Phil while we drove to the park. "He's been a bully his entire life, and everyone's afraid of him."

"You don't seem afraid."

"I'm not, and Phil knows that. Bullies don't challenge people unless they think they can win. He thinks he can whip you. He's a pretty good fighter."

"Do you think he can whip me?"

Boldin smiled, exposing his gold front tooth. "I don't know, but we're gonna find out."

At the park, the players circled around us like Phil and I were the main event at a heavy weight boxing match. I had to admit, I loved it. But I made one last plea to Phil. "Let's don't do this."

His body tensed and he clenched both fists. "You stupid hick." He threw a wild right cross at my face.

I ducked, then rammed my shoulder into his chest, putting him on his back. Straddling him on my knees, I smashed my right elbow into his forehead just above his left eye. The cut was deep and blood cascaded down his face. He raised his arms and crossed them, shaking his head.

I leaned over and whispered, "If you ever call me out again, I'll put you in the hospital. Make no mistake about it. I can and I will. Do you understand?"

He nodded his agreement, but something dark and sinister sat in his stare.

I didn't believe this was over. Not for a second.

CHAPTER 11

MOM HAD DROPPED OFF MY TRANSCRIPT AT SCHOOL AND enrolled me when we arrived in Belleville. On the first day of class, all new students met with Mrs. Wrenn, the school counselor. After the general meeting ended, she pulled me aside. "May I visit with you a moment?"

"Yes ma'am." I scratched my head, bit my lower lip, and wondered how I'd messed up on the first day of school. Mom wasn't going to be happy if I'd screwed up.

"I want to go over your class schedule. Your math grades were exceptional. I placed you in an advanced calculus class. But if that's not okay, I'll rearrange your schedule."

Whew! I tugged on the neck of my Polo shirt and took a deep breath. "I'd like to give it a try. Thank you, Mrs. Wrenn."

Leaving the counselor's office, I spotted Laura and walked faster to catch up. Why did I feel like a kid with a new bike every time I saw her?

She was talking with another girl. I tapped her on the shoulder.

"Hey, Jim, good to see you."

"I'm looking for Room 222. Math. Can you help me?"

She cocked her head to one side. "Is Mr. Chester your teacher?"

I nodded, "Yeah, that's him." Normally a new school year and a new math class were all I needed to be happy, but Laura added another dimension. Every time I saw her my legs felt like mush.

"He teaches Advanced Mathematics." Her tone said she was impressed. "You must be smart." She smiled.

That smile put me in orbit every time I saw it, but I didn't want her to know that. Calm down, you idiot. Stop reacting like a lovesick puppy.

Embarrassed, I fumbled with my schedule. "Are you in his class?"

She gave a soft, quiet chuckle, a chuckle of innocence. "Math's not my strong subject. I can barely solve basic algebra. Maybe you can give me some help."

Tutoring Laura? Whoa. I'd jump on that like a monkey on a June bug. "Deal, but only if you help me with English."

"Fair enough. Room 222 is down the hall. It's the last one on the left."

I adjusted the books under my arm. "I'll see you around." I walked a few steps, then turned to watch her move down the hall and around the corner.

When I got to math, my heart was heavy and light at the same time. Couldn't explain it.

Mr. Chester was visiting with some students at his desk. He saw me and motioned for me to come in. "You must be Jim Pepperman. Have a seat."

I supposed he already knew everyone from previous classes.

I found a seat in the back. Counted ten kids including me. What the heck had I gotten myself into? My palms began to sweat. This course must be impossible with so few students. I had been comfortable in Odessa because I knew my peers, but here it was new. I didn't want to make a fool of myself.

Mr. Chester welcomed us. "I'm excited about this class. I've personally selected each of you. The subject matter will be challenging, but I know you can handle the work."

If my legs hadn't been melted Jell-O, I'd have sprinted right out of there.

I didn't know anyone except Ken Hunter. He was a wide receiver on the football team. Mr. Chester had the class introduce themselves. The others were Ray Robinsky, Martha Kilpatrick, Glenda Barbie, Louise Hillin, Mike Webber, the twins Knox and Chloe Stenberger, and Jeff Langdon. Some of the last names were different than the ones in Odessa, not like Jones, Smith and Brown.

"Class, for the whole hour I want you to work on your own and evaluate the triple integral problem on the board. I realize you don't have much experience with integrals, but let's see what you can do." The way Mr. Chester sat on the edge of his desk, smiled, and spoke softly made me feel comfortable.

His choice of a problem was a stroke of luck for me. Three months prior to moving, my mentor, Tommy Birchwood, a geologist with Amoco Oil Company, had me work these types of problems. Coming up with the correct solution would be difficult, but I thought I could do it. This was a chance to prove myself. Didn't want to blow it.

I glanced around the room, and the others appeared to be struggling. I could see them erasing and starting over. Some scratched their heads while others squirmed in their seats.

"I think you left out part of the equation." Robinsky's tone sounded a little too confident.

Mr. Chester smiled as he rotated a paper weight on his desk. "No, Ray." He chuckled, "I don't think I did. Keep working."

After twenty minutes, I put down my pencil and looked up.

Mr. Chester noticed. "Jim," his voice apologetic, "if you need some help why don't you work with Ken?"

"I think I have the answer," I said.

The entire class looked at me in disbelief. Some shook their heads. Others snickered.

"Would you come to the blackboard and prove your work?" Mr. Chester moved to the side of the room.

I walked to the board with my scribbled notes. Breathing was hard. Every breath short and exaggerated. Sweat popped out on my forehead. I hoped the procedures to solve the problem were all correct. I had to get it right, or I'd make a laughing stock of myself.

There were ten steps to this particular problem, so it took me a while to write out the solution. Stepping back from the board, I placed the chalk in the tray.

Mr. Chester evaluated my work. The silence almost killed me. After what seemed an eternity, he turned to the class and with a look of surprise said, "Jim's answer is correct."

My lungs started to function again. Because of the mentoring I received in Odessa, I was a little bit ahead of my classmates. However, I had a feeling as the year progressed I would be challenged to keep up with this group.

After class Ray Robinsky approached me. "Jim, I'm Ray. Congratulations on solving the problem. I was on step five when you finished. You're fast."

"Thanks."

"Lots of kids call us conehead intellectuals because we take calculus. They think if people are smart, they're weird. But we're not any different from everyone else."

I guessed kids were the same everywhere.

He chunked a crumpled piece of paper at a trash can in the hall. It landed dead-center. "Swoosh . . . two points. Don't know why people label us. We enjoy most things other students like. We listen to the same music, watch the same movies, read the same books and enjoy the same sports. I don't like to be stereotyped, but what can you do?" He shrugged and walked away.

I leaned against a locker in the hallway. Robinsky made me feel welcomed, and that caused me to feel like this new school might just be okay.

I'd had a great experience with my first class. Now I had to get through the rest of the day and hoped the others went the same way.

CHAPTER 12

I'D MADE IT THROUGH THE FIRST SIX WEEKS OF SCHOOL. THANKS to Ken Hunter, the awkward transition of fitting in eased. We sat together at lunch and he introduced me to his friends. My Texas accent seemed to be an ice breaker with a lot of the kids.

My classes were going well, except for English. One day Miss Boyd gave an assignment to describe our favorite sandwich using as many adjectives as possible. I loved BLT's, but now I had a problem. I spelled phonetically, and unfortunately, phonetics weren't always correct. I grabbed a piece of paper, scribbled the word *bacin*, and slid it over to Ken who sat next to me.

"Do you spell bacin this way?"

He looked at me like I had wooden teeth. His return note said—*no, stupid, you spell it with an o, not an i.*"

I lowered my head, looked up at him, and whispered, "I'm getting you after class, you little punk."

When the bell rang, Ken ran out of English class like a ruptured duck. He avoided me the rest of the day, but I didn't forget his snide remark. I planned to get even.

By the end of the afternoon, I hoped Ken forgot about me being ticked at him. I hid behind the door leading from the school to the field house and allowed him to get ahead of me. I crept up behind him, grabbed his belt, pulled upward, and gave him a wedgie, a major wedgie. Although my spelling didn't improve, he never teased me again.

I found a groove in my classes, but our football season was on the rocks. We lost our first two games. We didn't pull together as a team. The players were divided because of the problem at the park between Phil Anderson and me. I tried to resolve our differences, but nothing I did worked.

Phil was skilled as a running back, but he was selfish. Whenever he didn't gain positive yards on a play, he blamed his offensive line. Not only did Phil complain about the linemen not blocking for him, he deliberately tried to divide the team by telling everyone I wanted the leadership role. Nothing could have been further from the truth, but he did manage to convince some of the players I was the cause of the problem. Coach knew the team was split between Anderson with his followers and the rest of the players. We seemed headed for a disastrous season.

One day in practice, our best lineman, Delmar Boldin, had enough of Phil's complaining. Following one particular play, Anderson jumped up and yelled, "Come on, Boldin. Can't you block better than that?"

Phil shoved him.

Bad decision. Boldin delivered a forearm to Phil's head, knocking him to the ground.

Anderson lost it. He turned to Coach Mancuso and flipped him off.

Coach had reached a breaking point with Phil. He kicked him off the team.

That caused quite a stir in the community. Many supported Anderson, but the town didn't know the negative impact he had on the rest of us. I admired Coach for taking a stand.

After Monday's practice, Phil no longer played for the Buccaneers. By Friday the coffee chatter at the diner had us losing our third straight game.

Anderson's replacement as running back was a little known sophomore named Terry Bensway. After the game, everyone knew Bensway Number 37. He rushed for a hundred and ten yards and four touchdowns. We won the game 35-0.

Ken Hunter made a great contribution to our success that year. He had the best hand-eye coordination of anyone I'd ever seen. He had a knack for finding the open spot in the secondary. However, as a wide receiver, he had one glaring weakness. He was slow. Painfully slow. When we ran fifty yard sprints after practice, Coach Mancuso gave him a ten yard head start, and he still couldn't win.

One day Coach gathered everyone around. "Men, we're running fifty yard conditioning sprints and today I have a special challenge for someone." He looked at Hunter with a lopsided grin. "Ken, if you win the fifty yard sprint today, tomorrow we won't run them."

Well, shoot, everyone knew that wasn't going to happen. Coach lined us up on the goal line. We got in our stance, ready for the whistle to blow. But he didn't blow the whistle. He motioned toward Ken. "You start on the twenty-five yard line."

We had a glimmer of hope. Maybe, just maybe, Hunter could win.

Coach blew the whistle and Hunter burst out of his stance like a snail on steroids. His legs were churning, but he was still slow.

I busted a gut laughing, but, by gosh, he beat us all.

The team gathered around him chanting, "Hun-ter, Hun-ter, Hun-ter."

I hoisted him on my shoulders, and we all headed toward the field house. Ken, the idiot, acted as though he'd won an Olympic gold medal. He blew kisses to an imaginary crowd and pumped his arms in the air.

As we reached the field house door, I unceremoniously flipped him off my back, and he landed on his. That show-off needed a dose of reality.

The coaches were tough, but they let us have fun too. I thought they enjoyed the Hunter episode as much as the players.

Eight straight victories followed. The Buccaneers made the playoffs.

I thought about Phil Anderson and his negative attitude. His dismissal from the team was a culmination of bad decisions. Our problems could have been worked out, but he was unapproachable. Although Phil and I had no direct contact, I had a strong feeling about him. And it wasn't good.

CHAPTER 13

Uncle Avin let me drive his 1950 two-door Ford. It was a trash can on wheels, but good enough to take Brook to the babysitter and me to school. Mom dropped Blythe at the junior high on her way to work.

On Tuesday and Thursday nights, Mom took accounting classes at a local community college. She fed the girls before she left to give me more time to study.

Glynna insisted that I eat at the diner. Debra Theesfeld, the evening manager, prepared me meals of pork chops, chicken, and once a week, a T-bone steak. Often I'd take some home to Mom and the girls.

I said to Debra one day, "The diner doesn't serve T-bones and thick cut pork chops. Who's providing this for me?"

She smiled as she flipped the steak, "Don't worry about it, Big Boy. You enjoy the meal."

After work I went straight home and started my homework. Mr. Chester's daily assignment consisted of five problems. It took me an hour and a half to work them, but math was fun, and I enjoyed the challenge.

English was another issue. My assignment usually made me so angry I could spit bricks. The people who developed our language had to be sadists. Homophones were a classic example. Spelling *r-a-q-u-e-t* described a piece of athletic equipment. Spelling *r-a-c-k-e-t* meant making noise. But they were pronounced the same. How dumb was that? If the guy who came up with homophones had been there, I'd punched him out.

Math dealt with absolutes. You added two plus two. It was always four, all the time. English? Not so much.

One Tuesday night after work I met Mom at the door. "Hi, Jim, I'm going early. Meeting with my instructor. See you when I get home."

I admired her for going back to school. Mentally, she was becoming as tough as a coal miner's lunch bucket. I hoped I had her desire to succeed.

Glynna gave me more responsibilities at the diner, and I had another job on Saturdays at a convenience store. Right now, my schedule was draining me mentally and physically.

I grabbed a Coke and sat down at the kitchen table and began to study.

Blythe slid around the corner, happy as a lark. "Mom said . . ."

"Not now Blythe," I snapped at her. "I have to study. Go back to your room. I don't have time."

With slumped shoulders and lowered head, she turned and walked away.

Thirty minutes later she came in the kitchen with a timid expression. "Brook and I are hungry."

"What?" I looked up from my books and softened my tone. "Didn't Mom feed you before she left?"

"That's what I was trying to say. Our supper's in the refrigerator. She won't let me light the burner so you need to warm the goulash."

I dropped the pencil and cradled my face in my hands. How could I have been so insensitive? Dad would never have yelled at Blythe.

I pushed away from the table, went to my little sister and hugged her. "I'm sorry . . . so sorry."

We called for Brook and all three of us sat on the couch for a long time. I held them tight.

Brook ended the silence. "Have we hugged enough? I'm hungry."

Laughing, I gave both girls an affectionate rub on the head, then warmed their supper. I made a decision to spend quality time with my sisters every night.

After dinner Blythe asked me to tell her and Brook about Dad and that skinny old cowboy with the black hat. They'd heard the story a hundred times and never got tired of it.

I settled on the couch, rested my forearms on my knees, and interlocked my fingers. Blythe and Brook sat cross-legged on the floor looking up at me. "I was seven when we moved to Texas. Dad and I were playing catch after his first day of work on the Texas oil rig. A dirty, dented white pickup pulled up in front of our house. I twisted my neck to see who it was and almost dropped the ball Dad had pitched to me."

The girls looked at each other and giggled. They knew what was next.

"The thin man climbing out of the truck wore a giant cowboy hat pulled down over his eyes. A real cowboy just like the ones on TV. Must be the guy from Dad's work. Mom nearly had a fit when Dad told her he'd invited him over for supper without asking her, but she calmed down after a kiss on the forehead. Mom never stayed mad when Dad kissed her."

Brook smiled and covered her eyes. I supposed the kissing scene was a little too much.

"The old man walked over and stuck out his baseball glove-sized hand. 'Name's Mimphord.' One of his front teeth was missing. Made him look like a train robber from the movies. 'What's yours?' 'Jim.' I inched closer to Dad as I slid my hand into the stranger's palm. 'Pleased to meet you, Jimbo.' He pumped my hand so long I was afraid my arm would fall off. "

The girls chuckled at this point of the story. Every time. Then they grabbed each other's arm and mimicked the pumping motion.

"He stopped shaking my hand when Mom came out carrying you, Blythe."

"I wasn't born yet, was I?" Brook interrupted.

Blythe leaned over and nudged Brook with her shoulder. "Shhh. Go on Jim."

"Mimphord took off his black hat and gently patted your curls, Blythe."

She grinned and dipped her chin toward her chest.

"He said to Mom, 'You must be the missus?' And when she welcomed him to our home, he placed his hat over his heart and leaned forward. 'Thank you so much. That's right kindly of you, ma'am.'"

"Right kindly," the girls repeated in their best cowboy accent and giggled.

I shifted on the couch, getting more comfortable. "Mom was warming up to Mimphord. She gave him that smile, the one she gave a good neighbor, and then told us to visit on the porch until dinner.

"I plopped on the ground in front of them. That's when I saw Mimphord's missing little finger. My heart began to pound, the beat so loud I was sure the stranger heard it. I wondered if one of those rattlesnakes like in the *Tom and Jerry* cartoon bit it off. Well, I thought I better get on the porch . . . just to be safe."

Brook inched closer to Blythe.

"The old guy turned his head, puckered his parched lips and spit a stream of tobacco juice through the gap of his missing front tooth. Then he wiped his mouth with the back of his hand."

"If Momma had seen that," Brook said, "she'd have made him wash his hands before he ate." Her grin was so broad it overshadowed her freckles.

"You're right. Mom would do that." I laughed and continued with the story. "Dad asked Mimphord what brought him to our parts and he said, 'I was a young man in Ohio. Work was hard to come by back then with the Great Depression and all. I read about how much money an oil field worker could make in West Texas, so I decided to give it a try. The Bowling Green paper reported there was a purty girl behind every tree, and that also sounded good to me. The only problem . . . there ain't no trees here!' Mimphord picked up his foot and slammed it on the concrete step, then laughed so hard his body shook.

"I jumped, not expecting the loud outburst. Dad leaned back, laughed, and tussled my hair.

"Mimphord coughed up his fur ball tobacco wad and pitched it to the side. He rested his elbows on his knees, leaned forward, and looked at me. 'What's your little sister's name, Jimbo?'"

"He asked about me?" Blythe asked.

"He sure did. I peeked around Dad's leg and said, 'Blythe.'

"The ol' deck hand scratched his head and looked at Dad. 'Pat, I gotta place for you to take the kids this weekend.'

"Just then Mom opened the screen door and told us it was time to eat. Although the old oil field worker was a little scary, I couldn't help but like him. I hoped he'd come back and eat with us again. After supper we walked him to his truck. Dad thanked him for telling us about the rodeo that Saturday."

Brook squinted and cocked her head, "Did Mom make him wash his hands?"

"I'm sure she did." I laughed and nodded.

"I was excited to see all the horses and those big ol' bulls. Blythe, you won't remember this, but your eyes lit up when you heard me say horses. You clapped your chubby little hands and said, 'Horsies, horsies.'"

She grabbed her cheeks with both hands as though she was embarrassed. "Did I really say that?"

I nodded again. "Well, the parking lot at the rodeo arena was packed that hot summer night with big pickups and long cars. The men and women wore cowboy hats. I thought I'd ask Dad to buy me one. Blythe, you were too little to have a hat and I thought a two-year-old would probably look dumb in one anyway."

Blythe scrunched her eyes and rounded her lips, then exposed the tip of her tongue.

"When Mom and Dad found our seats at the rodeo arena, a group of men and women on horses rode by carrying all sorts of colorful flags and banners. Everyone rose for the *Star-Spangled Banner*. What happened next was hilarious, a gut-busting hoot.

"A man on a tractor pulled a large cage to the center of the arena. He jumped down, flipped the latch and at least forty of the biggest rabbits I had ever seen bolted in every direction. They looked like donkey-eared cats with long hind legs."

Both girls laughed and echoed, "Donkey-eared cats."

"Blythe, you pointed your pudgy finger and said, 'Bunny rabbits, Daddy. Bunny rabbits.'

"Dad said, 'Those aren't bunnies. They're jack rabbits.' He bounced you on his knees, and your eyes were as big as butter beans.

"Then, a gate swung open and two men on horseback, twirling ropes over their heads, tried to lasso the rabbits. Critters ran everywhere. I'd never seen anything that funny. Not one hare was captured. By the time the riders threw their ropes, the rabbits were long gone, headed in another direction.

"Dad said jack rabbits had been clocked running as fast as forty-five miles an hour. They zigged, zagged, and then zigged again, never running in a straight line. Odessa, Texas had to be the only place to host a jack rabbit rodeo. That night made us feel better about our new home."

I finished the story, put my hands on their shoulders, and walked them to their room.

Tears gathered in Blythe's eyes. "I miss Daddy."

I bent on one knee and pulled her close. "Me too. Me too."

I returned to the kitchen to finish my homework. I failed Blythe when I scolded her about supper. It wouldn't happen again. I was determined to never put my needs before the girls. They would come first in my life—just the way Dad would have done it.

CHAPTER 14

I WAITED IN THE HALL BEFORE FIRST PERIOD HOPING TO SEE Laura. I stared at the Roman numerals above the doors of each math class. Wondered if that was Mr. Chester's idea.

My calculus class had some interesting people. Take Ray Robinsky — the best mathematical mind in the class and the guy who loved to challenge Mr. Chester.

One day Ray raised his hand. "I think the formula's wrong on problem number five."

"Okay." Mr. Chester removed his reading glasses. "Explain your position."

Robinsky argued a valid point, but Mr. Chester proved him wrong by pointing out a flaw in his reasoning.

The bell rang. Ray and I walked past Mr. Chester's desk and he stopped Robinsky. "May I visit with you for a moment?"

Ray paused and gnawed the inside of his cheek. "Yes sir."

"Have you ever thought about trying out for the debate team?" Mr. Chester sat on the edge of his cluttered metal desk.

Ray's eyes narrowed. "No. Why would I do that?"

"Well, you have a distinct way of presenting your point, and you're convincing in your argument."

Kudos to Mr. Chester. He recognized possibilities in Ray others overlooked. What a tremendous asset for a teacher. Ray took Mr. Chester's advice and made the debate team.

Ray was a good point guard and led the basketball team in scoring and assists. Morrison High was Belleville's biggest rival. The two teams had identical records going into the sectional championship. That game would determine who advanced to the playoffs.

Basketball wasn't my sport, but I liked supporting my school. I showed up early to the game—wanted a good seat behind the scorer's table.

With two minutes left in the game, the score was tied at sixty-six, and Ray dribbled the ball down the court.

An official called traveling.

Ray lifted his arms to plead his case. "Ref, I didn't travel."

"Careful, son." The referee cautioned him. "You're close to getting a technical foul."

Ray shook his head and appealed once more. "But . . . I didn't travel."

The referee turned to the scorer's table and signaled. "Technical foul on Number 15."

Ray slammed the ball down. The ball glanced off his foot hitting the official in the groin, and dropped him to the floor. The entire student section erupted.

Robinsky didn't finish the game, and Belleville lost by two points. Losing the sectional title was disappointing, but Ray's incident made the game worth it.

In math class, the Stenberger twins, Knox and Chloe, sat across the room from each other. Mr. Chester often challenged our class with speed drills and today wasn't any different. The twins raised their hands at the same time when they finished. This happened frequently. Mental telepathy, I supposed. The two rarely made mistakes, but when they did, their errors were identical. Spooky.

Jeff Langdon was unique. What you saw was what you got. He was tall, long-waisted, and had a big stomach. He wore sweat shirts, blue jeans, and tattered penny loafers. He might start the day clean, but didn't end the day that way.

I sat directly behind Louise Hillin in calculus class, and one day she turned to Jeff. "Is that a new red sweatshirt?"

"No." Jeff's response sounded annoyed and he pulled on his wrinkled, faded pants. "Why?"

"The red shirt you wore last week had a hole in the front."

Jeff puffed up his cheeks, then exhaled. "Louise . . . it's the same shirt. I put it on backward today." He turned around. "See." Ol' Jeff, the original Pig Pen.

Mr. Chester walked into class just as the bell rang. "For today I want you to work in pairs. You may choose your partner. See what you can learn from each other."

I raised my hand first and pointed to Jeff. "I would like to work with Hog."

"My name is Hawk. H-A-W-K, not Hog." Jeff tried to dispel his new nickname. Pretty smart. But it didn't stick.

Free spirited Jeff, a.k.a. Hog, loved practical jokes. One day he, Andy Mueller, and Phillip Johnston held Shorty Acorn by his feet out the second story window of Mrs. Bensway's chemistry class.

She walked in and freaked out. "What are you boys doing?" She ran to the window, telling the guys to pull Shorty back in. "Oh, my gosh. . . . Andy, Phillip, Jeff, principal's office now."

I usually got a kick out of his practical jokes, but not this one.

Jeff told me they were not reprimanded in a typical way. He said Mr. Timmons, our principal and Belleville's Chief of Police, Jeff's father, set the punishment. They had to report to the police station every Saturday morning for the next three weeks to clean the floors and toilets in the drunk tank.

Jeff admitted it was a stupid prank. Shorty could have been seriously injured or worse. Ol' Hog didn't stop with the practical jokes, but they were much less sensational.

Louise Hillin was the polar opposite of Jeff Langdon. Her attire was immaculate. Louise, like Hog, had the admiration of most of the students. They were voted senior class favorites. In calculus, the day before the yearbook photo shoot, Louise approached Hog, "Please don't wear one of your sweatshirts for our picture tomorrow."

"Why?" Jeff squinted.

I figured he wasn't going to like the answer.

Louise gave him a subtle smile. "Because it would look better if you had a shirt with a collar."

"Who said it would look better?" Ol' Hog was now on full defense.

"I said it would look better." Louise retorted with an exasperated whisper. "Just do it."

He mumbled something inaudible and took his seat, mastered by Louise's superior will.

The photo shoot took place at the Four Seasons Bowling Alley. I drove them there because Jeff's car was in the shop.

Louise examined Jeff's shirt to be sure there were no stains. "You look very handsome in your new oxford shirt. You should wear clothes like this more often." She patted him on the shoulder with a motherly coddle.

"This is ridiculous," Jeff grumbled to me. "I look like an Ivy League stooge."

As we entered the bowling alley, we walked past the snack bar to the lanes. For the picture Jeff held a bowling ball. Louise stood beside him. I'd never seen Jeff look so good.

At the end of school, we had a yearbook signing party in the gym. When Louise turned to the class favorites section, she slammed the book and shouted, "Jeff . . . I'm going to strangle you."

He heard her threats, and I saw him take a bee line out of the gym. Their picture was perfect except for the quarter size smudge right in the middle of his shirt. How the stain got there no one knew. It could only happen to Hog Langdon, Mr. Pig Pen.

CHAPTER 15

FIRST SEMESTER OF MY SENIOR YEAR WAS OVER. I'D PLAYED MY last high school football game, but wasn't ready for that part of my life to be over. I wanted to play at the next level.

College recruiting letters flooded the mailbox. Wisconsin, Rutgers, Syracuse, Ohio State, and Michigan State were big name schools that contacted me. I wanted a letter from the University of Texas. Blythe was dead set on me attending Texas Tech. The image of the masked rider and the beautiful black stallion had made a positive impression on her. Mom wanted me to stay close to home. Rutgers was her choice.

One evening in early January, Blythe met me at the door. "You got another football letter. You won't believe who it's from." I imagined the flywheel spinning behind those blue eyes.

It had to be the University of Texas. The coaches remembered me. Yes. Yes. Yes.

Mom leaned forward in her chair and, with a warm motherly smile, handed me the letter. I saw the return address—University of Oklahoma. Not Texas. Why would Oklahoma be interested in me?

I sat on the couch, slowly tore the end of the envelope, and removed the letter. I expected the typical accolades but was surprised when the letter was signed by Leon Fulton. He was the coach from the University of Texas who recruited me last year in Odessa.

"Coach Fulton is the linebacker coach at Oklahoma." I looked at Mom. "He wants me to come for a visit."

"Oh, well, you won't be going there. It's too far." She eased herself out of the chair and made a crossing motion with her hands. Her body language was unmistakable.

One evening the phone rang. Mom answered it, and I heard her talking but paid no attention.

A few minutes later, she came into my room, her shoulders tight and her mouth drawn in a thin line. "Coach Fulton wants to talk to you."

I set my pencil down, closed my math book, then looked into her eyes. "Do you want me to talk to him?"

"Oklahoma's a long way from home." She leaned over my shoulder and traced the frame of the only picture I kept on my desk. A picture of all of us, before Dad died. "A long way from us."

"I know, Mom." I leaned back in my chair.

Straightening, she stepped away. "Well, you'd better go see what he wants."

I pushed away from my desk and went to the phone. "Hello."

"Hey, Jim."

I heard muffled voices in the background. Maybe he was in the coaches' office.

"It's Coach Fulton from the University of Oklahoma. How are you?"

"Fine, Coach." Was Oklahoma still interested in me? What would I say if they were?

"I'll make this short. I'd like to come and visit with you and your mom about a football opportunity at Oklahoma. I could fly up next Wednesday. Would that be okay?"

"Yes, sir. I look forward to seeing you." I liked Coach Fulton, but Oklahoma – I wasn't sure.

I turned to Mom. She hummed her favorite hymn, *Amazing Grace*, when she was nervous. What did she think about him coming for a visit?

The day Coach arrived I made arrangements with Glynna to take off work. His flight landed in Newark at 1:30, and he would be at our house no later than 3:00.

Mom was in her recliner humming *Amazing Grace* again. I sat next to the window. Wanted to see him drive up. My right leg bounced up and down like a jackhammer. My hands rested on the arms of the worn vinyl chair, all ten fingers alternating thumps.

Blythe tapped her foot back and forth on the wooden floor making a popping noise with her heels. Brook, semi-reclined on the couch, chewed on a cherry Twizzler, and couldn't care less what was about to happen.

I saw the car pull up and told Blythe to let him in. She'd appointed herself the official greeter.

Coach Fulton barely had time to knock before she slung open the door.

"Coach, I'm Blythe, Jim's sister. Can I record your interview with him?"

That little knucklehead. She didn't tell us she was going to do that. I think it embarrassed Mom, and I know it did me.

"Blythe, go sit by Brook," Mom said in a calm tone. "I'm sorry, Coach Fulton. Please come in."

After the introductions, Coach went to the couch and sat between my sisters. "Blythe, do you like to interview people?"

"Oh, yes, especially football players. I know everyone on Jim's team and their numbers and have taped lots of talks with them. When I grow up I want to interview good football players, not like Jim."

Coach chuckled and patted her on the head. "When I finish visiting with your mom and Jim, would you like to interview me?"

Blythe's eyes lit up like fireworks. "Oh, thank you Coach Fulton. Thank you so much."

Brook took the Twizzler out of her mouth. "Sometimes I play tackle with Jim, but he's not very good. I knock him down all the time."

"I don't think you're giving yourself enough credit. You look strong. I bet you're tough, too."

Brook never said a word, but sat straight up and flexed her muscles, candy stick dangling from the corner of her lips.

Mom seemed to enjoy the interaction between Coach and the girls. From the look of things, he'd already won the hearts of my sisters, and I think he had a good start on Mom.

"Girls, Jim and I need to talk with Mr. Fulton. Why don't you go to your room and play?"

"I'll get my tape recorder ready." Blythe ran down the hall.

I started with a question. "Coach, why did you leave Texas?"

"The Longhorns hired a new head coach, and he brought in his own assistants. Fortunately for me,

Oklahoma needed someone to coach their linebackers. OU's head coach Pete Aderholt called and asked if I wanted the job. This was a good move for me, and I'm excited about being on his staff."

His baritone voice, the color of his hair, and the short-choppy sentences were just like Dad.

Coach shifted on the couch and crossed his legs. "I talked with Coach Mancuso and he said Belleville won the sectional championship with an eight and two record. Congratulations."

"Yes, sir, we had a good season. New Jersey doesn't have a playoff system like Texas. I wanted to play the winner of the other section."

After small talk about Belleville's season, Coach told us about a quality education, the campus life, and the usual stuff all recruiters talk about.

"I've seen a lot of game films since your junior year in Odessa. Your football skills are exceptional. Coach Mancuso said you're the best linebacker to ever play at Belleville. However, we look for character qualities as well as football abilities."

He leaned forward, moving to the edge of the couch. "I've watched some great high school linebackers, but after checking with teachers, principals, and community leaders, many don't have the character traits we're looking for. We are currently recruiting two middle linebackers this year. You are our top-rated prospect."

Coach turned his conversation to Mom. "I have a pretty good idea you would rather Jim play for a school close to home. Am I correct?"

"Yes," she answered. "I'd prefer for him to be closer to his family."

"I understand completely, but one of the things I do with every young man I recruit is make sure they write home to their parents every week. I look after these boys as if they were my own. I promise that's not a catch phrase. It's an honest assessment of how I feel about each one of my players."

Mom straightened in her chair and beamed a smile, a smile that was soft and gentle. I sensed that she was impressed with Coach Fulton, especially when he said how much he looked out for his recruits.

After our conversation, Blythe not only got her promised interview, Coach stayed for supper before he left.

"Did you like Coach Fulton?" I asked Mom as we dried the dishes.

"Yes, I do and I believe what he said, but Jim, Oklahoma is so far from home."

"I agree, and I want to look at other schools, especially Ohio State and Coach Woody Mayes. They have a good reputation for turning out great linebackers."

Mom didn't look at me, but continued drying the dishes.

I couldn't help but think about how much Coach Fulton reminded me of Dad.

CHAPTER 16

The third weekend of January I stepped onto the awesome Ohio State campus for a visit. The naked trees brought images of autumn's yellow and crimson leaves falling from the branches and drifting to the ground. That's what the campus would look like during football season.

Waiting for me by a leafless, gray-barked buckeye tree was Ed Paddington. That imposing red-haired, thick-necked, square-jawed lineman was assigned to show me around campus.

After we introduced ourselves, I tried to break the ice. "Is it true Ohio Stadium was the first horseshoe-shaped, double-decked facility in the United States?"

No response.

Tried again. "Is it true there are more girls enrolled here than boys?" I saw a half-hearted shrug. Wasn't sure if that was a yes or no. One last attempt to get this guy to open up. "Do all freshman football players have to write home every week?"

He never broke stride, turned both palms up, and shook his head. "Don't have a clue to any of those questions."

That was an awkward moment.

The center of the campus was The Oval, a beautiful open park-like area. The William Oxley Thompson Library was the only building within the Oval. The massive grayish white building dominated the landscape.

I was overwhelmed thinking about succeeding as an athlete. Could I face the challenge of getting a degree? Would I fit in socially?

After touring the Ohio Union, Ed planned to take me to the coaches' offices at the stadium. The sidewalks crisscrossing The Oval were filled with students going between classes.

We took a left and my shoe hit a crack on an uneven portion of the sidewalk. Almost in slow motion, my momentum thrust me forward just as a girl came from the opposite direction. With no time to dodge, her eyes and mouth widened, and she let out a scream. My outstretched hands landed on her chest, breaking my fall. She fell into a boy behind her, and he tripped the girl next to him.

Papers flew in every direction like wheat chaff in a windstorm. My runaway body must have traveled a good six feet.

I went to the girls, helped them up, and apologized. They were good sports and took the accident in stride, but the guy was ticked. He mumbled a few cuss words as he dusted himself off.

Ed's laugh was so loud it seemed to echo between the buildings. He stumbled to a bench and plopped down, head back, legs stretched in front of him. He had trouble catching his breath. When he finally regained his composure, his hand slapped his big thighs. "That was one perfect form tackle you put on that girl." He hesitated for a moment, and resumed his wild laughter.

I chuckled as I thought about telling Tony the tripping incident. He wouldn't believe me, but who could make up a story like that?

"The receptionist, Barbara Lockey, is a girl from my hometown." Ed walked up the flight of stairs toward the coaching offices. "We lived on the same street and started first grade together." He told me a few quick stories before we reached the door.

"Barbara," Ed said, "this is Jim Pepperman. I've told him about us growing up together. I also told him I make better grades than you."

Her eyes narrowed, lips straight, head tilted. "Well, I guess I should tell Jim I knocked out your front tooth when we were seven, and you ran home crying."

Ed snickered and gave her a big hug before he said good-bye to me.

I plunged both hands in my front pockets, feeling awkward. She was cute. "It's good to meet you, Barbara. Ed's a really nice guy."

Smiling, she cocked her head. "He's not just a nice guy. He's my best friend. I love him like a brother." She motioned for me to sit.

Still feeling uneasy about what to say, I struggled to find conversation. "What's it like being around the coaches, especially Coach Mayes?"

She put her hand up to her mouth, like she had to think about my question. "I don't think of them as just coaches. They're my extended family. Did you know Coach Mayes stresses academics? He makes a real effort to see that his players graduate. You need to seriously consider coming here." She glanced at the red light on her phone. "When Coach Mayes gets off the line, I'll let him know you're here. Would you like something to drink?"

"No, thanks." Wow. I was impressed. Barbara was recruiting.

Ed told me about the respect the players had for Coach Mayes, and not to let last year's record of four and five discourage me. He said Ohio State was going to have a great team and win lots of games. I began to buy in on the opportunity to play here.

While I waited for him, I sat in a big leather chair adjacent to Barbara's desk. I glanced down and noticed a huge scuff mark on the left toe of my new shoes. I covered the exposed leather with my right foot. Didn't want Coach to notice.

When he came out of his office, I stood to meet him. We shook hands. His little finger was crooked. Maybe a battle wound from his playing days? He was taller than I expected, and his erect posture demanded respect. His silver hair and gray-framed glasses reminded me of a history professor.

He took me into his office, and I sat in front of his desk looking at the pictures on the wall extolling the traditions of a great university. Pride swelled inside me. At that particular moment, I wanted to experience Ohio State — play for a school with a winning tradition.

Coach asked a few questions about my senior year, his eyes piercing me as I answered. With his arms crossed on the desk and his no-nonsense expression, he was a little intimidating. But I kept calm, answering every question.

Toward the end of our meeting, he leaned forward. "If you were the captain of the football team, how would you handle your role?"

I hesitated, wanting to think about my answer. "Help everyone play up to their ability."

"Would you treat everyone the same?" He tapped his fingers one at a time on the top of his oak desk.

I gave this a lot of thought. "No, sir." I hoped I said the right thing.

"Explain." He interlocked his hands and propped his elbows on the desk.

"We're all individuals. I don't think you can treat everyone the same."

"How would you treat them?" The pitch in his voice was elevated.

"Fairly. I would try to be fair to everyone."

"I believe the name on the front of the jersey is more important than the name on the back. What does that mean to you?"

I gripped the handles of my chair. I'd better get this right. "The team is more important than the individual."

He eased back in his seat. "Give serious thought to coming to Ohio State. I can't offer anything more in a scholarship than the other schools, but I can help you develop into the man your mom wants. I'll be fair to you. That's a promise."

We shook hands again and Coach showed me out of his office. He happened to look down as I walked through the door. "Son, how'd you scuff your shoe?"

I glanced away. "I was hoping you wouldn't notice." I felt the blood rush to my face. Please don't ask again.

He smiled and patted me on the back. "You have the leadership qualities we're looking for. We'll be in touch."

As I walked across the campus I thought about Coach Mayes. Rumors about his coaching style were legendary. You messed up—he held you accountable. You did your job—he noticed. That was fair and the way it should be.

I liked this school.

CHAPTER 17

AFTER MY VISIT TO OHIO STATE, I TOOK SEVERAL CAMPUS trips. All the schools had something to offer, but I narrowed my choices to Ohio State and the University of Oklahoma. Mom and I had set the date February 1 to make the scholarship decision, and that day had come.

I sat on the edge of the couch directly in front of her recliner. The situation wasn't tense, but the moment was anxious for both of us. My left leg bounced up and down on the hardwood floor. "It's down to two schools, Mom. Where would you like me to go?"

Across from me, the large vinyl chair engulfed her petite frame. A faded blue and white striped apron circled her waist. A dark hue circled her eyes. She looked drained. Exhausted. All the hub-bub about colleges was wearing on her, but she still had her "A" smile, and I trusted her to be honest.

She swallowed and cleared her throat. "Ohio State has everything that fits our criteria. Top education, a closer distance to home, good athletic programs. Oklahoma . . . so far from your sisters and me. But you were raised to make decisions with your mind, not your heart. You have to do what's best for you."

"I agree, Mom. My education is the most important thing to consider. Both schools have excellent academic credentials and top-notch football programs. Coach Fulton reminds me so much of Dad. He'll look after me. I know he will."

I choked up, then forced back my emotions. "This last year has been hard, but you've held our family together. You've sacrificed so the girls and I could have what we've needed. You're the greatest mom anyone could have, and I love you."

Tearing up, she pulled a tissue from her apron pocket and dabbed her eyes. "Your dad would be so proud. You've become the son he envisioned the day he carried you home from the hospital. I wish you had the memory of his face then, and I wish he could see yours now."

I knelt in front of her. She leaned forward and we hugged. The time had come. My decision was made.

"The University of Oklahoma is right for me."

CHAPTER 18

THE TUESDAY AFTER I MADE MY DECISION TO ATTEND OKLAHOMA was the official day for recruits to sign their football letters of intent. The city of Belleville had three major prospects prepared to announce their respective colleges. My high school coach and athletic director Ronnie Mancuso set up a time and place for us to sign our contracts.

I accepted Oklahoma's offer. Big ol' Delmar Boldin signed with Syracuse. Tony Helmsly, who attended Central High School in Newark, chose Notre Dame. The Belleville newspaper took photos of us with our families and ran articles about our schools of choice.

Mom, Tony's mother Glynna, and Mrs. Boldin planned a celebration party at the Knights of Columbus hall. Glynna fired up her smoker, and we had spare ribs, sausage, and brisket.

Delmar challenged Tony and me to a rib eating contest. I was the runt of the group, but held my own against the two bigger guys. Tony ate thirteen, and I had fifteen. Boldin took top prize, devouring twenty. Tony protested because he'd snacked on two burgers and fries before the party. He got no sympathy from Boldin or me.

Big Mamma Helmsly loved to cook. Nothing made her happier than seeing her boys fill their plates — more than once.

Besides working at Gloria's Diner, I had a second job unloading a beer truck and restocking the coolers at a local convenience store. The first Saturday after signing my letter of intent I was filling the cooler and discovered that the distributor made a mistake. He gave us one six pack more than what was on the invoice.

Wanting to drink my first beer, I stole the six pack. No one would miss it. I deserved a break from my problems with my sisters, school, and Anderson. Besides, I was going to college. Reason enough to celebrate.

I left the convenience store and drove to an isolated, wooded area of the city park. I opened the first can and took a sip. Holy Toledo! I'd never tasted deer urine, but that must be close. About halfway through the disgusting brew, I worried I might throw up. Beads of sweat broke out on my forehead. The bitter taste in my mouth was superseded by a moment of guilt. I took two more gulps, determined to finish my first can.

Popped the top of my second beer. The taste had improved, and my stomach settled. Now I knew why people drank this stuff. Made them happy.

After the third can everything changed. I stepped out of the car and almost fell down. My head spun like the tilt-a-whirl at the county fair. Then the disgusting liquid erupted from my stomach.

It started to get dark. I needed to get home, but driving was out of the question. I lay down on the seat and hoped to feel better.

A car pulled up and stopped. Startled, I sat up.

It was Chief Langdon. Steady. Had to get control of myself.

"Jim, are you okay? Is there something wrong?" He shined his flashlight on the beer cans in the floor board. "Son, I'm going to need you to step out of the car." His eyes filled with disappointment. "I'm surprised by this. You know it's wrong. Why would you drink this stuff? What would this do to your mother if she found out?"

I balanced against the car, then lowered myself to the ground. "It would break her heart."

"What would happen if that recruiter from University of Oklahoma knew?"

Placing my hand over my eyes, I clamped my lips and shook my head. "They would take away my scholarship."

"That's a likely possibility. I'll tell you what. We'll act like this never happened. You made a mistake, and I believe you're sorry. Am I correct?"

Still concealing my eyes, I nodded. "Yes, sir. . . . Chief Langdon. Are you going to tell Mom?"

He hesitated. "No. You're right, this would break her heart. She's gone through enough with your dad dying last year. And your sisters, what would they think of their big brother? Give me your keys. I'll drive you home in your car."

When he pulled in the driveway, Chief Langdon put his hand on my shoulder. "Son, we all make mistakes. The question is what do we learn from them? Think about what happened and turn it into something positive. Are you going to use this incident as a stumbling block or a building block?"

I managed to sneak through the back door and into my room without being noticed.

To the best of my knowledge Chief Langdon and I were the only ones to know about my blunder. I appreciated how he handled my mistake. Not only did he keep my secret, but he may have saved my scholarship.

I thought about Chief Langdon's advice about turning a negative into a positive. He made me realize I was responsible for my actions and how they affected others.

I'd worked hard for eight days trying to forget my first beers. Normally I didn't have a shift on Sunday nights, but Glynna asked me to come around ten o'clock to help until closing.

I'd never seen Glynna so happy. She learned the words to the Notre Dame Victory March — *Cheer, cheer for old Notre Dame* — and sang it so many times I knew the words.

I snuck up behind her and wrapped my arms around her broad shoulders. "Big Mamma, would you please sing another song? You're wearing me out."

Her jolly laugh echoed through the diner's kitchen as she patted my head. "I would sing the Oklahoma victory song if they had one."

Just before closing time the phone rang.

"Glynna, it's Tony."

She took the phone and slumped into her chair. "Lord, have mercy. What happened? Okay, I'll be home in just a minute."

"What's wrong?" I asked.

"Earl and Mary Nelle had an argument. Earl tried to kick her. He missed and hit the dining table. Tony thinks he might have broken his toe."

I placed one hand over my heart and laughed so hard my side hurt.

"I may need to take Earl to the emergency room. Can you close up for me?"

"Sure. Oh, by the way, just sing Earl the Notre Dame Victory March. I'm sure that will make him feel better."

She squinted, rounded her lips, and shook her finger at me as she walked out the back door.

At a quarter past eleven the diner emptied out and I turned the neon lights off. While I counted the cash and placed it in the safe, I had the weirdest feeling I was being watched. Eerie enough to prickle the back of my neck. It didn't last long. But just in case, I looked out toward the street. No one was there.

After sweeping behind the counter, I put the broom away and that prickle returned. This time it didn't go away. I slowly opened the back door. The outside light illuminated the rear of the building. A gust of wind rattled the tree branches, and the leaves swirled around the trash cans. The prickle intensified. I slammed the door and locked it.

My heart thumped so hard I could hear it pounding in my ears. I thought about calling the police, but what would I tell them—I felt like someone was looking at me. Come on. Pull it together.

I waited five minutes to assure myself it was okay to lock up and go home. I eased open the rear door. The alley light was out. A dog barked, not a normal I see you bark, but a don't tread on me sound. A shadow breezed around the corner of the building.

Before I could react, a man in a black ski mask pushed through the door, forcing me back. He swung a bat at my knees. I dodged the blow, but fell. I extended my arms to protect myself. He drew back to swing again.

Someone grabbed the bat before the attacker could strike. Twisted the weapon out of the assailant's hands as if he was taking a toy from a baby. It was Tony. With one punch of his right hand, he knocked the intruder against the wall, shattering his nose. Blood splattered the white paint.

The man crumbled.

Tony jerked the mask off the guy. Phil Anderson.

"What are you doing, you crazy bastard?" he screamed.

"Why, Phil?" I shouted. "Why would you do this?"

He wiped blood from his face with the back of his hand. "You ruined my life. I was the leader of our football team, and you got me kicked off the squad. I would have gotten a scholarship and had my picture in the paper, but you . . . you kept that from happening."

"That's not true," I said. "You're responsible for getting kicked off the team. You're accountable for your actions, not me. I tried to work things out between us, but you would have no part of it. You let the team down because of your selfishness. Coach had no choice but to kick you off."

Tony slapped Phil's head, not a hard direct slap, but a mocking one. "You egotistical punk. You couldn't get a junior high scholarship."

Phil lowered his head. His shoulders heaved as he sat on the floor. Blood still dripped from one nostril. He looked up. "Are you going to call the police?" His voice shook when he spoke. It made him appear small and weak.

Tony glanced at me.

My mind swirled while I decided what to do. As pathetic as Anderson was, he deserved a second chance. An assault charge would stay with him forever. "It didn't have to turn out this way. Now get out of here."

Phil got off the floor and stumbled toward the open door.

Tony grabbed him by the shoulder and spun him around. "Don't ever show your sorry face around here again. If you do, I'll finish the job."

Tony and I stood silent until Phil disappeared into the darkness. Still shaking from what had just happened, I took a deep breath and slowly exhaled. "Thanks, man, am I glad you came up here tonight. Why did you show up?"

"I was helping Mom with Earl's toe . . . had a strange feeling you needed help. Can't explain it."

I took a dish towel and wiped my forehead. "How's Earl?"

"His toe will be fine, but his backside is going to be sore tomorrow."

Little Earl helped to lighten a very intense night.

Looking at Tony, I said, "The first time we met I had a gut feeling I'd need a friend like you. Thanks, brother."

CHAPTER 19

APRIL 28, 1967, ONE YEAR AFTER DAD'S DEATH, THE DAY began with overcast skies, a perfect match for the sadness that smothered me. I sat down in front of his headstone, shivering in the misty rain. Cupping my hands around my nose and mouth, I breathed life into my numb fingers, then touched the engraved letters of his name.

I needed to be alone with him today. Both good things and not so good things were happening in my life. "The pressure of school and work is stressing me out. I can handle it most days, but I have to admit, there are occasions I just lose it. I'm trying really hard to keep my promise to take care of Mom and my sisters . . . being the man of the house that you'd want me to be."

I shifted on the damp ground, and whisked away a few dead leaves from around the marker. "We're doing okay. Mom has a good job, and I help her out with part-time work. Blythe and Brook are good kids, but it's hard for me to give them the attention they deserve. They miss you. I'll keep working at being a good brother. I always try to think how you would handle a situation. You were the best role model any son could have, and that was a blessing."

I paused a moment to sweep away the silky threads of a spider web from the headstone while I gathered my thoughts. "I'll be going to college in the fall on a football scholarship. I narrowed my choices to Ohio State and Oklahoma. The decision was difficult. I chose the University of Oklahoma. The linebacker coach, Leon Fulton, reminds me of you. He has a flat-top, chews on a cigar, and his laugh is so much like yours, but don't get me wrong, he's not you and never will be.

I picked up a pebble and chunked it as far as I could. Why did you have to die? Why? "Mom's a little disappointed because I'll be so far from home, but she also knows Coach Fulton will look after me."

I hesitated. "Got some studying to do. I'll talk to you soon. Love you, Dad."

Warming my hands once again, I traced over his name with my fingers. Suddenly a burst of cold rain splattered around me, and the wind picked up, but I felt at peace. Then my body warmed.

"Dad, you are here with me."

CHAPTER 20

Summer zipped by. I continued to work for Glynna at Gloria's Diner and exercised every chance I had to stay in top physical condition. Occasionally there'd been a date with Laura. I liked her more than just a friend—wished she felt the same.

Today I drove to Nanny's house for meatloaf and mashed potatoes. I tried to wrap my head around the fact that in two weeks I was moving half way across the country to Oklahoma. I was anxious, but looked forward to the next journey of my life.

The second I stepped out of my car, the scent of the freshly baked bread stirred feelings of family, love, and happiness. Her home cooking would be missed.

I entered the living room and Nanny stepped from the kitchen with a dish towel draped over her shoulder humming *In the Sweet By and By*. It wasn't the song that made me smile, but her high pitched tone. "Jimbo, I need some potatoes. Get my car and go to the store."

"Sure thing. How many do you want? But I'll take my car."

She shook her head. "No, take mine so you won't waste your gas. Let me get the keys." She strutted across the floor, chin up, and rummaged through her travel-bag-sized purse. "Oh, guess I left them on the floor board."

"What?" I chuckled. "You shouldn't do that. Someone could steal your car."

She squinted and scrunched up her button nose. "Okay, smarty-pants, I'll remember next time."

Feeling lucky to have a grandmother as neat as Nanny, I grinned all the way to her detached garage. She was a pistol. I raised the garage door to find a bright red '67 GTO. Whoa. Nanny got a new car. She told me she was looking for one. Man, she knew how to pick them. I double-timed to the back door, stuck my head inside. "You didn't tell me you got new wheels."

"I didn't." She continued to dry the dishes without looking up.

"Well, whose new GTO is parked in your garage?"

She laid the dish towel on the counter and turned toward me, her eyes sparkling like diamonds. "It's yours, Jimbo."

I edged my way to the kitchen table and sat down, stunned. "Is it really mine?" I asked in a choppy voice.

"Yes, it's yours." She nodded, her eyes full of tears. Her voice full of all the pride she had for me. "The day you were born your Granddad and I started saving for your education. You got a scholarship so that part is taken care of. I used some of the money to buy you a new car." She blotted her eyes on the dish towel. "It's a long way to Oklahoma."

Her tears were contagious. I swiped a tear with the back of my hand, stood, and gave her a bear hug.

"Put me down, you big rascal. You're squeezing me too hard. I can't breathe." She laughed and patted me on the cheek.

"Nanny, you're the greatest."

Her laughter stopped. She reached up and placed her hands on my face. "No, Jim, you are. Every grandmother wants a grandson like you."

Our eyes locked. True love spoken, and we never said a word.

"Oh, enough of this mushy stuff." She grabbed her purse, pulled out the keys, and jangled them. "Now go to the store and get those potatoes."

I gave her another big hug.

Her laughter returned and she smiled. "Stop it, Jimbo. You're giving me a backache. Now get out of here." She swatted my backside.

I ran to the garage and opened the car door. The rich smell of the tan leather seats stretched my senses like a taffy pull. I slid the key into the slot and turned it clockwise. Vroom. The sound breathtaking. I moved the four-speed manual gear shift into reverse and backed out. The 389-cubic-inch engine rattled the garage. I'd have to control myself. The power was more than I was used to.

Turned on the radio and wow. It was like a live concert. "The Letter" by the Box Tops blared through the speakers. Every time I heard those lyrics I vowed to think of this moment. Life couldn't be better.

I drove around the block to our house. Blythe and Brook stopped playing when they saw the shiny new car pulling into the driveway. As Blythe approached, I rolled down the window.

Her eyes were so big they dominated her small round face. "Whose car is this?"

"It's mine." I rested my elbow on the driver's side door.

Brook ran up and grabbed my arm. "Did you steal it?"

"No, silly. Nanny bought it for me."

Blythe ran into the house to tell Mom, who must've heard the rumbling of the engine, and met her at the door. Mom pushed her hair back, smiling as if she'd known all along about Nanny's gift. She came to the car and crossed her arms. "Nanny was happy she could do this for you. I hope you like it."

My mouth opened so wide I'm sure she could see my tonsils. "If I was going to pick out a car, this would be it. Oh, I almost forgot. Nanny wanted me to pick up some potatoes. Do you have any?"

"Yes, of course."

"Blythe, can you take them to her? Run down the alley. She needs them now. I want to test drive my new car."

The car was amazing, but not nearly as special as my grandmother.

CHAPTER 21

TWO DAYS BEFORE LEAVING FOR COLLEGE IN OKLAHOMA, KEN Hunter, Glenda Barbie, Laura Pomroy and I met at Gloria's Diner. We stayed late, and Glynna ran us off at closing time

While driving Laura home that night, very little was said. We parked in front of her house and she opened up. "Are you still going to major in math?"

"Yes, got my schedule lined up for the fall. How about you? Nursing still your focus?"

"Yes. The University of Pennsylvania sent me a letter yesterday recommending my first semester courses . . . crammed full of biology and human anatomy subjects."

We talked about school and keeping in touch. I wanted to tell her how I felt, but couldn't drum up the courage. After our conversation, she kissed me on the cheek, the kind of kiss a friend would give. Not what I wanted, but what could I expect? A friend was how she thought of me.

Not telling Laura my true feelings was probably best. We would be too far apart to develop a serious relationship.

The following morning I went to the Helmslys. Burl and Earl greeted me in the usual way. They busted out the front door wearing their Fighting Irish t-shirts and latched onto each leg. Roughhousing was standard protocol with the four-year-old twins.

"Big Boy, why can't you go to Notre Dame with Bubba?" Earl asked. "You need to go with him cause he's scared of the dark." His voice was high pitched with a hint of southern drawl he got from his mother.

I sat on the front porch with my two little buddies, watching them snack on Tastykakes. "Are you sure he's afraid of the dark?"

Earl wrinkled his forehead and tugged on my arm. "Yeah, Burl and me have to let him sleep with our teddy bears or he throws a fit."

"He's a big sissy baby." Burl nodded and poked a finger into his nose.

The twins had quite an imagination. That was for sure. Other than my family, I would miss them the most. I'd make a special effort to keep in touch.

Glynna told me a long time ago to come in the house like the rest of her kids. Walking into the living room, I noticed her motionless in the rocking chair, clutching a handkerchief in her limp hand. Her red eyes told the whole story.

I walked over, knelt on a knee beside her chair. "What's wrong, Glynna?"

She rocked, looking straight ahead. "I'm losing my big boys tomorrow. Tony's going to South Bend, and you're heading to Oklahoma." Glynna shifted in the chair facing me. "You're like a son, Jim. I didn't birth you, but that don't make no difference." Her chin quivered.

Our eyes locked. Mutual admiration was a given.

She patted my leg. "You've been a blessing to me and my family." She pushed herself out of the old wooden rocker. "I've got something for you in the kitchen."

She left me standing in the living room and returned with a large paper sack. "I made your favorite cookies. Three dozen coconut macaroons for your trip, and I'm giving you the green drinking glass you like. When you pour yourself a glass of milk, think of me." Big Mamma lowered her head.

I put my arms around her. "You are so special."

Big Mamma had given me a job when I moved to Belleville. How could I ever repay her kindness? Emotions were churning inside me, struggling to bust out.

She grabbed my shoulders and gave a gentle nudge. "Enough of this." Glynna pointed to the back door. "Tony's outside waiting on you."

From the kitchen I could see him sitting under a cherry tree. I pulled twice on the jammed door. "Hey, Tony."

"Hey, Jim, come on out and have a seat."

I sat next to him, mimicking his posture and pulling my knees to my chest and wrapping my arms around my legs. We stared straight ahead in silence, neither of us knowing how to say good-bye.

Tony turned his head. "You know I think of you like a brother."

"Yes." I met his eyes. "You know the same, right?"

Tony gave me a not-so-subtle tap with his right elbow. The niceties didn't last long before testosterone kicked in. "Yeah. You realize if Notre Dame plays Oklahoma, I'm going to have to take you out."

I placed my hand on his head and gave a gentle push. "You'll have to catch me first." We both laughed, and I extended my right hand. "Let's keep in touch, brother."

"For sure. I'll miss you, friend."

It wasn't his words that caught my attention, but the way he spoke them. His tone soft and caring.

I pushed up from the ground and walked back to the house. As I reached the door, I turned and held up my hand. He did the same. We were brothers. Always would be.

Race relations in America were bad. Whites against blacks. Black against whites. I supposed it had been that way for a long time. I didn't understand it. When I was with the Helmslys, I didn't see color. All I saw were good people — really good people.

The next day I was packed, car gassed up, and ready to leave. Telling my family good-bye was difficult. As I looked in the rear view mirror, Mom, Blythe, Brook, and Nanny stood on the curb waving. I knew they would be there until my new car was out of sight.

Dad's resting place was my last good-bye. My heart sad, I approached his grave. My feet shuffled along the ground. They were so heavy I could barely pick them up. Warming my hands, I touched his name on the cold granite marker.

"Dad, I'm nervous about leaving. Doubt is beginning to creep in. What if I fail? What if I don't finish my education? If you were here you'd assure me everything would be all right. You told me once that fear of failure is a great motivator. The fear I have is real, and I suppose time will tell if it motivates me to succeed. I don't want to let you down."

I paused for a moment. "I need someone to lean on right now. Mom tries to help, but it's not the same. I need you, Dad."

A feeling of calmness uncurled, first in my chest, then spreading outward. Warmth flooded my body as though Dad had wrapped his arms around me and patted my back. Couldn't explain it, but I felt it. On the walk back to the car, my confidence restored until my spirit felt unshakable. I would succeed in the next journey of life. For Dad.

CHAPTER 22

JEFF LANGDON, CHIEF LANGDON'S SON, RODE WITH ME TO Norman. It took us three days and fifteen hundred miles of hard driving to reach Oklahoma. Excitement and all-out fear bounced around inside me like a gunnysack full of gerbils. Had I made the right decision to leave my family, to play for a football powerhouse? Could I make the grades and graduate? I unloaded all my woes on Jeff during our trip, but he wanted nothing to do with my pity party.

"Good grief, Pepperman. You sound like a wimp who's leaving home to live on the other side of the moon. Wait . . . you'll be living in the South. That's worse than living on the moon. You poor soul, is there anything I can do to save you from a fate worse than death? Who's feeling sorry for you now? It ain't me."

I rapped him on the side of the head. "Thanks for coming with me. You're making the long trip seem soooo much longer."

Jeff reached in the backseat and pilfered through rumpled burger sacks and empty soda cans. "Did we eat all those macaroons?"

"You pot-bellied pig, you ate three-fourths of them."

He changed the subject. "Are you sure Oklahoma has a football team? Never heard of them?"

Shaking my head, I pursed my lips without a comeback. Jeff was too witty.

After a couple of nights in two-bit motels, we arrived in Norman, Oklahoma. The road trip with Jeff was good. It took my mind off fitting in with my new teammates.

After moving into the dorm, I had to take him to the airport. Walking to the car, I gave him a good-buddy slap on the back. "I don't want you to miss your flight." I opened the car door, put one hand on his neck, the other on his back pocket and shoved him into the car.

Jeff bumped his head on the car frame. "Ouch, you big dummy. You're so thoughtful." He gave me a look that would freeze water.

I stood in the terminal and watched until his plane disappeared. He was my last tie to Belleville. Now I had to face my challenges alone. Fifteen hundred miles from home, no friends, scared stiff. A sickening feeling smothered me like a truckload of wet sand. If Mom could see me now, she'd see a pale, lifeless, ball of insecurity. At that moment I wished I'd boarded the plane with Jeff.

Pulling into the dorm parking lot, I saw Paul McGlendon from Abilene, Texas. We'd played against each other when I lived in Odessa. Paul quarterbacked the Abilene Cooper Cougars. It was great to see someone I knew. It reminded me I wasn't the only freshman going through a change in life style, and it brought a little relief.

That evening I met most of the other freshmen athletes. A couple of the guys were from Lubbock and Midland. Being around West Texas guys lifted my spirits.

Football at the University of Oklahoma would be intense, demanding, and challenging. You make a mistake at the college level, your opponent beats you. You let your team down.

I remembered what dad said about fear of failure being a great motivator. My anxiety level couldn't be higher, but I knew one thing for certain — Jim Pepperman would succeed. Failure was not an option.

At that moment I felt emboldened, but how long would it last? Was I kidding myself? I would soon find out.

As the weeks passed, I got to know my teammates in the athletic dorm. James Morley had to be the most colorful. I called him J. Mo because that's what he called himself. His family moved to Florida from Jamaica. His father was a drummer in a rock band.

Life was a carnival ride to him. He wore bell-bottomed pants, flower-printed shirts, and at least three gold chains around his neck. His white patent leather platform shoes made a fashion statement. His Afro was the size of a number ten washtub pushing his 6' 3" frame to seven feet tall.

His ever-present smile exposed a gap between his two front teeth. One day at lunch he placed two straws in the cavernous gap, slapped his outstretched arms together, and made walrus sounds. J. Mo was secure enough to make fun of his physical appearance.

As personable as he was off the field, the opposite was true on the field. He played next to me at inside linebacker. When he put on his uniform for practice, you'd better be ready for contact. He never went half-speed. Dr. Jekyll and Mr. Hyde described his mixed personality.

Next to me in the dorm was Mike Podzinsky, a wheat farmer from Derby, Kansas. If you asked someone to describe a typical farm boy, he'd fit the stereotype. Big-boned, with hands the size of a one-way plow disc, he wore faded jeans, boots, and a sweat-stained ball cap. All the time. Mike drove a beat up, old Chevy pickup with tires that came to my thighs. It was the tallest dang vehicle I'd ever seen.

Podzinsky chewed Beechnut chewing tobacco and spit his chocolate brown saliva into empty Coke cans. One freshman player liked to sneak sips of other people's sodas. He only did it once to the farmer boy.

Eddy Olendorf, Mike's roommate, was a big ol' lineman from Dallas. His father, a cardiologist, once played professional football for the Green Bay Packers. Everyone on the team called Eddy "Pretty Boy" because his clothes were immaculate. Sorority girls loved him.

Mike and Eddy were definitely the Odd Couple. Mike's side of the room was a nuclear wasteland. He never made his bed and only changed sheets when the dirt mites made him itch.

Eddy always had clean sheets and everything was in its proper place. His shirts and pants were all lined up, short sleeves, then long sleeves. His pants were arranged by color.

One day I noticed two stacks of underwear in Podzinsky's closet. "Why do you have separate piles of underwear?"

"One is clean, the other dirty." He opened a pouch of Beechnut and stuck a fistful into his right cheek.

I hesitated before I asked, "Why don't you put the clean ones in your dresser drawer?"

He looked at me as though I had taken a bottle of idiot pills. "Because the drawer is full of my shotgun shells and fishing lures."

I grinned and shook my head.

How Mike and Eddy and their totally opposite personalities survived living together was more than I could figure out. Both liked to hunt and fish. I supposed, for those reasons, they put up with each other's quirks.

In calculus class, I met Brenda Claude, a girl from a small town in the Texas Panhandle. We tutored student athletes. I never admitted it, but she had a better analytical mind than I did. However, she had one minor flaw.

I told her, "The people you tutor would be able to learn more if you didn't talk so blasted fast. You are the only person I know who can spew out ten thousand words a minute."

She tilted her head from side to side in a sarcastic way. "The people I tutor don't complain. It must be your pea brain that can't comprehend more than a few syllables."

Never could get the last word on her.

I introduced Brenda to the best student athletic trainer ever. His name was Michael Dean. They made a good couple. She talked. He listened.

CHAPTER 23

MY FIRST YEAR AT OU WAS THE TOUGHEST. BEING AWAY FROM home was hard. Adjusting to my professors was a challenge. And making good grades was constantly on my mind. On top of that, the coaching staff red-shirted me. That meant my first year I had to work out and practice, but couldn't suit up on game day. It was like getting all dressed up for a party, then being glued to a dingy chair in a dark corner while everyone else had fun. But I would get five years of schooling and four years eligibility to play football.

Going to class, football practice, studying until midnight, sleeping, then repeating the same thing the next day was my entire life. More than once I thought about packing up and going home.

Coach Fulton had a sixth sense about my frustrations. His mentoring reminded me of the way Dad put life in perspective—take one day at a time and focus on the positive. Coach Fulton told me to keep my head up, be patient, work hard, and I might have a chance to play pro ball. He was a good man. A really good man.

The second year was a transformation. Athletically things clicked. I understood what the coaches told me to do. In practice, I would read the offensive guards on the field and react to the situation instead of thinking first and then reacting. I suited up for games, made the travel squad, and played mostly on kick-offs and punt returns.

I was aware of the clichéd idea that "Jocks are dumb." People who made those asinine remarks never put on a jockstrap. You couldn't be stupid and play football. It was like a chess match with one major difference — the knight on a chess board wouldn't fracture your jaw.

Once I figured out how to study, I actually had time to notice girls. Even dated a few. The girls at OU were knock-outs, but none compared to Laura. Her beauty and personality were my standards of what a lady should be. I missed seeing her, but letters every couple of weeks helped. She still treated me as her friend. But a friend isn't how I saw her. She was the only girl I wanted.

Warming the bench that second year taught me humility and patience — what Coach Fulton wanted me to learn. The next two seasons I started at inside linebacker. OU's record last season was seven victories, four losses, and one tie, and I was named to the All-Conference First Team.

The coaches and players were primed and ready for the upcoming year — my last as a player. Oklahoma was going to kick butt, and our team knew it.

CHAPTER 24

SPRING PRACTICE WAS OVER. THE ATHLETIC DORM WAS MOSTLY empty. All I had to do was finish my finals and head home for the summer.

Wham. Wham. Wham. My door shook.

I blinked at the glowing clock. 1:00 am. Stumbling out of bed, I stubbed my big toe on a chair and limped toward the door. More than a few cuss words crossed my mind, but I bit them back.

I eased open the door. The bright hall light forced me to squint. "What the . . . ?" Good lord, it was Olendorf and Podzinsky looking like they'd been caught stealing pies from their mothers' window sills. Podzinsky chomped on his wad of tobacco. Juice caked in the corners of his mouth like he had been eating mud. Olendorf's Cheshire grin made me suspicious.

Podzinsky shoved his dirty ball cap to the back of his head and belched so loud it echoed down the dormitory hall. He didn't say a word, but his ridiculous smile said enough.

"My last final's at 9:00. This better be important." My body was slack. My tone low and distinct.

"We went to the Oklahoma City Civic Center to see country star Uncle George," Olendorf said. "On the way home Pod decided to run over all the reflector poles on the side of the road."

The goof-balls looked at each other and cackled like teenage girls.

I wiped the sleep from the corner of my eye. "What happened?" Although I wasn't sure I really wanted to know.

"It was the last reflector pole on I-35," Olendorf said. "The one at the Norman turnoff. We got it good." He yawned and cupped his hand over his mouth. "The problem is—Pod's truck is stuck on the pole. We can't get it off. You know how many poles we ran over between The City and Norman?" he boasted. "Thirty-four of 'em."

Podzinsky looked at Olendorf, then spit his murky spew into a paper cup. "Thirty-three."

Olendorf shook his head and waved his hand from side to side. "Thirty-four."

I pounded my fist into the door frame. "I don't give a bull's rip how many you knocked down," I shouted. "What do you want me to do?"

"Help us get my pickup off the reflector pole, of course," Podzinsky quipped with a lemon-slice grin.

Olendorf tugged on his shirt until the wrinkled tail was exposed and yawned. "Ya'll go get the pickup. I've walked too far tonight. I'm going to bed."

I grabbed him by the collar as he turned to walk away. "I don't think so. Get your tail in my car. You're going with us. Why would you run over reflector poles in the first place?"

Podzinsky turned his cap backward and shoved it snug onto his head. "Small town Derby, Kansas. Saturday nights. That's what you do."

"You better hope Coach Aderholt doesn't find out, or he'll tear you a new one."

Olendorf and Podzinsky looked at each other and made the my-lips-are-zipped gesture.

Most of the time I loved those guys. Tonight I wanted to chunk them out my second-story window. "Meet me in the parking lot. I've got to get dressed."

Putting on my Levis and wrinkled t-shirt, I imagined those two clowns in that monster pickup, clipping the reflector poles and snapping them like toothpicks. I envisioned the amber reflectors popping loose and flying through the air like clay pigeons flung from a skeet shoot. Falling back on the bed, I laughed so hard the frame shook.

We piled in my car and drove to the scene of their screw-up. I got behind the wheel of Pod's pickup and made them lift and rock the back of the vehicle. I gunned the truck and it popped loose from the pole.

After pulling the pickup forward, I went back to my car, started it up, and stuck my head out of the driver's side window. "Do you think you can find your way back to the dorm?" My tone was sarcastic and loud.

"Yeah, sure, Jim. Thanks," Olendorf said.

Pod waved good-bye with his middle finger.

I watched the two bozos in my rearview mirror. It looked as though they were arguing, probably about the number of reflector poles they destroyed. I'd do anything for those guys. They'd do the same for me.

After a very short night I managed to ace my 9:00 o'clock final. Maybe I should have the Odd Couple interrupt my sleep before all my exams. Or — maybe not.

CHAPTER 25

AFTER MY LAST FINAL, I WENT BACK TO THE DORM, PULLED out my State Farm road atlas, and planned my trip to Belleville. The interstate was my usual route home, but this time I wanted to see more of the countryside.

The phone rang. It was Mom. She sounded happy. I thought she must be ready for me to get back to New Jersey.

"Hey, Mom, what's up?"

"Just checking to see what time you're leaving and remind you not to speed."

Mom's tone softened and she whispered. "Brook got into trouble at school. I've already grounded her, but I want her to tell you what happened. Whatever you do, don't laugh."

Oh, boy, this should be interesting. My little sister had creative ways to demonstrate her personality. "Okay. Put her on the phone."

"Brook," Mom shouted. "I want you to tell Jim what happened at school."

I could hear her running down the hardwood floor hallway singing. Couldn't make out the words.

"Hi, Jim. How's Coach Fulton?" Brook deflected. Her usual tactic when she messed up.

I settled back in my chair, crossed my legs and waited for the I-can't-believe-mom-is-so-upset excuse. "Hi, Brook. Want to tell me what happened at school?"

"I can't believe Mom's so upset because I hit a boy in the stomach."

Ah ha. I was right. "Why would you do that?"

Brook exhaled, apparently frustrated. Much ado about nothing. "Dawson cut in front of Susie in the cafeteria line."

I gathered my thoughts and spoke in my best fatherly voice. "What did the principal say?"

"She said it was okay."

"Now, Brook, did she really say that?" I bit down on my lower lip. Couldn't wait to hear the rest of the story.

"No . . . but she was thinking it because Dawson's a bully."

Now was the time to use a dad-ism. "Do you think there was a better way of handling that situation?"

After a long hesitation, she said, "Yes."

Excellent. Thinking how Dad would have responded worked. "Good. What should you have done?"

"Hit him in the nose?"

My cheeks puffed up as I struggled to choke back a gut bustin' laugh. "Eight-year-old girls shouldn't hit people."

"Blythe said when we lived in Odessa, you hit people all the time when they did the wrong thing."

I circled the inside of my cheeks with the tip of my tongue. "Put Mom back on the phone."

"Okay. Bye. Love you. Mom," she yelled. "Jim wants to talk to you."

I heard Mom tell Brook to clean up her mess in the kitchen. Brook messy? That wasn't hard to believe.

Mom's little pitter-patter footsteps increased the closer she got to the phone.

She cleared her throat. "You didn't laugh, did you?"

"No, but it was all I could do not to. She had a comeback when I tried to reason with her."

"She's bull-headed just like the rest of the Peppermans." Mom chuckled. "Her arguments are persuasive. Hope she becomes a lawyer."

Unable to contain myself, I hee-hawed like I was watching a Dean Martin and Jerry Lewis movie.

"We are so ready for you to come home. I think Brook is acting up because she wants to see her big brother."

"I'm leaving in a couple of hours. Still have some packing to do."

"Drive carefully."

After hanging up, I sat at my desk and gazed out the window. Being a father figure to Blythe and Brook was difficult. My thoughts swirled. Had I done everything to help my sisters develop into responsible people with goals and aspirations? The big brother part was easy, but substituting for a father was a big challenge.

I'd been fortunate. The girls were good with just a few problems I couldn't handle over the phone. Our weekly calls helped, but it wasn't the same as being there. From time to time I wondered if staying closer to home would have been better for them.

I talked to the girls about making good choices and showing respect for others. Dad had a way about him when he taught me right from wrong. He asked me questions and let me come up with the solution. If the answer wasn't what he expected, he rephrased the question. I remembered the time Father Aguilera scolded me for running down the aisles after Sunday mass. Dad asked questions until I said it didn't show respect for God in his house of worship.

Brook had to learn better ways to handle her emotions.

As I continued to stare out the window, beads of sweat broke out on my forehead. My skin was clammy. Why, Dad, why did you have to die? What if I fail to keep my promise?

CHAPTER 26

THE DRIVE HOME AT THE END OF THE SCHOOL YEAR WOULD give me time to think about my grades. I'd maintained a 3.8 GPA in math, my major, but my blasted English courses brought my overall grade point down to a 3.2. The knuckleheads who developed our language were either drunk, on drugs, or sadists.

My English professor said my spelling proficiency was barely at a sixth-grade level. I hoped he was kidding, but in all honesty, the English language and I were mortal enemies.

Graduating with a Bachelor of Science degree in math next year would be a major accomplishment. Figuring out a way to pay for my sisters' educations would be next. Blythe would graduate from high school in two years and Brook in ten. Being drafted by the National Football League was a priority. The university provided my education, and professional football would allow me to pay for theirs.

Spending the summer with family and friends in New Jersey would be a welcomed break. And I needed a few weeks away from football.

I pulled out of Norman at five o'clock in the afternoon. After driving several hours, I was in the back country of Arkansas. It was a beautiful state with lots of trees and lakes. I drove through Delton, a small, one-stop-light town and noticed Jeff's Hardware Store. It reminded me of my high school buddy, Jeff Langdon. We usually talked three or four times a semester, but, for some reason, hadn't connected the past few months. I'd look him up when I got home.

I thought about Laura Pomroy. I'd decided to see her as much as possible during the summer and make an effort to share my true feelings. She was the only one for me. I was excited and nervous at same time. What if she still just wanted to be friends? Not sure I could handle the rejection.

Coming off my finals, a lack of sleep, and driving late into the night, I'd had enough. The Manson Motel just outside of Little Rock wasn't the New York Plaza, for sure. But it was about all I could afford. The paint-chipped run-down building had a neon sign that flicked on, then off, then on again.

My horror movie imagination told me to get the heck out of there, but my body made me stay. The picture on the faded lime green wall looked like it was painted by a first grader on a sugar high. The mattress was short and lumpy. I didn't care. I passed out on the blue, germ infested bedspread.

On the way out of town the next morning, I stopped at Joe Bill's Pancake House. The drive to Knoxville, Tennessee would be a challenge, but at least home would be closer. First priority — food.

The fresh smell of bread reminded me of Nanny's homemade goodies. I slid onto a red vinyl-covered stool and propped my elbows on the counter.

The lady who waited on me could have been Big Mamma Helmsly's sister. "What can I get you this morning, hon?"

I glanced at the plastic-covered menu, but already knew what I wanted. "One sausage biscuit and a large cup of orange juice to go."

She peered at me over round glasses perched on the end of her round nose. "Is that all? A big guy like you. Figured you more for a short stack, six slices of bacon, and three fried eggs." She put her hand on her hip. "That little ol' biscuit won't last to the stop light."

I folded my hands and broke out in a grin—a grin that said I like you lady.

She cocked her head. "What's you grinning about, son?"

I leaned forward. "You remind me of someone special back home. It's the highest compliment."

She turned her head and gave me an aw-shucks wave. "That's so sweet, sugar. Now, what's you wanna eat?" Direct and to the point. She'd make a good football coach.

"Just the sausage biscuit and orange juice. I have to hit the road."

She squinted her soft, caring eyes. "Where you going?"

"Back home to New Jersey."

She placed one hand on her plump hip. "Where you coming from?"

"Norman, Oklahoma."

Her voice shifted and excitement burst out of that jovial body. "Norman, Oklahoma. You're big. I bet you're a football player."

"Yes, Ma'am, I play for Oklahoma."

She reached over and latched onto my shoulder with a grip that could crush rocks. "Lord, have mercy. I have a son in junior high who loves the Sooners. That's all the boy talks about. He has OU caps, sweatshirts, and jackets. Is that a good school?"

I nodded. "Absolutely."

She turned her order pad over and plucked a pen from behind her ear. "What's your name and number?"

"Jim Pepperman. Number 55."

"I'm gonna tell my boy we met. I'll bet he knows about you. Jim, are you any good?"

I began to chuckle. "Well, I guess that depends on who you ask. What's your son's name?"

She gave me a smile that would melt a snow cone. "His name is Billy . . . Billy Simmons."

Talking with this wonderful lady started my day right. I realized I never asked her name. But I knew she worked at Joe Bill's Pancake House in Foster, Arkansas. I'd write her son a letter. Who knew, he might play for the Sooners one day.

With one hand on the steering wheel, the other wrapped around my breakfast, I headed out of town. Just ahead, the road snaked around a small hill. The sun was positioned dead center in the highway. Directly in my eyes. "Wow, that's bright." I could hardly see a thing. I slowed down, flipped the visor, and patted the seat feeling for my shades.

Pow! Plunk, plunk, plunk. The car began to shudder.

"Dad-gummed flat tire." I pulled over on the shoulder of the narrow, two-lane road. Getting out of the car,

I noticed the bottom half of the left rear tire was indeed flat. Remembered that from a joke Olendorph told about a cowboy on a dirt road near Marfa, Texas.

I placed my hands on my knees and stared at the wilted rubber mess.

The blast of a truck horn froze me. The swerving big rig pelted me and my GTO with gravel.

The next moment happened in slow motion. My arms and legs flailed. Mouth wide open, air escaped my lips, but I heard nothing. The ground came up to greet me. Had I been hit? Was I dead? What happened?

The next thing I knew, a man in overalls was crouched over me. "Hey, you all right? You okay?" He was inches from my face. His short-cropped gray hair sparkled.

Was he an angel? Then I smelled the stale odor of coffee and the undeniable stench of cigarette smoke. I managed to sit up. Blood dripped from my elbow. My Levis were dusty and my shirt torn. In shock, I muttered, "I'm . . . I'm all right."

The trucker dragged the back of his hand across his mouth. "Thank goodness. I came around the bend in the road and could hardly see anything. The dang sun blinded me. I couldn't tell whether I hit you or not. My truck barely missed your car. Are you sure you're not hurt? Can I get you some water? Gosh. I'm so sorry." Both palms of his hands were turned upward, seeming to beg for forgiveness.

"I'm fine. I'll take some water."

He started to walk to his truck, then turned facing me. "When I blasted my horn, you were flat-footed, then dove head first over the trunk of your car and landed a good six feet on the other side. That was the dog-gond-est thing I'd ever seen. How'd you do that?"

I shook my head. "Don't know . . . guess it was adrenalin." I watched the driver go to his eighteen-wheeler for the water. I tried to gather my thoughts. What really did happen?

The trucker asked if he could change the flat. The Good Samaritan helped me replace the tire and wished me a long life before he left. The burly Teamster didn't ask me again about the bizarre flight that launched me into the ditch.

But he was wrong. I didn't dive over my car. Something latched on to me and lifted me out of harm's way. The peacefulness was surreal, almost indescribable.

And I'd heard a voice. "I've got you." It sounded like Dad.

CHAPTER 27

Now that I was home for the summer, I looked forward to spending time with my sisters. Taking the girls fishing, spending afternoons at the water parks, and enjoying the watermelon feast after the Fourth of July parade were some of my favorite summer activities.

I made myself a bologna sandwich and handed Mom the mayo to put back in the fridge. Through the kitchen window I noticed Brook turning cartwheels in the backyard. She wheeled too close to the fence and her foot busted through one of the wooden slats. Oh, great. Now I had to go to the lumberyard and buy a new board.

I opened the screen door. "Brook, you okay?"

She dusted herself off and shouted, "Yeah, I'm fine."

"Come over here. I want to talk to you about something." I was curious what she'd tell me about punching the boy in the stomach.

She hopped on one foot, trying to put her shoe back on. "Are you going to talk about the boy I punched?"

With a mouth full of sandwich, I muffled out, "How did you know?"

She cocked her head to one side and exposed the tip of her tongue. "The only time big people want to talk to little people is when the little people mess up."

As usual, her logic was right on target. "Okay, smarty pants, let's talk about you imitating Muhammed Ali."

"Well, I don't hit someone unless they're doing something they shouldn't do. Do you remember when I hit Johnny Powell in the stomach when we lived in Odessa? I was four, but I could hit. Do you remember who taught me to punch?"

I jostled my jaw from side to side and puckered. The little scamp was working an angle. I was forced to answer. "Me."

She patted my shoulder. "That's right. You're such a good brother." Her tone was sarcastic.

I wanted to pinch her little head off.

Brook knew she'd worked me into a corner and could blame me for any wrongdoing when it came to fighting. How was I going to get out of this? I hated it when she spun things to her advantage.

"Do you remember when Callie Hobbs rode her bike up in our front yard and told me about Johnny Powell spitting on her? She was my friend and needed help."

"Yes, I was working on my truck and you were sitting on the sidewalk playing jacks, but that's no reason to punch someone."

"Ah . . . that's not what you told me when I went to Johnny's house and doubled him over. You said it was the right thing to do. He deserved it."

Shoot. . . . She remembered everything. Quick. I had to think of something.

"Do you think there's a better way of settling differences besides fighting?" That's what Dad would say. Hoped this worked.

Sitting on the top step of the back porch, she placed her elbows on her knees and cupped her face between her hands. I could tell she was thinking about my question. "Can I ask you something?"

I could almost see the wheels in that eight-year-old brain spinning two hundred miles an hour. "Ask away."

"If one of your friends was getting the tar beat out of 'em, what would you do?"

I had an answer. Gettting good at this Dad stuff. "Well . . . first I would separate the two and tell them fighting never settled anything."

"Did you tell Phil Anderson fighting never settled anything before you beat him up?"

I snapped my head around so fast a piece of lettuce fell from my mouth. "How do you know about Phil Anderson?"

She smiled, exposing her one missing front tooth. "Everybody in town knows you beat up that mean bully."

Oh, shoot. Now she'd backed me into a corner— again. "That was different."

She tapped her index finger on her lips and squinted. "How?"

I racked my brain to come up with a good answer. Didn't have one. Time to deflect. "If Mom finds out you've been in another fight, she'll ground you again. You know she will, probably longer than the last time.

She looked at me with a straight, tight grin, blinked three times, to let me know she'd just got the best of me— again. "Okay, now can I go turn cartwheels?"

Hmmm. Either she didn't think she'd get grounded or she didn't care. The little snoot. Mom was right. Brook needed to go to law school. Chuckling, I wished Dad had been here for this learning session. He would've gotten a kick out of Brook besting her big brother.

I walked back in the house and picked up my car keys to go to the lumberyard. As I was leaving, Blythe came in. "Hey, do you want to ride with me to the lumberyard?"

She scrunched up her nose. "Okay, but why are you going there with mayo in the corner of your mouth?"

I did a quick swipe. "Getting a slat for the fence. Brook kicked one out when she turned a cartwheel."

"Are you kidding me?" Blythe stammered. "She turned one in the living room last month and broke a lamp. Mom sent her outside to flip around. Now, no place is safe from the little snoot."

"That's what I just called her. The name must fit."

We drove to the lumberyard, and Blythe turned on the radio. I glanced over at her. "I'm really proud of you for writing the sports column in the high school newspaper. Not many girls would get that opportunity."

"Some of the students didn't want a girl to be the sports writer. They didn't think I could do the job. Heck, I've learned more in sixteen years about sports, especially football, than most boys."

"Mom said you got an award for writing an article about my high school coach Ronnie Mancuso. What did you write about?"

"Most of the article portrayed Coach as a positive role model for his players. He's tough on them, but fair. Did you know he still talks about you?"

"Really?" I checked the rearview mirror before changing lanes. "What did he say?"

"He said you would charge hell with a bucket of ice water if one of the coaches asked you to. What does that mean, anyway?"

I smiled. "It means I'd do whatever it took to win." Coach Mancuso was a true mentor. The players respected him. We played our guts out for the man.

"Enough about me. What about you? Mom said you want to be a TV reporter for college football."

She nodded. "Yes. That's what I'm going to do." She changed channels on the radio—a sports network no less.

I started to tell her sports reporting was exclusively for male broadcasters, but I thought how Dad would've responded to her dreams. "Blythe, that's great. Nothing would make me prouder than seeing my little sister on the sidelines interviewing players and coaches. That job's a perfect fit. You practiced on me for years. Just think, Blythe Pepperman, the first female sideline broadcaster in history. Go for it."

There was nothing I could have said that would have boosted her ego more. My responsibility would be to keep that desire burning and make sure her dream came true. I worried about being so far from home and missing opportunities to talk about her goals. Phone calls helped, but it wasn't the same as being there.

About a mile from the lumberyard, we passed two joggers on the side of the road. Blythe put her right hand out the window and airplaned. "I'm going to lay out a running program for you and Tony Helmsly. Follow my routine, both of you will be in great shape. Now, I know weightlifting is important, but you and Tony need to stretch before and after you lift. If you don't, you won't be flexible. Oh, and you must run at least three miles every day to improve your cardio-vascular system. Just so you won't cheat, I'll ride my bike along with you."

How did she know all this?

She reached over and tapped my shoulder—make that a poke. I think she wanted my attention. "I need to remind you of something."

An annoying tire advertisement came on the radio. I turned it down. "Okay, what is it?"

"You're going to be at Nanny's this summer, and she'll feed you homemade bread. You can't eat too much of it, or you'll be overweight when fall practice begins. Coach Fulton won't like that."

I scratched my head and laughed. "Did Coach tell you that?"

"Of course not. I just know what you need to do to control your weight."

Maybe she needed to be a trainer instead of a sportscaster.

Several hours after my conversation with Blythe, I drove down Passaic Avenue past the high school. Senior year memories flooded my mind. I thought about Laura Pomroy and my heart quickened. I'd already called her and we were going to the lake tomorrow with a group of friends. One guy had a boat and water skiing was planned. I had to be careful and not get hurt. No fancy tricks, just straight line skiing.

But first on my list was to see Glynna Helmsly at Gloria's Diner. Pulling into the parking lot, I could see the small strip of grass needed some TLC. Brown spots indicated someone didn't do their watering job. And, sticker heads were popping up. Big Mamma would never have let that happen when I worked there.

One week when I hadn't cut the grass, Glynna set me straight. "Big Boy, you didn't mow last week. You know better than that. Now get out there and do it." She popped me with a dishtowel and laughed. Although she made light of my dereliction of duty, I knew Big Mamma was dead serious.

Entering the diner I spotted Debra Theesfeld behind the counter talking to a customer and pouring his coffee. She pointed to the kitchen. I peaked around the corner. Big Mamma had her back to me as she took rolls of paper towels from the top of the cabinet. She was doing her best impression of Aretha Franklin singing "RESPECT." She was jiving and moving her hips, shoulders bouncing up and down, tapping her feet.

I came up behind her quiet and stealthy and placed my hands on her shoulders.

She whipped around and let out a scream that seemed to rattle the windows. "Lord, have mercy, Jim Pepperman." She placed her hand over her heart and did a little pitter-patter. Then she smiled and opened her arms. "Give your Big Mamma a hug."

Before I could get my arms around her, she lifted me off the floor and gave me a bear squeeze. Keep in mind, I hovered around two-hundred-fifty pounds. Big Mamma was one strong woman, and I loved every ounce of her.

Mom was my first resource when it came to helping raise Blythe and Brook, but Glynna helped too. Sometimes the girls had acted horrible when I'd kept them while Mom was at night school. Glynna said,

"Honey, they just want attention. Give them some of your sweet time." Big Mamma was right. The girls just needed my companionship. Glynna understood children and their emotional needs — another reason I admired this woman.

I left Glynna's. Jeff Langdon was next on my list of friends to see. I knew without a doubt, he'd have more off-the-wall stories to tell than a barber on Saturday morning.

CHAPTER 28

Driving down Washington Avenue I saw Jeff Langdon coming out of the police station. Sloppy sweatshirt, faded jeans, and worn out shoes were still a trademark for ol' Hog. Jeff's dad was still the Chief of Police in Belleville. I pulled over to the curb, leaned out the car window, and hollered, "Hey, did you just get out of jail?"

Jeff angled his head and squinted like he'd never seen me before. "Do I know you? You sound like some country bumpkin from Oklahoma."

"Get in the car. I'll make you think country bumpkin."

We went to O'Reilly's Pub to catch up. Jeff was a National Merit Scholar and could have gone to any university in America, but he chose Yale. He was the antithesis of most of the preppies attending that Ivy League school. I think he made his selection just to tick off the upper crust.

After ordering a couple of Budweisers, I kicked back in my chair. "So, what's been going on? I haven't heard from you in a couple of months. Fill me in."

Jeff took two large gulps of beer from the frosted mug, leaving froth on the end of his nose. "My GPA dropped so I had to study more. My National Merit Scholarship wasn't in jeopardy, but my grades needed to improve. And . . . I had to see the Dean of Student Affairs."

I cupped my hand over my mouth to hide my grin, knowing this was a story to enjoy. "Okay, what stupid thing did you do?"

Jeff's body stiffened. "It wasn't stupid. Actually, I was quite proud of myself."

"Go on."

"Mid-terms were coming up, and I had a C in Economics. I had to make an A on the mid just to pull a B."

I shook my finger at him. "You got caught cheating, didn't you?"

"I'm not an imbecile. I don't have to cheat."

He took another gulp of beer and then belched. It was two-toned, high and low pitches that seemed to harmonize. I had no idea how he managed to do that.

Jeff continued. "I went to study in a tavern around the corner from my apartment. The oldest bar in New Haven. The benches gave you splinters in your rear if you crossed your legs." He stretched his neck upward and belched again. That absurd eruption was more mellow, not as robust as the other one.

"Dang it, Jeff. Quit belching. It wouldn't happen if you'd stop guzzling."

He poised his chin in a pious way. "I need to belch."

"Why?" I asked.

"It keeps me from passing gas."

I took a deep breath, stared at him, and shook my head. "Get back to your story. You're still as crude as ever."

Jeff tapped his finger on the side of his mug. "Two hours passed and my notes started making sense. I even took time to memorize the label on the Budweiser bottle. I learned it verbatim. Do you want me to recite it for you?"

"No, stupid."

"Too bad. 'This is the famous Budweiser beer. We know of no brand produced by any other brewer which costs so much to brew and age. Our exclusive beech wood aging produces a taste, a smoothness, and a drinkability you will find in no other beer at any price.'"

"How many beers did you drink before you learned it?"

"That's not the point. What you must understand was Budweiser boosted my brain power. I aced the exam and made a B in the course. I also realized if I'd gone to class and turned in my work, I wouldn't have been in that predicament."

I extended both hands, pushing outward. "Whoa. You had to see the Dean for studying in a bar?"

Jeff began to squirm. His body language told me something really dumb happened. "No. I told two of my classmates the omnipotent powers of Budweiser. Then a stroke of genius came over me. I decided to form a social club known as the *Knights of the Golden Nectar*.

"To be a member you had to recite the Budweiser label verbatim, and you only got two tries. Now, the initiation part. You had to save all your beer cans and put them in the back seat of your car. When the empties were level with the front seat, you were knighted and sworn into the *Knights of the Golden Nectar*."

Chuckling, I continued. "Didn't the car start to stink after a while?"

Jeff tilted his head, brows arched in a condescending way. "Not if you like the smell of beer."

I couldn't hold back any longer. I crossed my arms in front of me, laid my head down and busted out laughing so hard my jaws cramped. After getting my face straight I said, "Tell me about the swearing-in ceremony."

"Get this, Pepperman. I made a perfect sword out of a broom handle, black electrician's tape, and ten beer cans crushed firm against the shaft. Trust me, it was an artistic masterpiece. The Knights were then dubbed into the order of the Golden Nectar. It was my proudest moment."

Jeff continued. "Next I took the pop-top rings and made me a crown. My design for the headpiece was outstanding. I wove several black shoestrings in and out of the pop-top holes, making two rows of metal rings that fit my head. Then . . . picture this. I attached two pop-tops together end-to-end and glued them four inches apart all the way around the band. It was magnificent. Do you want me to make you one?"

I lowered my head. "I . . . don't . . . think . . . so. Okay, where does the Dean of Student Affairs come in?"

"I'm getting to that." Jeff talked on. "Two weeks after the economics test, I was driving back to my apartment from class when a dump truck pulled in front of me. I swerved to prevent a collision, hit the curb, and launched my car toward a house. Cans flew everywhere. It reminded me of flies swarming around honey. Have you ever been hit in the back of the head by thirty or forty airborne cans?"

"No. Go ahead."

"Well, I slammed on my brakes, and the car came to a stop just before I hit the house. A little old lady on the front porch fell out of her rocking chair. She got up, shook her fist at me, and hobbled into her house and called the cops."

"What happened next?" I questioned even though I had a good idea.

"When the campus cops arrived, they asked if I'd been drinking after they saw all the cans. As you know, I don't drive when I drink. One cop removed his sunglasses and asked what I was doing with all of those cans. I said I couldn't tell him. I was sworn to secrecy. He stared at me for a long time."

I gawked at Jeff as he continued his story.

"The other policeman asked me what I had on my head. I told him it was my crown. He said it looked like beer can pop tops linked together. I lifted my head and told him it was. In a voice dripping with sarcasm, he called me Your Highness and asked my name. I told him King Jeffrey. They were so peeved they took me to the Dean of Student Affairs."

I had to ask. "You did take your crown off before you went to the Dean's office, right?"

Jeff looked insulted. His eyes widened and his lips parted. "Of course not."

"Why would you wear that thing into his office?" I asked.

He looked at me quizzically. "I've already told you. It was a thing of beauty."

I slapped my hands together and laughed so hard I almost peed my pants. The bartender waved a towel. "Hey, Pepperman, quiet it down over there. You're not in a pasture in Oklahoma."

I raised my hand indicating I understood, then whispered, "Okay, tell me about the Dean."

"The police officers had me sit outside his office for about five minutes. One of the policemen motioned for me to come in. The Dean was sitting behind a large oak desk. He had a big, bushy red moustache and wore round wire-framed glasses. Dean Schrib was a combination of Teddy Roosevelt and Wyatt Earp. I didn't know if he was going to counsel me or shoot me."

By now I was thoroughly engrossed in this melodrama.

"Dean Schrib stared at me. The look on his face was not conducive to a pleasant outcome. He motioned me to sit directly in front of him. He asked me to explain in my own words what took place today. Then he instructed me to remove . . . his words . . . whatever that thing was on my head."

Jeff waved two fingers toward the bartender to order more drinks. "I told the Dean everything . . . the reason for the beer cans, the Knights of the Golden Nectar. No detail was left out. As the story unfolded Dean Schrib had a slight grin. He looked amused, but said I was disrespectful when the officer asked for my name. I agreed. Then he asked me to consider what would have happened if I'd had an at-fault accident, and the newspaper found out about all the beer cans in my car."

Jeff balanced his chair on the two back legs. "I told him it would have been a poor reflection on Yale. Dean Schrib nodded and said I was correct.

"The Dean lowered his head and peered at me over his wire-framed glasses. He said he wouldn't put me on disciplinary probation if I agreed to pick up trash around the campus for two weekends. He wouldn't even tell my parents. I thought that was fair."

The suspense was more than I could take. "What about the pop-top crown?"

Jeff stood, raised both arms straight up making a touchdown signal. "Dean Schrib took it. I think he wanted to wear it that weekend."

My face turned red, my teeth clinched, trapped air gathered in my bulging cheeks. I gasped from lack of oxygen. Jeff's life was one hilarious stunt after another. I'd been blessed by this fun-loving character.

Someone told me the difference between a person with a low I.Q. and a genius was one brain cell. I thought Jeff just proved that theory was correct. One less brain cell and he would have been an idiot.

CHAPTER 29

ON THE WALK UP TO LAURA POMROY'S HOUSE, MY KNEES quivered, my heart rate quickened, and sweat popped out on my forehead. I stumped my toe on the porch step and almost fell down.

I'd loved Laura since the first summer we met four years ago. I loved her and she needed to know why. I couldn't imagine the rest of my life with anyone else, but we needed a serious dating relationship first. Telling her would be a monumental challenge. A challenge I didn't know if I could handle. What if she shot me down? My ego could take it, but could my heart?

We'd seen each other several times the past few weeks, but always with friends. At Gloria's Diner, the lake, Casale's Lemon Ice.

What was wrong with me? I faced the biggest and toughest football players in the country every week and never got jitters this bad. She was just one little ol' girl, and I was so nervous I couldn't think straight.

I looked at her front door. Snap out of it, Jim. Man-up. Push the darn doorbell.

Mr. Pomroy met me at the door. He was a nice guy, and I couldn't help smile. He looked like the dad on *Leave it to Beaver*.

"Hey, Jim, come on in and have a seat."

I plopped onto the sofa in their living room, still working out how I would say what I needed to say to Laura. How would I get her to understand how much I cared for her and wanted a future with her?

Mr. Pomroy sat across from me in a lounge chair adjusting his glasses. "How's your summer going? Are you working out and getting ready for this fall?"

"Yes sir. I've been running and lifting weights." I patted my gut. "Eating my grandmother's homemade bread all summer won't make the coaches happy."

"Maybe you should eat less or run more."

His small talk wasn't doing anything for my nerves. "I hate running for conditioning. Cutting down on the hot rolls may be my best option."

Laura's dad filled his pipe bowl and lit the cherry wood aroma tobacco. "Who does Oklahoma open with?"

"SMU." My tepid voice cracked. I bet that impressed him. This was going so well already and Laura hadn't even come out.

"Is OU going to have a good team this year?"

His questions felt like an interrogation. "Yes, sir. We're going to be good."

Laura walked into the living room, her summer tan set off by a white blouse and blue shorts. Her toes peeked out of a pair of white sandals. Miss America couldn't have looked better. My heart was going ka-boom, ka-boom. Her dad's questions forgotten, I couldn't keep my eyes off her.

Laura greeted me with a smile. I couldn't tell if she missed me, too.

I stood up to greet her, and my belt snagged a button on the couch cushion, and it came with me when I stepped toward her.

Mr. Pomroy exhaled a puff of smoke and grinned. "I like you, son, but not enough to let you have my sofa."

Laura placed the tips of her fingers on her lips. Her eyes sparkled, obviously amused.

Why was it when I tried to impress her, I made a fool of myself? I tried to unhook the cushion, but needed Laura's help. I couldn't get us out the house fast enough.

I watched her as we walked to the car. "Your dad must think I'm a total spaz."

She hooked her arm in mine. "Dad thinks you're the best football player he's ever seen."

I drove us down Union Avenue to Casale's Lemon Ice and tried to calm my emotions. We talked, but for the life of me, I couldn't remember anything either of us said.

Once inside Casale's, I tried to be calm, but my anxiety returned. The rapid heartbeat pounded in my ears. I picked a booth near the back for privacy, and we sat facing each other. The soft lighting gave her an angelic look. I was mesmerized by her beautiful, brown eyes. She had character and self-confidence. I couldn't find a single flaw in her. I'd dated pretty girls at OU, but none ever stacked up to Laura.

"How's nursing school this year?" My legs bounced like a jack hammer.

She pushed her hair to the side. "It's going well. I love the medical field."

"What do you like best?"

Laura put her elbows on the table and rested her chin on the top of her hands. "Surgical nursing. I didn't think I would like the operations with the blood, but once I got past the initial shock, I found it fascinating."

"Okay. That was an easy question. What do you dislike about nursing?"

"Bedpans."

We both laughed. Laura's chuckle was a perfect match for her personality, cute and sweet.

"My turn. What do you like best about football?" She took a sip of her soda.

I scraped the top of the Lemon Ice with my spoon. "My teammates. The brotherhood I have with those guys is special. The hard work, the disappointing losses, and the victories develop a bond that's unique."

She angled her head. "Okay. What do you dislike about football?"

"Displeasing my coaches, especially Coach Fulton."

Laura bit down on her lower lip. "That's an interesting answer, but why Coach Fulton?"

I felt more relaxed and leaned back against the booth. "He reminds me of my dad, the way he holds me accountable for my actions, and he's always there for me if I need to talk."

Laura nodded. "What do you want to do after college?"

"If I'm fortunate enough to be drafted by the NFL, I want to give professional football a try. I'll graduate with a math degree, but want to go back and study civil engineering."

"I think you'll be drafted. When you play on television, I'll point at the screen, tell my friends that I know that guy because we went to high school together." She clasped her hands and smiled. "Becoming an engineer is something you can definitely do. You have a bright future. I'm sure of that."

My hands rested on the table. She reached over and touched them.

Perfect time for me to speak up. My anxiety mellowed, "Laura, I want to tell you something about—."

Laura pushed her drink to the side and softly clapped. "Oh, I've got something to tell you first."

"Okay, shoot." Man, I was ready to tell her what had been bottled up inside me for years. Be patient. Be patient.

"I'm seeing a guy at school, and I really like him."

Whoa. What did she say? Another guy. That couldn't be happening. I placed my doubled up fist under the table.

"He has a slow southern drawl that I love, and he's such a gentleman. The first time I met him, he reminded me of you."

He reminded her of me? She ripped my heart out. All this time I've been nothing but a friend. How could I have been so foolish to have fallen for her? My disappointment was replaced with anger. Had to get control of myself. Calm down.

"Jim, sorry I cut you off. What were you going to say?"

I took a deep breath, licking my lips. "It was nothing." I shook my head. "Nothing important. Just . . . Oklahoma's Engineering School. Boring stuff."

I'd only felt this low one other time in my life, and that was at Dad's funeral. It was time for me to move on.

The date didn't last long.

After taking Laura home, I was too ticked to go back to my house. I drove to a picnic area in the city park and chose a table by a tree, next to a street light. But I couldn't even sit. The park was quiet, too quiet, except for the chirping of crickets and a single car passing by with music escaping from a rolled down window.

Steam built inside my chest like an old boiler ready to explode. I left the table and walked through the playground, flinging the wooden seat on the closest swing. The chain clanked on the support pole and wrapped around it—twisted, like my relationship with Laura.

She was playing with my heart—teasing me—leading me on. Why didn't I see what she was doing? I took her snapshot from my billfold where it had been since I left for college. I gazed longingly at first, then despised it. I tossed the photo in the trash can. Laura Pomroy was out of my life for good. With a kick from my right foot, the trash can absorbed the force of my disappointment.

I got to my car and jammed the key into the ignition. Then it hit me. I'd never so much as hinted to Laura my true feelings. I was a jerk, thinking only of myself, and blaming her for our friendship not developing.

I stared in the rear view mirror. My reflection seemed to say "You're a fool, Jim Pepperman, and you got what you deserved. Get out of the car, go find the picture, and thank God for bringing Laura into your life."

I picked up the rubbish and the dented can, regretting my stupid, juvenile actions, and searched through the trash. But I couldn't find her picture.

Something drew me to the picnic table and when I walked over, there was her picture, on the table, illuminated by the streetlight. How had it gotten there? I knew I'd watched it flutter into the trash container.

A cool breeze slashed through the night air and rattled the tree branches with one, short burst. I'd felt that breeze so many times at the cemetery.

"Dad . . . are you here? Did you put the picture on the table?"

Laura didn't know about the park incident. No one knew, except maybe Dad. If it had been him there that night.

CHAPTER 30

TONY HELMSLY AND I HAD SPENT MOST OF OUR SUMMER together running, lifting weights, getting prepared for fall football practice. We followed Blythe's workout schedule. We had no option. She was with us every day.

Our college football careers would finish at the end of this season. Tony had already been named All-American from Notre Dame, and I was certain he'd be drafted by the NFL. It was important for me to have a great year and be selected by a pro team. How else could I pay for Blythe and Brook's college?

When summer ended, I was more than ready to head back to Norman for fall semester of my last year.

The first day of practice each player had to weigh in. I was concerned what the scales would reveal. I'd backed off my training and was afraid my diet wasn't what it should've been. Hope I didn't have to pay for being stupid.

I eased onto the scales in the locker room, cutting my anxious eyes Coach Fulton's way.

The veins popped on his neck. His face turned scarlet and one fist was doubled as he slapped the balance weight on the scales. "Pepperman, two-hundred-sixty-pound linebackers won't cut it. You are one biscuit away from being a defensive tackle. You're with me after practice every day until you lose ten pounds."

I knew what that meant. This wasn't going to be a casual jog in the park.

The players behind me he-hawed and snorted. Jerks.

My actual weight was two-fifty-six. Coach rounded up, and from that day forward my teammates and coaches called me Biscuit. Olendorf and Pod took it a step further and dubbed me Dough Boy.

The first day after practice Coach Fulton's eyebrows knotted, and he hissed through his clenched teeth. "Stadium bleachers."

The first time up my breathing was heavy. Then my calves cramped, hard as rocks, and my thighs burned, pleading for relief. Going down, I caught my breath, but the pain persisted.

Olendorf, J. Mo, and Pod followed me to the bleachers. "Ten pounds, Dough Boy. Ten pounds." They laughed their buns off as I struggled to run the steep incline of Owen Field.

I thought my buddies would be more supportive. I wouldn't laugh at them. Well, maybe I would. Olendorf and Pod could stand to lose a few pounds. Why wasn't Coach making them run?

The third day of my weight-loss routine Coach Fulton caught up with my three hecklers, "Okay, Bozo's, you think it's funny? Why don't you join Biscuit the next time he goes up? Olendorf, you go down to section 2, Podzinsky, section 4, J. Mo, 6."

I'd never seen anyone high-tail it to the field house as fast as those three stooges. They reminded me of the 1920 Keystone Cop movies running in fast forward.

Coach laughed at my buddies. "I never intended for them to run, but I wanted to get them off your back."

After four days of running steps, my weight dropped under two-fifty, and I think Coach Fulton's blood pressure returned to normal.

The seniors entered our last football season. We had talent, but talent alone doesn't win games. The team had to prove itself again every single Saturday.

All of us knew something special awaited the 1971 Sooners. My advice to all of our opponents — strap it on tight. We were good, butt-kicking good.

The brutal autumn practices began. The coaches pushed us beyond our limits — or — so we thought. We ran exhausting sprints across the field. The ninety-degree weather and high humidity made my lungs want to collapse. The contact drills were vicious. The intensity of these workouts caused fights to break out, and the coaches had to separate the combatants.

By September 10th, the date of our first game against SMU, we were tired of beating up each other in practice. The Crimson and Cream took it out on the Mustangs. Sooner victory, 30 to 0.

We won our first three games over SMU, Pitt, and USC and were on a roll. Paul McGlendon quarterbacked our offense to perfection, and our defense played equally well. But, Coach Fulton, being a consummate perfectionist, would rail against the defense if we allowed two first downs in any given series.

James Morley, a.k.a. J. Mo, was the other inside line-backer next to me. He was tough as rawhide and could run like a deer, but he couldn't catch a football. He'd had opportunities in the games against Pitt and USC to intercept passes, but he muffed every attempt.

Although things were tense during games, there were some light-hearted moments in practice. One day J. Mo dropped a pass thrown right to him. Coach took off his cap and slung it across the field. I swear it made a whoosh, whoosh sound, like a helicopter.

"J. Mo," Coach Fulton bellowed, "You're the only human on earth to have hands made by U. S. Steel. Why can't you intercept the frigging ball? When it hits your hands it reminds me of a bullet ricocheting off a Sherman tank. You . . . you're going to cause me to commit Hara-kiri."

J. Mo looked at me, shrugged his shoulders, and asked in his Jamaican accent, "What's Hara-kiri?"

The Monday following the USC game we lined up to stretch. I glanced at J. Mo and did a double take. I couldn't believe my eyes. He wore round-framed sunglasses under his helmet. He looked like one of the *Three Blind Mice*.

"What the heck are you doing?" I asked.

"Not to worry, mon," J. Mo proudly said. "My ortho-dontist said the sun was too bright for my eyes. That's the reason I'm not intercepting the passes."

I laughed and we continued to stretch. "First of all, your eye doctor is not called an orthodontist. He's an optometrist, you bonehead."

He spat through his face mask, exposing his snaggled-toothed grin. "Whatever, mon. I have a note from him explaining my problem."

I poked him on the arm. "You better take those things off before Coach sees you, or he's going to explode."

After warm-ups, we broke into position groups. J. Mo and I stood behind three other linebackers when Coach Fulton noticed him. Coach squinted and licked his upper lip. "J. Mo, take off your helmet."

Slowly, he did as Coach asked. His Afro sprang upward like a thousand tightly coiled springs.

Coach Fulton lowered his head and folded his arms. "I know there must be a reason you're wearing those sunglasses, so why don't you explain."

J. Mo beamed as he placed his helmet under one arm. "You see, Coach, my sunglass doctor, Dr. Shades, said I missed all those interceptions because my eyes were sensitive to the light. He said I would never drop another pass if I had my special glasses on."

"I see," Coach said as he rubbed his nose with his index finger and thumb. "Where did you find out about Dr. Shades?"

The free-spirited Jamaican adjusted his dark glasses. "He has a commercial on TV every night."

Fulton removed his hat, scratched his head. "Now that Dr. Shades helped your eyesight, did he recommend Dr. Steelfingers to help you catch?"

"Really, Coach, is there such a doctor who can do that?" He put his hands in the air and flexed his fingers like the Tin Man from the *Wizard of Oz*.

Coach Fulton exhaled, shook his head, and grinned. "Give me those glasses. Line up for drills." Coach gave J. Mo a friendly pat on the helmet.

A couple of guys snickered. Some started to chuckle. Soon everyone laughed so loud the guys across the field stopped what they were doing and looked in our direction. I'm sure they thought we were crazy when we patted each other on our helmets like Coach did to J. Mo.

There was no Dr. Shades. J. Mo made that up just to put a burr in Coach Fulton's underwear. Being around J. Mo, you'd think he'd been down on too many kickoffs and had brain damage. When actually, he was smart. Smarter than most of the team.

We all loved the wild Jamaican, especially Coach. J. Mo's infectious attitude motivated us for our game the following Saturday. Heated rivalry. The University of Texas. Time to turn it up a notch.

CHAPTER 31

THERE WAS A CHILL IN THE AIR AS I WALKED TO THE DORM AFTER the team practice. I snapped my letter jacket and thrust my hands into the pockets. Leaves swirled around my feet and crunched under my shoes. Autumn football weather.

Game week—arch rival—The University of Texas. I loved this game.

I headed to my room and flipped on the radio to Rock and Roll channel 1520 AM, KOMA in Oklahoma City.

The D. J. was talking about Saturday's contest. "Sooner fans, here's a little trivia. The first game between OU and Texas was in 1900. Just a thought . . . was the Cotton Bowl in Dallas the original site of this contest? Let's ask the sports guru here at the station."

There was a pause.

"No, the guru confirms the Cotton Bowl wasn't the original site. Well, when was the first game played there? He's looking it up. . . . 1932."

I laid my jacket on the bed and turned up the volume.

The disc jockey continued. "The loser of this game has to wait a full year to get even. Make no mistake, bragging rights are significant. Enough talk, here's a tune you guys have been requesting all night. It's an oldie, but goodie. Chuckles, Chuck Berry and *Johnnie B. Goode*."

The D. J. was correct. Bragging rights. It was time to break the losing streak against Texas. We had to win. The OU-Texas weekend was a big deal. If you didn't believe me, try to get a hotel room or a dinner reservation in Dallas.

The game was called the Red River Rivalry because the Red River separated Oklahoma and Texas. To say the two universities didn't like each other wouldn't be strong enough — hate was a more accurate word.

The teams always spent the night in Dallas before the game. Our hotel location was supposed to be a secret to the public. But some Longhorn fans discovered the site and drove by all night honking and shouting "Hook 'em Horns."

I didn't sleep much. Not because of the loud noise. Because of nerves.

Fear of failure tied me in knots so tight I could barely breathe. I was afraid I'd let my teammates and coaches down. I wished Dad were here. He'd know how to settle me down.

My stomach was queasy as I boarded the bus taking us from the hotel to the stadium. One last chance for me to beat Texas. What if we lost again?

No, no, had to think positive. Get rid of the negative stuff. Dad would've told me to believe in myself. I choked back my anxiety with a hard swallow and deep breaths.

It had rained earlier that morning, and the temperature hovered just above freezing. Both squads used the same tunnel from the locker rooms to the field. OU was the visiting team. We exited the lockers first. Texas followed. Once both teams hit the field, verbal taunts and insults erupted.

A big Texas lineman stared me down. "Fifty-five, you SOB. I'm taking you out."

I flipped him the bird.

OU jogged to the north goal posts to warm-up. The flags in the stadium whipped around the steel poles. The Cotton Bowl reminded me of the Roman Coliseum, and I felt like a gladiator preparing to do battle. Those warriors faced death. My situation might be a little less fatal, but that didn't alter my anxiety.

Jeers from the Texas fans intensified the knots in my gut. White puffs steamed from my nose and mouth. My mind flashed back to watching the Texas Tech game when I was seven and the black stallion snorting his breath into the cold air.

I remembered how much I'd wanted to play for Texas. Longhorn paraphernalia filled my room and closet. The rips in my burnt orange Texas sweatshirt resulted from backyard football games with my buddies on Saturday afternoons. But life was fickle and led me instead to Oklahoma.

I looked up at the press box as the team stretched. A small patch of fog engulfed the structure. The low hanging cloud dimmed the lights and made the silhouettes inside appear ghostly.

I took a deep breath and tried to relax. If I could make it to kick-off, my overloaded nerves would calm.

After warm-up, we had to weave our way through the Longhorn band to get back to the locker room. Coach Fulton and I always came off the field together and discussed defensive schemes, but the band separated us.

I searched the locker room but couldn't find him. I needed to review my formation calls. We had ten minutes before returning to the field. Questions cluttered my overactive mind.

"Pepperman, get over here." Coach Fulton's raspy voice came from the entrance to the locker room. His pants were dirty and soaking wet. Muddy grass covered the top of his clipboard.

I hurried over to him. "Coach, what happened?"

He brushed the excess moisture from his jacket sleeve. "I bent down to tie my shoe and a blasted Texas tuba player tripped and fell on top of me." Coach picked up a towel to blot the water from his play sheet.

My teeth clamped onto my lower lip. I wanted to bust out laughing but knew better. "Are you okay?"

"Yeah, but that guy was big. I think he busted my rib."

I imagined every time I looked to the sideline to get our signals, I'd picture my linebacker coach getting pancaked by a Longhorn tuba player. That was funny. Bust-a-gut funny.

The first half both offenses controlled the game. If we wanted to win, we had to do a better job of executing our defensive strategy. The game would be determined by the team who forced the most turnovers and made the fewest mistakes.

With 3:29 left in the fourth quarter, OU led 41-27. A comfortable lead. But, another Texas touchdown would put them back in the game. They needed a first down to keep their drive alive. Our defense needed a stop. I wasn't going to let them come back and beat us. Not this year. No way.

On third down their quarterback dropped back to pass. Ol' Steelfingers J. Mo drifted into his zone coverage. I watched the ball as it left the quarterback's hand.

Time slowed.

The ball spiraled toward a wide open tight end. Just as the Texas receiver was about to make the catch, J. Mo stepped in front of him. His hands were in a perfect position to make the interception.

"Catch it. Catch it," I shouted.

The ball went through J. Mo's outstretched hands, bounced off his helmet, careened upward about ten feet, turning end over end. He raced to the out-of-control ball to make a second attempt to secure it. And caught it. At the twenty-five yard line, he tucked the ball under his left arm and sprinted down the sideline.

"Seventy-five yards away. Run, you brick-fingered Jamaican! Run!" I raised both arms and sprinted toward him. My fists were pumping up and down like pistons in a Formula One racing car.

Clods of mud and grass flew from J. Mo's water soaked cleats. He left a trail of would be tacklers behind. Was he fast enough? Could he do it?

My adrenalin spiked so high I was surprised my heart didn't explode. "Score, J. Mo. Score."

As he reached the seven yard line, a Longhorn player drove him to the ground. Our entire team jumped up and down, screamed, and slapped each other on our shoulders. Even though Texas stopped him, if we could control the ball for the next three minutes, we'd win. The chains of defeat that had shackled us for the past few years would be broken.

I unfastened the chin strap of my helmet and raced to Coach Fulton, picked him up and shouted, "We did it, Coach. We did it."

J. Mo ran over too. "Coach Fulton, see Dr. Shades' glasses conditioned my eyes to make the interception."

"Yeah, and thank God, the ball took a favorable bounce off your helmet." Coach laughed and gave him a bear hug.

Three plays later McGlendon scored on a quarterback keeper assuring the victory. So far, that was the proudest moment of my college career. Oklahoma-48. Texas-27.

CHAPTER 32

We all knew the importance of our Thanksgiving Day showdown with the Nebraska Cornhuskers. Not only the Big Eight title awaited the winner, but the #1 national ranking in the polls was at stake. The Cornhuskers were defending National Champions and ranked #1. The Sooners #2. If we won that game and went undefeated the rest of the season, the top ranking would belong to us, and maybe the National Championship.

The buildup to this year's contest was huge. Reporters had filled the Student Union and interviewed many of our players. A Sports Illustrated reporter spent a great deal of time talking to me, his questions stupid. Did I think OU would win? Did I have respect for the Nebraska players? Was I nervous?

The truth was the hype wasn't intimidating. Our team was confident, but that didn't diminish the respect we had for Nebraska.

Head Coach Aderholt entered from the back of the room. His strong gait commanded respect, reminding me of those World War II movies when a high ranking officer addressed his pilots before bombing raids over Germany.

"Men, I don't have to tell you the importance of this game. You know what we have to do. I have no doubt the outcome will be a victory if we focus every minute of every workout leading up to Thursday's kickoff."

Coach Aderholt took off his glasses and laid them on the podium. "We have home field advantage and our fans will be loud. If you can't get excited about this game, you're dead and don't know it."

His comment brought a chuckle from the team.

"Listen up.´ He cleared his throat. "The news media has been here all week. You've handled that distraction well. I have an advanced copy of this week's Sports Illustrated I want you to see." He held up the magazine.

The cover was a picture of me nose-to-nose with Nebraska running back Joe Orsen. The headline read: Irresistible Oklahoma Meets Immovable Nebraska.

I could feel my face flush and sensed everyone looking at me. That wasn't right. The game wasn't about me. I shouldn't be on the cover.

Coach Aderholt continued, "I want to get this distraction out of the way. Being fair to the team, this game's not about one individual. Jim, I know you had nothing to do with this. Sports Illustrated asked if they could use one of our guy's pictures on the cover. I drew your name out of a hat."

"Biscuit, Biscuit," the team laughed and shouted. This put a light mood on the team meeting. Just what we needed.

Coach picked up a piece of chalk and turned to the blackboard. "There are three things we have to do to win." He wrote:

1. Control the line of scrimmage on offense
    and defense

2. No mental errors

3. Force turnovers

Coach Fulton took the defense to our separate meeting room. He was usually in a lighthearted mood on Sundays and joked around, but not today. Coach turned on the projector, and we studied the Cornhusker offensive personnel. It didn't take us long to realize these guys were great athletes and well coached. To beat them would take our best effort.

Thanksgiving Day No. 1 versus No. 2. The sports writers called it the "Game of the Century." Every college football player lived to take part in a game like that.

Our fans stomped their feet sending vibrations into the stadium. Their piercing screams reverberated through the stands onto the field. The guy next to me said something. I saw his lips move, but the words never reached my ears. My heart pounded so hard I could feel throbbing in my neck.

This battle was more colossal than I anticipated. How was I blessed enough to play in a game of this magnitude?

Nebraska won the coin toss and chose to kick off.

Our first possession McGlendon and the offense failed to make a first down. We punted.

John Roberts, a brilliant Nebraska receiver, caught the ball and returned the punt. In his attempt to run up the field, he changed directions at least three times, evading the Oklahoma tacklers. He burst through the middle of the field for a seventy-two yard run.

Touchdown Nebraska.

When our defense took the field for the first time, I looked across the line of scrimmage. Their linemen had thick ankles, huge calves, and legs that looked like telephone poles. Their heads completely filled the helmets. When they snapped the ball, the guard charged out to block me. We made contact.

After the play, Nebraska's No. 60 grunted. "You're in for a long day, Pepperman."

"I ain't going anywhere," I fired back.

That guy was quick, strong, half-man, half-monster. At two hundred fifty pounds I matched up with most of the competition. But, today this player gave me all the trouble I wanted and then some.

OU took the lead on McGlendon's passing and running skills the first half. We walked to the locker room, and my body was drained of energy. My legs felt like rubber and cramped up. I grabbed a Gatorade. I didn't remember ever being this tired. My chin dripped blood because of #60's relentless attacks. My thoughts drifted back to the gladiators and their struggles in the arena. God, give me the courage to finish my battle. Half time — OU 17, Nebraska 14.

During the third and fourth quarters, the Huskers relied on their power running attack and went ahead 28-17. McGlendon and the potent Oklahoma offense retook the lead 31-28 with 7:05 left to play. The Sooners kicked off, and the Cornhuskers started their march to win the game.

After they made a first down, #60 bumped into me. "Told you it was going to be a long day."

"Hey, how's your nose?" I countered. "Having a hard time breathing?" At some point in the third quarter the Nebraska guard got his nose busted. Blood dripped out of both nostrils and stained his white jersey.

Ol' big boy liked to jaw. He tried to break my concentration by razzing me. It didn't work. I tried to break his concentration. On the next play I smashed my forearm to his facemask making him grimace. That didn't work either. He was a warrior, and his pain threshold high.

Oklahoma called time out and Coach Fulton gathered the defense around him. "Men, this is gut-check time. Don't let them drive the ball down the field. Suck it up for seven minutes, and we win this game."

Nebraska had possession at their own thirty-six yard line. Our defense refused to give up big yardage, but the Huskers still moved down the field. A referee called time out because of an injury to a Nebraska player.

I huddled the defense. "Okay, they're trying to run it down our throats. I'm not going to let that happen. We're going to stop these guys right now. Are you with me?" Every player accepted the challenge. I was proud to play with these brothers. I would fight for them, and they'd do the same for me.

The Nebraska offense moved the ball to the Oklahoma forty-eight yard line. Our defense prevented long runs, but they chipped away with short yardage gains.

I looked at J. Mo. "You're doing one heck of a job. Keep it up for five more minutes."

"No problem, mon. We've got this game won," he responded with his nonchalant attitude.

The Huskers broke the huddle, and No. 60 and I made direct eye contact. Come on, big boy. Give me your best shot. Come my direction, and I'll stuff your big tail right where you stand. I couldn't read his mind, but as sure as I stood on this field, he planned to do the same to me.

As he got down in his four-point stance, I noticed his body wasn't leaning forward like on previous running plays. He didn't have pressure on his hands and actually leaned back on his heels. He was going to pass protect for the quarterback. "Watch the pass. Watch the pass," I shouted to the secondary.

The ball was snapped. The quarterback faked to the running back and set up to throw to their best receiver, John Roberts. He caught the ball, broke several tackles and ran all the way to the fifteen yard line.

Now they had great field position. We had to hold them. This was our last chance.

The clock ran. Two minutes fifty seconds left in the "Game of the Century." Did we have it in us to stop them? The Nebraska offense broke the huddle, and I once more looked at #60. He kept his head down, but the way he dug in his cleats showed determination. Both exhausted teams were putting everything on the line.

Their center snapped the ball and the quarterback handed it off to their best running back Jack Tinney. He only made a couple of yards.

Three more chances. We could do this.

Tinney again carried the ball. His knees were churning as he ran at me. Ol' #60 reminded me of a ticked-off rodeo bull. He aimed directly at my chest. I lowered my body position, aligning my pads under his. I stopped his charge. After straightening him up, I pushed him aside and made contact with Tinney. We met head on. Wham! The contact sounded like a shotgun blast. He went down like a cow on ice.

Blurred vision resulted from the head-on collision. Shaking my head from side to side cleared the cobwebs. I turned to my teammates. "They're going to run the ball two more times. Suck it up, guys. Suck it up."

They ran toward J. Mo. He warded off the blocker and made a game-saving tackle on the one yard line. Fourth and one. Nebraska's last chance. Could we hold them?

In the background the crowd screamed, but I barely heard them.

The ball was snapped. Tinney took the handoff and swept around our left defensive end. More than one defender made contact with the tough ball carrier. The defense was drawn to the runner like steel to a magnet. Did he make it across the goal line?

The official tried to untangle the mass of humanity. He pulled and tugged on the players to see if the ball crossed the goal line. An eternity passed before he made a decision. Did we stop him?

The referee stood up, raised both arms above his head. Touchdown Nebraska.

I felt like I had been stabbed in the heart. We didn't do our job. Looking to the sideline, I could see Coach Fulton. He bent down on one knee, slammed his clipboard to the ground, snapping it in two. We let Coach down, and I didn't want to face him. I jogged off the field, head hung low.

Coach Fulton ran over to me. "Get your head up, son. You and the rest of the defense fought, fought hard. Sometimes you win the fight. Sometimes you lose. You've nothing to be ashamed of. I'm proud of you guys. Really proud."

With two minutes to go, OU's offense had one last chance, but failed to score. OU 31, Nebraska 35.

Football's a strange game. For three hours we battled our opponent, and then it was over. I sought out No. 60 and found him at the fifty yard line. "One heck of a game. Congratulations."

With a crooked nose and swollen eyes he looked at me. "Game could have gone either way. Today was our day, and we were fortunate. You are one bad German."

Shaking hands, we parted. As two gladiators, we faced the ultimate challenge on the football field, and both of us stood proud.

A sports writer from the Omaha World Herald said it best. "Neither team lost. Nebraska just scored four more points."

CHAPTER 33

WHAT AN UNBELIEVABLE YEAR FOR THE 1971 OKLAHOMA
football team. Coach Berry, the OU offensive coordina-
tor, perfected the wishbone offense that led the nation
in scoring and rushing yards. Our only loss came at the
hands of Nebraska. On New Year's Day, the Sooners
faced Auburn in the Sugar Bowl and won 40-22.

I continued my weight training and conditioning
program to prepare for the upcoming professional football draft. I needed to play at the next level to pay for
Blythe and Brook's college, and I wanted to play pro
ball because I thought I could. Make that, knew I could.

The weight room was unusually warm today. Sweat
trickled down my back and soaked my t-shirt as though
I'd been caught in a rain storm. I had a love-hate relationship with lifting. I knew it was necessary, but during
every workout, my body threatened to revolt from the
intense, hard work.

A graduate assistant approached me in the middle of
a bench press workout to let me know Coach Aderholt
wanted me in his office. Glad for the interruption, I
slipped on my warm-ups and headed upstairs.

Coach Fulton was seated on a crimson leather couch
next to the door. Aderholt waited at his desk, polishing

his glasses with the end of his tie. His serious blue eyes focused on me.

"Have a seat, Jim," he mumbled and pointed to the chair in front of him. "I have some news."

Icy prickles rippled through the back of my neck. Did something happen at home? Was one of the girls in an accident? Was Mom okay?

An easy smile broke out on Coach Aderholt's face, a total departure from when I walked into the room. He eased his glasses onto his narrow face. "The Associated Press released the All-American Team for 1971. You're first team linebacker."

I sat motionless. Numb. All-American? Really? Holy Toledo! The news hit hard and a flood of adrenaline washed away the numb, pushing me higher than a twelve-story window washer.

Coach Fulton got up from the sofa and gave me a man-hug like Dad would have done. "Proud of you, son. Congratulations."

Coach Aderholt shook my hand so hard it cracked my knuckles. "This is a great day for you, Jim, and the University of Oklahoma."

I stayed for a few minutes as the accolades continued. I couldn't wait to call Mom and the girls. My chest swelled. I walked with a confident swagger out of the coaches' office, my body almost levitating down the hall.

I ran down the stairs skipping every other step, showered, dressed, and stormed out the door. Inside my car I slapped the dashboard and shouted, "Yes! All-American!" Then sped out of the parking lot, probably a little too fast.

All-American. How many people could say that? How many football players could say that? The pros would be calling. I was good, really good. I'd be drafted in the first or second round.

A vision of Dad flashed in front of me. I sensed his presence, slowed down and pulled to the curb. It was as though Dad was warning me to back off with my ego rush.

My mind shifted to gratitude. I recalled the coaches who'd influenced my life. Coach Mancuso and Coach Fulton had a big part in my athletic development. My teammates at Oklahoma—there was no way for me to receive such an honor without them. I had been blessed with athletic abilities, but God deserved the credit for my accomplishments. He made all this possible.

I parked the car and ran to the dorm to call Mom. On a scale of one to ten, my excitement blew out of my chest at a fifteen. My hand shook as I dialed the number. "Come on, come on. . . . Answer."

"Hello." Mom's muffled tone sounded as though she was chewing on something.

"It's Jim."

Mom chuckled. "Yes, I recognized your voice."

I pushed back my chair and plopped my feet on the desk. "I made the Associated Press All-American Team. Coach Aderholt and Coach Fulton just told me."

Silence. Silence so loud it startled me.

"You made the All-American Team?" Mom's voice quivered. Then she screamed so loud I had to rip the phone from my ear. I heard her tell Blythe and Brook my good news.

Blythe's yell made it sound as though she was in my room. She got on the phone. "Jim, don't be kidding us. Really, did you make All-American?" Without giving me a chance to answer, she continued. "I want you to give me an interview and . . . and come to my school and sign autographs . . . and go to the newspaper and have your picture taken."

I lowered my legs and propped my elbows on the desk. "Whoa, Blythe. Okay. Now let me talk to Mom again." I heard another glass-breaking shriek as she handed the phone to Mom.

"Jim, I'm so proud of you." I sensed she was trying to muffle her sobs. "Hold on. Brook wants to talk."

"Hi, Jim. Blythe said you were an All-American. What does that mean?"

I wasn't sure what to say so that she would understand. I'd pass the buck to Mom. "Ah . . . ask Mom."

I overheard her say in a sassy, high pitched tone, "Jim doesn't know what an All-American is. He told me to ask you. I thought we were all Americans. What's the big deal?"

Leave it to nine-year-old Brook to put me in my place — the little squirt.

CHAPTER 34

THE 1972 NFL DRAFT NEARED. MY EMOTIONS SOARED HIGHER than Mount Everest. But what if I didn't get drafted? Or what if I got picked but wasn't good enough to make the team? I rode one emotion to another—having loads of confidence to none. Regardless, on Tuesday, February 1st, I'd have some answers.

Mom made my arrangements to fly home and watch the professional draft on TV. I made sure Coach Aderholt gave all the NFL teams my phone number in Belleville.

I called Mom to confirm my flight schedule to New Jersey. "Hey, Mom, my plane lands at Newark on Monday at 3:45 p.m."

"Okay. I'm taking off at noon." Papers shuffled in the background. Maybe she was anxious, too. "Oh, the Helmslys are coming over on Tuesday to wait for the calls. Glynna and I visit every day wondering which teams will pick our boys."

I looked at my watch. Time for class. "Mom, did Tony give the pro teams our number so they'll know where to contact him?"

"It's all been taken care of. They'll know where to reach him."

"Good. Got to go. Calculus in ten minutes. See you Monday. Tell the girls hello."

I woke on draft day to a loud *bang, bang, bang* on my bedroom door at home. I rubbed my eyes and tried to focus on the fuzzy green numbers on the clock. 7 a.m. I yawned and rolled over. "Blythe, give me a break. Stop pounding on the door."

"How did you know it was me?" she yelled outside the door.

"Who else would it be?" I shot back.

"Mom said to get up. What do you want for breakfast?"

I pulled the covers over my head, "Pancakes, ham and eggs, and a bowl of oatmeal."

"Hey, this isn't Gloria's Diner. You only get one choice." Her high pitched sarcasm was not appreciated.

I stretched. "Ham and eggs."

"We don't have any ham."

"Good grief. Whatever Mom cooks is fine."

"She's not cooking, too nervous."

I shook my head and chuckled. "Then why did you ask what I wanted if you knew Mom wasn't cooking?"

Silence. . . . "All we have are cornflakes and bananas," came a soft reply.

I picked up one of my shoes and hurled it at the door. She got my drift and scampered loudly down the stairs.

Mom arranged with the schools to let Blythe and Brook stay home for the draft. Glynna did the same for her clan. According to the newspaper and TV reports, the entire town was excited about the possibility of Tony and me being drafted.

I was a hundred percent sure Tony would be selected. I hoped the same for me. Tony said Pittsburgh and Denver had shown interest in him. He wanted Pittsburgh because it was closer to home. I didn't care what team wanted me—I wanted them. Any signing bonus would be enough to get the girls a start on their education.

At 11:45, the Helmslys pulled into the driveway. Burl and Earl were the first out of the car. I hid behind the door to wait for my little eight-year-old buddies. They busted through hollering, "Big Boy, where are you?"

I grabbed the two from behind, and wrestled them to the floor, surprised with their size and strength as they tried to get away.

"Stop, Big Boy, I'm about to pee my pants," Burl pleaded.

Belinda and Mary Nelle ran directly to Blythe and Brook's room and slammed the door. I went outside to help Tony and Glynna bring in the food. I could smell those smoked pork ribs before I got to the car. That aroma would make a grown man weep and a hunting dog howl.

"Big Mamma, let me help." I wrapped one arm around her shoulder and squeezed.

"Oh, there's my boy," Glynna patted both my cheeks. "You and Tony go on inside. I'll get the food."

"No, Mamma, we'll help you." Tony waved her off and picked up the metal tray. "Besides, Jim and I might want to sneak a few of your pork ribs."

She snatched the pan out of his hands with the quickness of a cheetah. "Lordy, you two would eat all four slabs. I'll get the meat. You get the beans and potato salad."

We did as Big Mamma asked, but when she put the ribs on the kitchen table, he and I grabbed three or four of 'em and headed up to my room. "Tony, I'm a little shaky about this draft. What if I don't get selected? Do you think I have the right stuff?"

Tony licked his fingers and reached for another sliver of paradise. "No problem, man. You'll get a call. Good linebackers are always a top priority. Just relax. It will happen."

Burl pushed through the door and dove on my bed, "Bubba, do the pros wear jock straps?"

Tony almost choked on a mouthful of pork. "Yeah. Why are you asking?"

"'Cause Earl said only guys with little winkies wore 'em."

Tony grabbed him by the seat of his pants and gave him an affectionate swat. "Get outa here, knot head. Jim and I have some talking to do."

Mom hollered up the stairs when it was time to eat. We all gathered around the table.

Mom looked around the dining table. It was crowded, but we managed. "It's nice to have the Helmslys over to share this wonderful day. Who would like to say the prayer?"

Earl took a sip of soda, choked and spewed a light mist across the table, hitting Mary Nelle in the face.

She gasped and shouted, "Mamma, did you see what Earl did? I'm going to punch him out."

Everyone laughed, except Mary Nelle. She pinched her lips and blinked her eyes.

"Oh, calm down, girl," Big Mamma said in a gruff, half laugh. "Earl, go wipe the soda coming out your nose. Mary Nelle, go wash your face."

After the Earl drama with Mary Nelle, things settled down. Mom said the prayer, and the food was passed around the table. Amazing how a meal could turn constant chatter into complete silence. I noticed how fast everyone ate. Nerves, probably, but grabbing a prime seat in front of the TV was important.

Mom turned on the tube at 1:00 p.m. I sat in a recliner, Tony at the end of the couch next to me. The NFL Commissioner welcomed the audience. My heart rate spiked. My heels bounced up and down like oil-field pump jacks.

I looked at Tony. His laidback demeanor puzzled me. How could he be that calm?

One hour passed. No calls. Then two hours. Still no calls. My nerves were more frazzled than J. Mo's Afro.

The girls got bored and left the living room, with the exception of Blythe who appointed herself official receptionist to answer the phone—if it ever rang.

Burl and Earl lay spread-eagled on the carpet in front of the TV, snoring like two bear cubs.

The first round of the draft was coming to an end.

Ring, ring, ring. We all jumped like our chairs were hotwired.

Blythe answered. "Hello . . . yes, he's here. He can't talk right now. He's busy. Bye."

I popped up like tightly coiled bed springs. "Blythe, who was that?"

"It was a reporter from the Belleville newspaper." She sounded disappointed.

Was this day ever going to end? I couldn't take much more. Ring, phone ring.

Another thirty minutes went by with no calls.

Then the phone rang again.

Blythe rushed to it. "Hello . . . yes, he's here." She took the receiver from her ear and cupped her shaking hand over the speaker. Bouncing up and down, she clasped the phone to her chest. Her blue eyes beamed. "Tony, it's Coach Charles of the Pittsburgh Steelers."

Tony sprang from the couch and reached for the telephone. "Hello . . . yes sir. This is Tony . . . yes sir. Thank you, Coach, for selecting me. I'm thrilled to be playing for the Pittsburgh Steelers."

I reached Tony first, almost mowing him over with my hug. "Congratulations, brother. No one deserves this more than you." While I was happy for him, somewhere deep down inside me, envy reared its ugly head and clawed at my guts.

Big Mamma turned into a middle-aged cheerleader. She put her arms straight out, then made a circular motion, and moved her hips from side to side, and chanted, "My Tony, my Tony, my Tony."

The twins jumped from the couch to the chairs all the way around the room and never touched the floor. They continued romping until Big Mamma noticed. "Quit running on the furniture, you little hooligans. Tony, give me your belt." Both jumped off the couch in a nanosecond.

The girls had come back to the living room for chocolate chip cookies. They made a circle, locked arms around each other's shoulders, jumped up and down screaming like a bunch of teenagers at a Beatles concert.

Mom, however, had the most composure. She sat in her lounge chair, placed her hands over her nose and mouth, and silently wept. What a classy lady.

As the celebration continued, I walked out the back door. Had to get away. My confidence was lower than whale barf on the bottom of the ocean. What if no team chose me? I couldn't stand the humiliation. I paced to stay warm and to keep from going crazy as my future without football passed before me.

Even with a house full of family and friends, I felt alone.

Blythe opened the back door. "Jim, where are you? It's Coach Thomas of the Dallas Cowboys." She slammed the door and ran back to the living room.

Oh, my gosh. Oh, my gosh. I bounded up the steps, pulled on the door knob and the blasted thing came off in my hand. Son-of-a-gun. I tried to put it back on. Didn't work. I ran around the house through the front door. Blythe handed me the phone. I gave her the door knob.

"Hello, this is Jim . . . yes, sir. I'm very happy to be a member of the Dallas Cowboys." The fear that consumed me minutes before had evaporated. I did a one-handed tug boat horn pull. "Thank you, Coach Thomas." I hung up.

The festivities and congratulations were similar to Tony's. Mom was more animated. She raised both arms in the air, jumped up and down, and screamed "Yes, yes, yes." Tears of joy trickled down her cheeks.

Burl and Earl once again ran the furniture obstacle course, but this time Earl's foot stuck between the couch cushions. Burl, following behind, had no time to stop. The two collided, turned over the couch and an end table. Knowing their mother would be asking for the dreaded belt again, the twins bolted out the door like scalded dogs.

February 1st was a fabulous day for Tony and me and our families. What were the odds of two guys from Belleville being drafted the same year? Nothing could be better than this. Nothing could top our happiness. Nothing.

About an hour after my conversation with the Cowboys, the telephone rang again. Probably the Belleville newspaper wanting an interview.

Blythe answered. "Hello . . . yes, he's here." She turned to me. "Jim, it's Coach Charles of the Pittsburgh Steelers."

I shook my head and pointed. "Blythe, he wants Tony."

"No, Jim, he said you."

"Coach Charles, this is Jim. . . . Yes, sir, I understand. This is official, isn't it? . . . Thank you for calling." I slowly lowered the receiver and stared into space. All the air was sucked from the room.

Mom stepped from the kitchen, drying a plate. "What's this all about, Jim?"

"Coach Charles said the Cowboys traded me to the Steelers for an undisclosed draft pick next year. Tony and I will be teammates."

All of us looked at each other without saying a word. The situation was surreal.

Tony broke the silence. His laughter bellowed throughout the house. The sounds of delight resonated with each outburst.

When I said nothing could top our happiness — I was wrong. Two rookie Pittsburgh Steelers in one room went beyond happiness to euphoria.

CHAPTER 35

I WOKE EARLY THE NEXT MORNING AFTER DRAFT DAY. MY FLIGHT to Norman didn't leave until 9:00 p.m. A light dusting of snow made the morning crisp, but the gray, overcast sky looked threatening, and there was more snow slated in the forecast.

I hoped the weather wouldn't affect my flight. Coach Aderholt had scheduled a press conference on Thursday afternoon in Oklahoma for me to answer questions about the draft.

I drove Mom to work and took the girls to school. Mom had a glow about her that let me know how proud she was of me.

Blythe was still pumped and her cinnamon-freck-led skin seemed to sparkle. "Jim, I'm going straight to Coach Mancuso's office. I want to know what he thinks about you being drafted, and I'm going to start writing my op-ed for the school paper . . . and . . ."

I reached over and placed my hand on her head. "You need to get out of the car. I still have to take Brook to school."

She fumbled with her books, dropping one on the floorboard. "Okay, I'm so excited."

"I would never have guessed." I beamed a crooked smile, stretched across Blythe to open the door, and gave a gentle nudge with the back of my hand. "Out."

She squinted and eased the tip of her tongue through tight lips, her way of letting me know she still liked me, but not to be too pushy.

Pulling up to Brook's school, I looked in the rear view mirror. She was sound asleep in the back seat. I reached behind me and pushed on her chubby knee. "Hey, Brookie Bear, wake up. We're at your school."

Without opening her eyes, she scrunched her limp body between the door and the seat. "Are you sure we're here?" she mumbled.

"Yes, I'm sure."

Forcing the door open, my little sister slid down the car seat onto the snow-covered sidewalk. Her first step mimicked a new-born fawn attempting to walk. Arms flailed, legs oscillated in and out. Fortunately she fell backward, and the car stopped her from busting her backside.

I rolled down the passenger side window, laughing so hard my temples ached. "Are you okay?"

She stuck her head through the open window, and raked a chunk of blonde hair away from her light blue eyes. She gave me a fingertip wave goodbye, then stuck out her tongue.

The tongue thing must be an inherited trait of the Pepperman girls.

From the school I drove to the cemetery. A blast of north wind rocked the car, and swirls of snow pelted the windshield. I wrapped a scarf around my neck, tucked the ends inside the overcoat and buttoned the collar.

Approaching Dad's grave, my steps were slow and choppy. I felt like a steel blanket was anchored to my chest. It was difficult seeing his cold, lifeless marker. Kneeling, I traced my finger over each letter of his name.

"Dad, it's been tough, but I made it. I'm graduating this spring. Can't really explain how it makes me feel." I closed my eyes and drew a deep breath. My lips quivered. I had to pull in my emotions.

The wind picked up and slammed me from behind. I squeezed my shoulders together and tightened the scarf. "Dad, I was named to the All-American team this year. Remember that Texas Tech game you took me to when I was seven? That was the day I decided I loved football. And . . . yesterday I became a member of the Pittsburgh Steelers. Your son's going to be a professional football player. Now I can pay for Blythe and Brook's education.

"Dad, Dad, why did you die? I wish you could see me play pro ball. My life hasn't been easy, but you said trials in life were blessings that made us stronger. You were right. I wish I could stay longer, but I've got to go now. Just wanted to give you some good news."

I traced my fingers over his name again, then returned to the car and sat a few moments to savor the experience. Tears formed, but didn't fall. Joy filled my soul. I knew Dad was walking with me through this amazing journey.

CHAPTER 36

THE 1972 STEELERS TRAINING CAMP WAS HELD IN LATE JULY at Saint Vincent College in Latrobe, Pennsylvania, a small town about forty miles southeast of Pittsburgh. The new guys were required to arrive two days before the rest of the team.

Nervous rookies, Tony and I arrived a day early. Didn't want to be late.

As we walked up the park trail overlooking Saint Vincent, the afternoon was misty with a light fog. The view from the rolling hills reminded me of pictures I'd seen of Scotland. I could almost hear bagpipes playing. For some reason I thought about how much Laura would like this place. She filled something in me, and since we had been apart, that space in me felt empty. I should write her.

I gave Tony a tap on the shoulder with the back of my hand. "Did you know Arnold Palmer is from Latrobe?"

"You're kidding." He tugged on his right earlobe. "How'd you know?"

"Saw it on *Wide World of Sports*. You ever think about taking up golf?"

He looked at me. "You ever think about taking up the violin?" His voice was thick and sarcastic.

Hmmm . . . guess that was a no.

Before leaving the hilltop overlooking the campus, Tony gave me a nudge. "I know why they chose this place."

"Why's that?"

He pointed his finger and pumped it up and down. "I can count the number of traffic lights on two hands. There's nothing to do here except eat, sleep, and think football."

"Well, that's all a big dumb lineman like you needs. Anything else and you'd lose focus." Before he could ring my neck, I ran a few yards ahead.

"You little piss ant." He quick-stepped after me. "You'd better run."

I did my best boxing shuffle to stay away from the big guy.

After scoping the town, we came back to the dorm and unloaded our cars. Tony was bunking down the hall from me, near the fire escape.

"Hey, Jim, come here," Tony hollered.

I took an apple from the sack of goodies Mom had packed and headed to his room. My mouth full, I poked my head through his open doorway.

Tony's hands were outstretched and his eyes were droopy. "There's no air conditioning."

I was laughing so hard my belly shook. I wanted to tell him he looked like a Tennessee bloodhound with his sad eyes and slack jaw, but I knew better. I'd kidded him enough today and barely gotten away with it. Didn't want to stretch my luck.

But then — stupidity latched onto me like sucker pads on a frog's foot. I couldn't resist saying something to rouse him one more time. "As fat as you are, you'd better go get two electric fans." I took another bite of the apple.

He made a strangling gesture with his hands.

I ran down the hall and slingshot into my room, my feet barely keeping up with the rest of me.

It was almost midnight. The first team meeting was at seven a.m. But I was too wound up to sleep so I decided to write Laura. I wanted to at least keep our friendship intact.

Hey Laura,

Tomorrow is my first big day. I'm excited. A little nervous. Hope I've got the stuff to make the squad. I've met several other rookies. All seem to be good guys. Don't have much to say except wish me luck. I'll keep you posted. We'll be here for four weeks.

Tell your dad I'll bring him a workout t-shirt like he wanted.

Later,
Jim

I laid the pen on the table, folded the letter. I'd have to buy an envelope and stamp tomorrow.

Laura and I clicked the first day we met at Gloria's diner in Belleville. She made me feel welcomed, just moving to a new town. I needed that support.

Dang, why hadn't it worked out for Laura and me — the way I wanted it to.

CHAPTER 37

TRAINING CAMP PROVED TO BE A BIGGER CHALLENGE THAN I'D expected.

Over the month, I had great days, good days, and some days I wondered how I'd even gotten there. The physical stress was a given, but the mental aspect overwhelmed me. Professional football was an unforgiving business. You learned to adapt or you failed.

On the upside, there weren't any serious injuries for me or Tony.

Being drafted didn't mean you made the team. There was no option of not proving myself. The alternative was to go home. Fear of failure motivated me to work hard for a chance to succeed. But what if I didn't make the cut? How would I take care of my family? What else would I do if I couldn't play pro ball?

The last day of training camp at St. Vincent College left me drained. I sat in front of the open dorm room window. Birds were chirping, and a light breeze rushed over my face. Everything seemed calm and under control, but my world was turning upside down with uncertainty and fear.

I picked up the phone and called Mom.

"Hello." Pop, smack, smack.

"Blythe?" Next to scraping a fingernail on a blackboard, the smacking and popping of gum was a major irritation to me.

"Hi, Jim." Pop, smack, smack.

"Are you chewing. . . ." I scratched the end of my nose. "Never mind. Is Mom there?"

"Sure." Blythe yelled for Mom. "Here she is."

I could still hear Blythe's mouth music as she transferred the phone.

"Hello." Mom's voice was perky and upbeat.

"What's with Blythe and the gum?"

"She's trying to learn how to blow a bubble inside a bubble. She's got two or three pieces of Bazooka jammed in the side of her jaw. It wouldn't be so annoying if she was the only one, but Brook's trying to learn too. Their actions are nuttier than a Snickers bar."

I smiled, remembering the time bubble gum ended up in my hair after I left it in my mouth one night when I was ten.

Mom shuffled the phone, probably moving to a quieter part of the house. "How are you tonight?"

"This is final cut day." I got up from the chair and paced the room as far as the phone cord would allow. "Tensions are high. If I can make it till two a.m., I'll be on the team." I checked the clock. Eight agonizing hours to go.

"Two a.m.? What happens at two a.m.?" Her tone slid into confusion.

"If you don't make the team, a coach will knock on your door before 2:00 a.m. and ask for your playbook. The players call him the Grim Reaper. If that happens, I'm done."

"Okay, but why the middle of the night?"

"It's Coach Charles's way of being sympathetic to the players who don't make it. They can save face by leaving before anyone else gets up."

"That's a nice gesture." She paused. "But it won't happen to you." Her tone went from confused to confident.

Confidence that might be misplaced. "You don't understand. There're some really good athletes who'll be released. No guarantees. I just wanted to prepare you if things don't work out."

"Stop. I'm not going to think about it. You'll make the team. You will, you will." She said it like she had a magic wand waved over me through the phones.

But her confidence didn't help. I had to sweat it out just like the rest of the guys.

I shifted from the chair to my bed and propped a pillow behind my head. "I don't want you to worry. Don't tell the girls about the Grim Reaper. No need to get them involved. One way or the other, I'll know tomorrow. Mom, honestly, I think I won't get cut. Just wanted to let you know it could happen. Get some rest. We'll talk in the morning." I placed the receiver on the base next to the table lamp.

I lied. I had no idea if I'd make the team. Didn't want her to worry.

My old fashion alarm clock ticked, ticked, ticked the minutes away. Too fast. Too slow. The clock hands turned to ten. Four more hours. I felt like a death row inmate sweating out the last few hours before time was up.

At 12:30, I heard a knock. Then another. The door across from my room squeaked open.

I placed my hands over my eyes and took a deep breath and said a prayer. I couldn't take much more. When would this be over?

I tried to stay awake, but fatigue got the best of me. My eyelids sprung open.

The clock read 3:30.

And no one had knocked on my door. I doubled both fists and air punched. The Steelers playbook lay on the chair next to the window. I reached over, grabbed the binder, and gave it a big kiss. Tony, what about Tony? Did he make it?

I ran down the dormitory hall, and anxiety got the best of me. I paused. Then knocked—tap, tap.

No response.

Tap, tap.

Nothing.

Oh, God, please let Tony be in there.

Slowly the door eased open. "Dang, Jim, you scared the bejeebers out of me. I thought you were the Grim Reaper. What time is it?"

"It's 3:30." I grabbed Tony's shoulder and shook him. "We made the team. We did it!"

Tony grabbed my arm and pulled me through the doorway. "Get in here."

My small burst of excitement dimmed in the shadow of the past few hours. Mentally, I was kaput. We sat on the side of his bed like a couple of zombies.

"Congratulations." Tony's thin-slice smile was a welcome sight.

"Same to you, Brother." We shook hands.

We were Pittsburgh Steelers.

CHAPTER 38

Being a member of a long-established football franchise was a dream come true. Just suiting up in the Steelers uniform made me proud. Tony was penciled in as the starting left offensive tackle. The coaches listed me second on the depth chart behind a three-year veteran middle linebacker. I also played on the kick-offs.

Our team had a bunch of characters—men with unique personalities. Stefan Meitler, Pittsburgh's new kicker, was a classic. One of the coaches had noticed him on TV playing for the German National Soccer team. He could nail a ball like no other. I was positioned next to him when we lined up for kick-offs. We developed a competition challenging each other to see who would get down the field first.

His athletic ability didn't make him unique, his aggressiveness did. Normally, a kicker hung back as a last-resort tackler. Not Stefan. He sprinted down the field and ran head-on into the first opponent in his way. The guy caused a major train wreck. No problem if you were 6' 4" and weighed 250 pounds, but this guy, at best was 180 and stood 5' 9". The coaches told him he wouldn't make it to the end of the season with his Kamikaze approach. He either didn't understand or chose not to listen.

The fans loved our fearless kicker. He soon became an icon in the Pittsburgh area. Before games, the crowd chanted, "Meitler . . . Meitler . . . Meitler." He had superstar status, no doubt about it. The sports writers gathered around his locker requesting interviews, and he didn't shy away from the attention.

Stefan and his wife, Wilhelmina, were accepted without reservation by the Pittsburgh community. According to a reporter, Wilhelmina was too hard to spell so the press nicknamed her Billie. She was a well-known international actress, a celebrity in her own right. Rumor had it Billie held the title of "Miss Germany" a few years earlier. Didn't know if it was true or not.

The sixth game of the season, the New England Patriots came to town. The Steelers won the coin toss, and Coach Charles decided to go on defense first. By now, the opposition was familiar with Mr. Meitler's suicidal tactics. The crowd went bananas, chanting the likeable German's name. When he teed up the ball, the roar from the stands intensified. I imagined the Roman Coliseum in its heyday.

The official blew his whistle and pointed to Stefan. He slowly approached the ball. And boom. The ball was high and relatively short. The New England runner caught it and started up the field. Every eye focused on Stefan. One big Patriot lineman had a bead on him. The two played a game of chicken, however one resembled a Mack truck, the other a Volkswagen beetle. The closer they came, the more the tension built. The collision was imminent.

Meitler lowered his head, resembling a medieval battering ram.

The New England player did something very uncharacteristic. He side-stepped Stefan. Too late for the wild man. He launched his body and flew through the air like a bottle rocket. He landed flat on his stomach and slid at least two yards.

Grass flew as though it was tossed in a wind tunnel. The field looked like it had been plowed with a John Deere tractor. The stadium erupted with a loud "Ooooh."

Ol' Meitler knocked the wind out of himself. The trainers helped the gutsy German to the sideline. When our team realized Stefan wasn't seriously injured, our laughter morphed into all-out bedlam.

The Steelers defense took the field. Our veteran linebacker had sprained his ankle against Houston the week before. That gave me the opportunity to prove myself as his replacement.

Fear and excitement wrapped their tentacles around my chest. I threw up three times before kickoff. After the game started, I settled down and had a decent outing with four unassisted tackles and three assists.

The only major blunder happened in the second quarter. I stepped on an official's foot. Our trainer examined him, and his big toe was broken. I hoped he wouldn't hold a grudge the next time he officiated a Steelers' game.

We beat the Patriots 33-3. Our record stood at four and two, but our team performance was lackluster. All of us played hard at times, but didn't stay focused through all four quarters.

After looking at the game film, the coaches demanded we concentrate more on our individual responsibilities

and be more physical. In other words, man-up and per-
form like professionals or spend the rest of the season
watching someone else play.

CHAPTER 39

WINNING THE NEW ENGLAND GAME WAS GOOD. BUT SEEING Mom, my sisters, and the Helmsly crew who'd made the long trek from Belleville to Pittsburgh was better. On the way to the restaurant after the game, Mom told me there was a bit of excitement before kickoff. My intuition told me the twins were involved.

The story started when Glynna bolted out of her chair in the stadium like she'd been shot out of a circus cannon. Mom got animated as she told the rest.

Glynna asked, "Mary Nelle, where're Burl and Earl?" Mary Nelle chewed on a bite of hot dog and swallowed. "Remember they went to the concession stand for popcorn."

Glynna tapped her watch and said they'd been gone fifteen minutes. She placed both hands on her cheeks, looked up and rolled her eyes. "Somebody got my babies. Where are my babies? Get the police. Oh, I should have gone with them."

Mom happened to glance down on the football field, then tugged on Glynna's arm and told her to look under the goal post. Burl and Earl. Glynna cupped her hand over her mouth and pitter-pattered her feet. "My little sugar bears. They're okay."

When a large security guard approached the two, Glynna's joy turned sour. "How did those pumpkin heads get down on the field? Belinda, give me your belt."

"Don't have it," she said.

Mother Bear Helmsly stomped down the concrete steps toward the field, on a mission. She marched right up to the security guard. Through the whole conversation, she moved her hands, head, and sometimes her hips, like a contortionist at a Shriner's Convention. Then she grabbed the twins by their hands and pulled them inside the tunnel leading to the locker room.

"I knew the procedure when the twins messed up." Mom closed out the story. "I'd seen it on numerous occasions. Glynna would give 'em a swat on their behinds, then hug 'em, and demand an apology." She said Burl and Earl minded their manners until kick-off. After that, Big Momma had her hands full.

Mom loved traveling with the Helmslys. She said being with the twins was like a who-done-it movie. You never knew what would happen next.

After each home game, the Steelers provided a dinner for the team, their families, and guests. Tony and I shared a table with Mom and Glynna. The girls and the twins sat behind us. The conversation started with the game, but Glynna couldn't wait to tell about the runaway boys, even though she knew Mom already told us.

She rocked her head from side to side, definitely a negative sign, about the boys getting into trouble. I thought she would blow a gasket reciting each and every detail. Glynna glanced over her shoulder at the kids table. Burl and Earl were gone. She squinted, rolled her lips into a circle, and scoured the banquet hall. She spotted them flanked on each side of Coach Charles.

Glynna tapped, tapped, tapped on Tony's shoulder. "Give me your belt!"

He wiped his mouth and laid his napkin on the table. "Momma, I'm not giving you my belt. I'll go get them."

"No. Sit down." She pushed her chair away from the table and stood, heading toward Coach Charles. Her first few steps were slow and deliberate. Then her pace picked up and her arms pumped back and forth like a locomotive building steam. Faster, faster, faster.

Burl and Earl noticed their mom when she was halfway across the room. Both dropped their ice cream spoons and sprinted for the door.

Coach acknowledged Glynna with a wave and pointed toward the exit. He tilted his head back and laughed. By the grin on his face, he loved the interactions between players and their families.

It may be cliché to say the Steelers were like one big family. We lived for one another. All for one, one for all.

CHAPTER 40

COACH CHARLES CALLED THE TEAM TOGETHER AFTER HE'D watched the film of our November 26th game against Minnesota. "Men, it's almost December and we've had a great season. You're champions of the AFC Central division. No Pittsburgh team before you could make that claim. I'm proud of you . . . darn proud. However, we have some unfinished business. When we beat Cleveland on Sunday, our record will be 9 and 3. A victory will provide momentum for the playoffs. Do your job this week in practice. Stay focused. I repeat, stay focused."

He turned to the assistant coaches. "Get with your guys. Give them the scouting report on Cleveland. Let's go to work."

I spent time everyday in the training room after we beat Minnesota. A chop block by one of their lineman did some minor damage to my meniscus and my knee ached. The swelling was noticeable, but the injury didn't limit my mobility. The trainer gave me an ice pack for home.

I entered my messy apartment. Clothes, towels, and food containers were everywhere. Looked like a West Texas twister ripped through my living room. I tossed my keys on the table, plopped on the couch, and placed the ice bag on my knee.

The loud ring of the phone startled me. "Hello." I adjusted the cold compress.

"It's Laura." She didn't have to tell me. I knew her voice.

"Hey. How are you?"

"Good. You okay?" Her tone sparkled, like she cared for me.

"Fine, I've got a few nicks and bruises, but other than that I'm hanging in there."

"I've watched you on TV. You're playing really well. The announcers call out your name a lot."

Water dripped all over the couch and made little puddles. Shoot. The stupid ice pack had a hole in it. I placed a towel over the wet spot. "Appreciate the compliment. Hope Coach Charles agrees."

Our conversation steered to talk about her job, then back to mine.

Even if she didn't feel the same about me, I still cared for her in a special way. Maybe even loved her. But I wasn't sure. I felt happy when I talked to her and broken-hearted when I hung up.

"I'm going to be in Pittsburgh this weekend and wondered if I could get a couple of tickets for the game," Laura blurted out, catching me off guard.

I could feel my grin spread from ear to ear but didn't want to sound too excited. "Sure," I said, my voice cool. "I'll leave them at the Will Call window." And casually tossed in, "Oh, after the game would you like to come to our team dinner? The meal's pretty good, and it would give us time to visit." But inside I was a bundle of ricocheting nerves.

"That would be great. Is it okay if my friend joins us?"

"Why not? I'll meet you outside Gate Five."

I hung up and jumped at least two feet off the ground screaming, "Yes . . . yes . . . yes." On the third jump I came down at an angle and tweaked my sore knee. No matter. Laura would be here this weekend.

In my excitement, I forgot to ask Laura who the second ticket was for.

The twelfth game of the regular season. Winners of our division. Laura Pomroy. Couldn't get any better.

What would Laura look like? Would her hair be long or short? What would my reaction be when I saw her for the first time in over a year?

Whoa, back up. Concentrate on the game. Seeing her wouldn't mean as much if we lost. One thing was certain. I intended to play the best game of my life. Pumped didn't begin to describe my state of mind.

The Steelers dominated Cleveland. Coach took me out near the end of the fourth quarter. My knee held up fine thanks to the PT treatments and the tape job.

Players talked about being in a zone when everything went right. This was one of those games for me. My personal stats were good—four unassisted tackles, one pass deflection, and a fumble recovery. My best performance. If Laura provided the spark needed to play at this level, she'd be coming to all the home games. At my expense.

The last three minutes of the fourth quarter seemed like an hour. The team was blown away after winning our ninth game of the year 30 to 0 and advancing to the first round in the playoffs. The champagne shower was fun until the bubbly got into my eyes.

Coach Charles passed out game balls to those who played well. I received my first one. It was a badge of honor. My chest swelled to the size of a fifty-five gallon drum. The ball was going smack dab in the middle of my fireplace mantel.

"Men, what you've done for the community can't be measured in words." Coach took the opportunity to congratulate us. "Steelers fans now have hope. Something that's evaded the people of Pittsburgh for twenty-five years. But . . . we're not finished."

The team went nuts. Shouts filled the dressing room. Coach Charles got his champagne shower too. He looked like a water-logged beagle.

Our confidence level was a solid ten. Mine was a twelve. I had a feeling the Steelers Nation would be proud of this team for many years to come. We would be NFL champions soon. If not this year, then next.

I was the first one in and out of the showers. The trainer stopped me halfway to my locker. "Pepperman, you need to soak your knee in ice water before you leave."

"Come on, Doc. I'm in a hurry. I'll ice it down when I get home tonight and come in tomorrow for the cold water treatment."

He hesitated and rolled his lower lip as though he was thinking about my offer. "Okay, but you have to be here by eight in the morning."

I was as nervous as a June bug in a chicken coop. Gate Five was the location for families and friends. At least fifty people jammed the area, but spotting Laura was a snap. We made eye contact, and I forced myself to slow down. Didn't want to appear too eager. Her smile and that beautiful face illuminated the dark shadows of the stadium. This was going to be a fun night.

A thought zipped through my mind. Who was the other ticket for?

CHAPTER 41

A COLD FRONT HAD MOVED IN AFTER THE GAME AND THE TEM-perature dropped. That winter in Pittsburgh had been brutal. Cold clamped down on your bones and wouldn't ease up.

Laura stood shivering next to a tall, skinny guy in a black top coat with a gold Steelers scarf.

Had she brought a boyfriend? I wanted to ring his scrawny chicken neck.

He stepped in front of her and patted my back like I was his best buddy. "Great game today, Pepperman. You did an excellent job deflecting that pass in the third quarter. A sure touchdown for Cleveland. No doubt about it."

What a joke. This bean pole was not her type.

"Excuse me, sir." Laura edged her way in front of the man and placed her arm around my waist.

He wasn't with her. My heart slowed when I realized they weren't together. My wide eyes and open mouth must have been a dead giveaway to my wrong assumption because Laura looked amused.

Her smile was all I needed to feel good.

"Congratulations on the win. You played awesome." Laura's brown eyes seemed to sparkle as she adjusted the collar of my coat.

The lady next to Laura acted as though she knew me. She was small, and her cute face was framed by a short, brown Afro.

"Jim, I want you to meet Tai Lynn. We're nurses at University of Penn Hospital."

"I'm sorry," I said. "Is it Tay Lynn?"

"Close. It's Tai, like pie, Tai Lynn."

Both women looked at each other and grinned like they knew something I didn't. Laura placed her thumb under her chin and rested her forefinger under the lower lip. "Tai Lynn is a big fan of Tony's. Would you introduce her?"

"Sure, if he hasn't left. Sometimes he's out of here before I am." I glanced toward the gate and spotted him. "Tony, over here." My extended arms crisscrossed to get his attention.

Tony walked over and flashed his school-boy grin, the kind of grin most women swooned over.

"Bubba, an old friend is in town."

"Hi, Laura, it's been awhile." He bent and gave her a gentle hug.

"You get bigger every time I see you."

His baritone chuckle seemed to get everyone's attention. "It's the coat, Laura. It's the coat."

The long, brown, furry jacket did make him look like a full-grown grizzly. Glad he was my teammate.

Laura took Tai Lynn's hand and guided her in front of Tony and introduced them.

Tai Lynn tilted her head as far back as possible, mouth wide open, eyes fixed.

My mental image—Tinker Bell meeting the Jolly Green Giant.

Tony extended his hand. "I'm Tony Helmsly."

I held back a laugh. Whatever you do, brother, don't break her fingers.

She continued looking up, mouth still wide open, saying nothing.

Helmsly angled his head, sporting a puzzled look. "Tai Lynn, that's a beautiful name. Is it Asian?"

"No, it's from Queens, New York. I mean . . . I'm from Queens. My name's from . . . I mean the origin of my name . . ." At this point she just shrugged her shoulders. "I really don't know. I was the last of seven kids. What can you expect?"

The name thing seemed to relax everyone. I asked Tony if he wanted to join us. It was the beginning of a fun evening. After the team dinner we went to Klevon's. Tony had to have his sweets. It didn't matter how cold it was he'd eat vanilla ice cream with chocolate syrup and call it Buff Dessert. Don't know where that came from.

Tai Lynn's chin quivered as she inched the spoon of the frozen cream toward her. She was so focused on the big guy sitting across the table, she actually missed her mouth and ice cream dribbled down her chin.

Tony, too busy slurping down the vanilla treat, never noticed. The goof ball.

Laura and I talked about the summer we met and the long conversations we had driving around Belleville. Being with her felt right. Like we belonged together. I wondered if she thought the same thing. She had put her arm around my waist. That had to mean something, right? Should I tell her how I felt? I didn't know what to do. If she felt the same way, fantastic. If she rejected me, I wasn't sure I could stand it.

Tony and Tai Lynn seemed to hit it off. I'd never seen him so confident. His shy demeanor around women was not evident that night, not by a long shot. There was definite chemistry between the two.

I wished the same could be said for Laura and me.

CHAPTER 42

THE STEELERS FIRST PLAY-OFF GAME WAS AT HOME AGAINST the vaunted Oakland Raiders. The skill level on the Raider team was top shelf. Two words summed up their defense — bad news.

The practice sessions leading up to the Sunday game at Three Rivers Stadium were intense. Some of the drills came with pushing, taunting, cussing. The focus in practice paid off. Steelers 12 – Oakland 7. The battle decided in the last few seconds.

On Monday after the game, Tony and I went to the Quaker Steakhouse on North Shore Drive and ordered our usual rib-eye and baked potato. The ritual had begun five weeks earlier after our victory over Cleveland. We told ourselves superstition had nothing to do with where we ate, but we lied. As long as the Steelers won, we would eat the same thing at the same restaurant served by the same waiter.

The temperature was in the teens, not unusual for Pittsburgh in December, but it was unusual for a restaurant to be open Christmas Day. Tony took off his coat and scarf as we slid into our booth. "Can you believe their quarterback scored with a minute and seventeen seconds left in the game and put us behind 7 to 6? I wanted to choke him."

The waiter had our usual cups of coffee ready. I cupped cold hands around the hot mug. "I have to admit, doubt crept in, and I thought we could lose. I didn't give up hope, but it didn't look good." A chill spiraled its way up my spine. The building was warm, but my body hadn't adjusted.

Tony tapped his index finger on the table. "We've got the best quarterback in the league. Terry Bradburn's a winner. We all knew a pass play would be called with only twenty-two seconds left to play. He told us lineman if he got sacked, he'd beat the tar out of every one of us." Tony and I chuckled. "Our quarterback couldn't whip his grandmother."

I blew over the top of my coffee. "The defense was all bunched together on the sideline. We looked like rubber-necked penguins trying to see the next play. Terry had two defenders coming at him. He released the ball just as he took the hit. Frenchy was wide open. I knew he could catch it, but would he score?"

Tony folded his arms and leaned toward me, his eyes the size of ping pong balls. "When the Raider defender collided with Frenchy just as he was about to catch the ball, it was the craziest thing I'd ever seen. It sailed end over end backward and good ol' Harper scooped it up just before it hit the ground."

Helmsly pounded his left fist on the table, sloshing coffee everywhere. "Can you believe he ran it in for a touchdown with five seconds left on the clock? Harper ran for a touchdown . . . with five freaking seconds left. He wasn't even supposed to be anywhere near the ball. He's got to be the luckiest dude ever." He smiled and placed both arms on the back of the booth.

"Tony, talk about a miracle. It was the miracle of all miracles. I'm telling you, Pittsburgh's headed for greatness this year. Mark my words."

The Steelers beat those West Coast bad boys. We couldn't make up a better ending to a game. I rested my leg on the cushion of the booth. My knee continued to swell, and it hurt a little, but I didn't care.

Tony rarely was injured, but even monsters like him got banged up in a tough game. The fingers on his right hand looked like bratwurst sausages.

I laughed as he tried to cut his steak. Because he couldn't get a grip on the knife, he dropped it three times trying to slice the juicy meat.

His frustration peaked. "The heck with it." He looked at the steak, one that was large enough to give a vegetarian a migraine, picked it up with his good hand, and took a bite.

I glanced around to see if anyone was looking. "Hey, you're going to get us thrown out of here."

Tony never said a word as he ate every bit of the rib-eye without a fork.

Even though Tony and I couldn't go home, we shared this snowy Christmas Day together.

Sportswriters labeled Harper's catch the Immaculate Reception. They could pen whatever words they wanted to describe the play, but to our team, it was an early present. Holiday or not, we were forced back to work.

Our next opponent — the undefeated Miami Dolphins.

CHAPTER 43

THE STEELERS WERE POISED TO PLAY IN THEIR FIRST AFC Championship. We'd beaten the Oakland Raiders the previous week. Everyone had been on a high, but on December 31, 1972, the Miami Dolphins derailed our dreams 21 to 17. We'd be watching the Super Bowl from home. So much for being a team of destiny.

Sleep evaded me after the game. My mind swirled with what ifs. What if I'd made the tackle on third and three? What if our receiver hadn't dropped a touchdown pass in the fourth quarter? What if Bradburn hadn't been sacked on our last drive?

I had to get away from the city. Going home to Belleville for a visit would take my mind off the disappointing loss.

New Year's Day, I arrived at Pittsburgh International Airport an hour-and-a-half before my 3:00 p.m. departure to Newark. The terminal was eerily vacant. I supposed people were still recovering from yesterday's late night revelry.

A sports bar was handy, and I wanted a Coke. Just as the bartender set my soft drink in front of me, a guy in a Dolphin jersey took a seat three stools down. He was a thick-set guy that looked about two-forty. His belly garnered most of his bulk.

He clasped his hands together and rested his forearms on the bar. "I'll have a Budweiser draft." Taking a cigarette from his pack, he started a conversation with the bartender. "What's your name, barkeep?"

The bartender removed a white towel from his shoulder and cleaned the area in front of the Dolphin fan. "J. B."

"One whale of a game, wasn't it? The Steelers have a good team, but not quite the caliber of Miami." He lit the tobacco and blew a perfect smoke ring.

J. B. gave him a sour stare, apparently annoyed by his comments. "You're wearing jersey No. 56. Who's that?"

"Jesse Howell, the best linebacker for the Dolphins. He played at West Texas State, a small school in Canyon, Texas."

"Why do you like him?" J. B. pulled the Budweiser draft handle and slid the beer in front of the man.

"He's hard-nosed . . . a head hunter. I used to play linebacker, so I know what I'm talking about."

The bartender gave him a stink eye. "You played linebacker in college?"

"No, two years in high school. I hit people so hard the coaches made me quit." He nervously rolled his lighter between his fingers, then took a long sip of beer.

J. B. rested his palms on the bar and lowered his head at the guy. "Wow, too bad. I'm sure you would've been a great player for some college." The sarcasm sailed right over the goober's head.

"Such is life. You have to roll with the punches." He took another drag and blew smoke out the corner of his large blubbery lips. "The Steelers' middle linebacker is overrated."

What? This guy was talking about me. Steam built inside my chest until I was ready to explode. No. I took a deep breath and calmed myself. I wouldn't let some self-inflated jerk push my buttons.

The bartender crossed his arms and leaned back against the cash register. "Why do you think he's over-rated?" I could tell J. B. was about fed up with this blow-hard, even though he hadn't recognized me.

"Too slow and shies away from contact."

Okay, enough was enough. I gripped the Coke so tight the ice jiggled in the glass. No. Had to keep my cool. It wouldn't be good for a Pittsburgh player to thump a Dolphin fan.

"I think the guy played at Oklahoma." The Miami know-it-all made a limp wrist gesture. "Anyway, the Sooners usually turn out good players, tough guys. I think this little puppy's name was Pepper, Pepperidge, or something like that."

The bag of puke didn't even get my name straight. Blood pounded in my jugular. A nervous twitch developed in my left leg. This bum had gone too far.

I looked at the pompous fool and snapped. "Pepperman. The guy you're talking about . . . his name is Pepperman."

"Yeah, okay . . . whatever." He took a sip of brew and smiled at me. "You're a big guy. Did you play any ball?"

I spun my stool around to face him. "Yeah."

"Oh? Interesting. Did you play in college?"

I nodded, making direct eye contact.

"Where would that be?"

I hesitated. "The University of Oklahoma."

"Okay," his forced laugh indicated he didn't believe me. "You should try out for the Steelers." He extended his right hand. "I'm Barney Franks. What's your name?"

I got off my stool and stepped over to him. The muscles in my forearm tightened. "Jim, Jim Pepperman, and I don't need a tryout. I'm that over-rated middle linebacker you've been bad-mouthing."

The loser's mouth dropped and his skin turned ashen. I placed my right hand on his shoulder and squeezed. "You need to be careful when you talk about people. You never know who might hear."

His hand shook as he lifted the glass to his lips. Some of the beer sloshed onto the bar.

Ol' Barney Franks looked straight ahead and never said a word, but perspiration streamed down his left temple like a punctured water balloon.

I handed the bartender five dollars to pay for my Coke. He tipped an imaginary cap and slid the money back. "It's on the house. You just made my day."

CHAPTER 44

TWO SEASONS LATER WE WON OUR FIRST SUPER BOWL, AND the team knew we had the make-up to repeat as World Champions. The Steelers played at a remarkable level and achieved greatness—three Super Bowl titles in five years.

You didn't wake up one morning and decide to be the King of the Hill. It required total team dedication. I had to bring my best game every week. I spent hours during the season in the weight room and watched so many game films of opponents, I'd dream about their tendencies.

The off season was no different. I studied constantly to improve my knowledge and skill. The injury I sustained the first season continued to nag me until I had to have a couple of surgeries to repair the meniscus in my right knee. On top of that, I went back to OU during the summers to work on a master's degree in civil engineering.

I had zero life. I dated sporadically when I needed someone to go to an awards banquet, but that was about it. Brook told me I was a hermit and needed to get married before I got so old no one would want me.

Laura managed to come to at least one game every season. We both seemed to enjoy our time together. But, her job as a nurse in Philadelphia was just as demanding as mine. She was instrumental in staffing and managing a new In-Hospital Nurses Training program.

What I always dreaded happened on the last home game of my career. Laura brought a friend. Dr. Neal Sullivan, a surgeon from Philadelphia. I invited them to the team dinner and noticed Laura slip her hand into Neal's as we walked through the restaurant parking lot.

When Neal went to the restroom, Laura said, "We've been dating for several months. I've totally fallen for him."

Didn't need to hear that.

He seemed like an okay guy, but even though he was a doctor, no way was he good enough for Laura. He couldn't care as much for her as I did. She was the sweetest person on earth. No one was like her.

But she loved him so my thoughts were irrelevant. I knew it was time for me to move on. I just didn't want to.

CHAPTER 45

THE STEELERS' SUPER BOWL XIII WIN OVER THE COWBOYS last week had been my last game. After seven years of professional football, it was time to retire. My body gave me signals that I needed to quit. The morning pain and stiffness in my knees was a daily reminder.

After I announced my retirement, ABC Sports did a segment on my career. When I arrived at their studio in New York City, I was greeted by a huge make-up artist, sporting jet black hair accented by a white stripe down the middle. The lady motioned with her tattooed right arm for me to sit in the swivel chair. Never saw a makeup artist with tattoos. She gave me a sour eye as she noticed the remains of a shiner I'd received in the Cowboys game.

"Hmmm . . . some bad boy did a job on you. I have some makeup that will hide that beauty and keep you from sweating under the lights. She stood in front of me, angled her head, and rolled her lips. "Why do grown men get pleasure out of beating up each other on Sunday and calling it a sport?"

The question caught me off guard. I didn't know if she was teasing or not. "That's a little judgmental, don't you think?"

She placed her hand on her raised hip and tapped all four fingers on her Spandex pants. "You bet it is, Bubba."

I could abide most things, but self-righteousness wasn't one of them. "Before I answer your question, I have a comment. Last week the lead news story in Pittsburg reported two female hairdressers squabbled, and one stabbed the other with a pair of scissors. Would you consider hairdressing a violent business?"

Her expression said my question was stupid.

"I've played football a long time, and I've never heard about a player stabbing another while a game was being played."

"What's your point?"

"I'm not interested in your opinion. I don't recall asking what you thought of football. You can have your view about my profession. That's not an issue, but to openly denigrate the way I make a living in front of me is wrong."

Her cold, blank stare gave me the impression she didn't care about my point of view. She put down one jar of make-up and picked up another. I guessed she'd chosen the wrong one.

Later, I felt bad about my comments. Usually those kinds of remarks didn't set me off. I needed to remember the Biblical truth and be slow to anger. Being respectful of others was an honorable trait Mom and Dad had taught me.

Tim McKay, the *Wide World of Sports* celebrity, greeted me in the green room, next to the studio. "Jim, it's great to have you on the show today. You did get a list of questions I'll be asking?"

"Yes. I appreciate you giving me a heads up."

"Before the session starts, be aware, the lights on the set are brutal. I'll have Reneau get us a mug of ice water. Feel free to take a sip anytime during the live broadcast. Are you nervous?"

"A little, but I'll be fine." My gut was doing the cha-cha the way it did before every kick-off.

He gave me a thumbs-up. "Good. Just be yourself and picture us having a conversation at a coffee shop."

Easy for him to say. Interviewing was his job.

The director signaled for the program to begin.

"Good morning, sports fans." Tim looked at the camera. "Today our guest is Jim Pepperman, the great middle linebacker for the Pittsburgh Steelers. Unfortunately for the Steelers' organization, he just announced his retirement. We wanted to get his comments about playing for the World Champions." He turned towards me. "Welcome, Jim."

"Thank you. My pleasure to be here." The jitters faded, just like after a kick-off.

"Let's start the interview with your impressions of being the first team to win three Super Bowls?"

I paused to get my answer right. "When you consider how far the Steelers have come in a short period, it's nothing less than remarkable. Remember, the first time this team won a playoff game was 1972, my rookie year."

"You bring up an interesting point. Why retire at the peak of your career? Pittsburgh is playing the best ball in Steelers' history.

"I've seen guys try to extend their playing time. Two knee operations in seven years told me it was time to hang it up." Boy, the lights were hot. I started to sweat. The lady said the make-up would prevent that.

Tim straightened in his chair and leaned forward. "Besides winning Super Bowls, what are some memorable moments for you?" He seemed genuinely interested in my answer.

"That's a tough one, but two incidents immediately come to mind. The story behind the Terrible Towel was something unique."

"Tell me about it."

I shifted my body in the chair, uncomfortable in the heat. "In 1975 we played Baltimore in our divisional playoff. Local sportswriter, Myron Pope, encouraged the fans to bring a yellow dish towel to show support. The gimmick, intended to be a one-shot deal, became a Steelers tradition. To see thousands of fans wave the towels gave us our mojo. We felt unbeatable."

McKay crossed his legs and placed his question sheet in his lap. "That tradition started in Pittsburgh. Other teams copycatted the idea but never pulled it off. I suppose it was a gimmick that only worked for you guys. Shifting gears, was there a particular game that you'll never forget?"

"Absolutely, the 1972 game against Oakland. The Immaculate Reception has to be the most miraculous play in all of football. Harper scooped up the ball just before it hit the ground and scored with five seconds left. The moment was surreal. Few, if any, sporting events can match that comeback victory."

"I agree. That had to be special for a rookie."

"Yes, sir, without a doubt." The room grew hotter by the second.

"What Super Bowl games stand out most?"

"The two wins over Dallas, especially the game this year. I'm fortunate to have played against great teams like the Cowboys."

"Why those two games?"

"Dallas is a nationally known powerhouse with tons of tradition. Every Steeler player knew it would take the ultimate effort to beat them. We were prepared and played our best game both times. The Cowboys were talented, and we had a lot of respect for them."

"Would you say those two victories were the proudest moments in your career?"

"No. When the sportswriters declared the 1976 defense the greatest in NFL history that pleased me the most. I would do anything to help those guys, and they'd do the same for me. We were a special group . . . had a bond that wouldn't be broken."

Tim nodded and pointed the eraser end of his pencil at me. "I was one of those writers. I do believe we may never see a comparable defense. Only twenty-eight total points given up in the last nine games. Remarkable."

The studio felt like the inside of a Pennsylvania coal furnace. I wiped the sweat from under my eye and noticed makeup on my finger. Why wasn't Tim perspiring?

He reached over and took a sip from his mug, and gave a startled look. He cleared his throat. I didn't think much about it until I took a big swallow. It took my breath. What I expected to be ice water was vodka. Someone had played a practical joke. It was difficult to keep a straight face for the rest of the interview. This was the type of prank a football player would pull. The *Wide World of Sports* crew was a loose bunch. I liked that.

Regaining his composure, McKay set down his drink. "The Steelers started the 1976 season with one win and four losses. What turned it around?"

"Numerous things, but during practice after our fourth loss, I watched great players just going through the motions preparing for the next game. That had to stop. Coach Charles went a little crazy in the middle of a workout. He screamed, 'We're a better team than what we're showing.' I won't repeat the language, but the point was, we weren't taking care of business."

Tim put his pencil next to his lips. "Are you saying the attitude had to change in order to win?"

I nodded. "We had the talent. Everyone knew that. The mental approach to the game had to improve."

McKay laid his notepad on the side table next to the vodka mug and turned to the camera. "Let's look at some of those Steel Curtain defensive plays. Roll the tape." We watched highlights of the '76 defense. "Jim, it's easy to see why you were All-Pro five consecutive seasons."

"Well, let's give credit where credit is due. See No. 75? Mean Joe Steen. It's easy to make tackles when that guy keeps blockers off you. He'll be in the Professional Football Hall of Fame before long."

"Jim, let's reflect a bit. What will you miss most about the game?"

"Wow . . . there are so many great memories, but I touched on those earlier. I'll miss my teammates. An old War World II veteran once told me the men fought for each other. That's how I felt about my teammates. We were a family. We had each other's back."

"What will you miss the least?"

I rested my elbows on the arms of my chair, interlocked my fingers, then laughed. "Two-a-day practices at summer camp. It was like working on a West Texas chain gang in 105 degree heat." Like it felt in the studio.

"Let's get away from football for a moment. On a lighter side . . . what's your favorite meal?"

"Hands down, Big Mamma Helmsly's meatloaf, the best ever made."

"Is that Tony Helmsly's mom?"

"Yeah, next to my mother, this lady had the greatest influence on me."

"How so?"

"She gave me a job at a diner in Belleville, New Jersey, when I was seventeen. She taught me to be accountable for my actions, that hard work pays off, and never to give up."

"Good advice for anyone," Tim nodded. "What's your plan after football?"

"I've gone back to OU in the off seasons and worked on a Master's in Civil Engineering. I received my degree last year and have an interview with Phillips Petroleum next month."

"Congratulations. You've prepared yourself for life after football. Many of your fellow players haven't done that. Last question. Which would you say gave you the most enjoyment, winning three Super Bowls or making All-Pro five consecutive years?"

"Neither." I rested my forearms on the chair and took a deep breath. "My dad died in an oil field accident when I was seventeen. I felt responsible for my family. Pro football allowed me to send my two little sisters to college. I helped my Mom go back to school, and now she's a CPA. I'm more proud of them than any football accomplishments."

"You are a man of honor and character, Jim. I enjoyed the interview. Thank you for sharing your time with us. I wish you the best of luck in your new career."

As soon as the cameras were off, McKay jumped out of his chair and yelled, "That blasted Reneau put vodka in our mugs." Tim laughed all the way down the hall as he searched for the prankster.

After the closing shots, I pushed out of my chair. Felt like I'd been locked in a sauna. An assistant handed me a large glass of ice water which I promptly poured over the top of my head.

Then I headed to the restroom and stared in the mirror. I'd sweated off all the makeup and looked like a bad actor in a class B movie. The black eye couldn't have been more obvious.

I grinned. Dad always told me never to take myself too seriously and try to find humor in bad situations. By changing the sweat-proof make-up to something different, ol' Skunk Hair got the last laugh.

I was the butt of her joke, but had to admit, it was a good one.

CHAPTER 46

In March of 1979, looking at my football career in the rearview mirror, I flew from Pittsburgh to Tulsa, rented a car, and drove forty-five miles to Bartlesville, Oklahoma, for a second interview with Phillips Petroleum Company.

The session went well, and they offered me a position. My career path changed. Excitement abounded. Along with the new challenges of being a civil engineer.

Before my flight back to Pittsburgh, I scrambled to get enough coins to call Belleville from the terminal "Mom, they want to hire me. I'm taking the job."

"Oh, I'm so proud. Do you have a title?" Mom's voice cracked and I sensed she was tearing up.

I covered my other ear to muffle the airport noise. "New systems engineer."

"Okay . . . in English, what will you be doing?"

I forced a grin, weary from the fast trip. "The environmental agencies are starting to clamp down on oil refineries to reduce emissions. I'll help develop systems to control pollutants."

"Emissions, pollutants, environmental agencies. I shouldn't have asked. Come home soon. The girls want to see you and so do I."

I checked my watch. "Talk to you later, Mom. We're boarding. I'll fill you in when I get to New Jersey in a few days."

On the trip back to Pittsburgh, emotions overwhelmed me about retiring from professional football. The sport had been part of my life for so many years. It was hard to give up. The hard work, championships, and victory parades were part of me. Giving up my ties to the Steelers would be difficult. Not being around my teammates was an even bigger issue than missing the game itself, but I couldn't have one without the other.

After the long flight and lack of mobility, my stiff, achy knees convinced me I'd made the right decision.

The next day I was cleaning my apartment in Pittsburg in preparation for the move when the phone rang.

"Jim, it's Laura. How are you?" Her tone was fractured and uneasy.

"Fine." I hesitated. "I was about to call and let you know Phillips Petroleum offered me the job."

"Oh." Her voice deadpanned. "Are you going to take it?"

"Yes." I untangled the cord on the wall phone and moved to the couch. "I'll be moving in two weeks."

"How's your mom dealing with you moving back to Oklahoma?"

"About like she was when I accepted the scholarship to OU, not happy about the distance, but happy for me."

Then silence. I sensed bad news.

"Jim, I'm getting married in six weeks." Laura's voice was soft and low as though she didn't want to break the news.

Her announcement ripped my guts out with a claw hammer. I sank onto the sofa and placed my hand over my mouth to gain composure. "Is it Neal . . . the surgeon in Philadelphia?"

"Yes."

I swallowed and tried to fake a sincere response. "He seems like a great guy. If you're going to marry him, I know he'll make one heck of a husband. I'm happy for both of you."

I'd had a feeling it was serious when Laura introduced us after a Steelers game. I did my best to not like him, but it didn't work. He was friendly, self-assured, and cared for Laura.

"Will you come to the wedding?"

I rubbed the bridge of my nose. "Sure. Of course I will."

"One other thing," she said. "I need to tell you something."

After Laura's lengthy one-sided conversation, I took the phone from my ear and set it beside me. A cold, clammy sweat broke out on my forehead. I was stunned and had trouble digesting what she told me.

CHAPTER 47

I NO SOONER ARRIVED IN OKLAHOMA TO START MY NEW JOB, when my supervisor told me to board a company plane to the Texas Panhandle town of Borger. He wanted me to meet J. F. Briscoli, Phillips Petroleum's chief civil engineer specializing in emission controls. The man would be responsible for my initial training.

As the plane approached Borger's municipal airport, I looked out the small round portal. The topography looked barren—hills sparsely covered with small bush-like trees. The soil had a grayish-tint which reminded me of a forest after a fire. Rocky hills highlighted a dry creek bed and bleached sand after years without flowing water.

Inside the terminal, a large, heavy-set man approached me. His broad shoulders and huge legs were characteristic of an NFL lineman. His shirt was partially tucked in, a cigarette dangled from the corner of his mouth, and his five o'clock shadow reminded me of Paul Bunyan. He stuck out his hand. "You're Jim Pepperman, I'm guessing."

I nodded. "I am."

He removed his smoke, tilted his head back, then exhaled. "I'm J. F. Briscoli. Glad to meet you. Guess the flight was okay?"

"Yeah, a little bumpy at times."

"I keep telling the big shot corporate bean counters to get a larger plane, but the eggheads don't listen. If they were as big as you and me and had to fly on those little puddle jumpers, they'd get a decent sized plane."

I immediately liked him. J. F. appeared to be a no-nonsense guy, kind of like Coach Charles.

"Jim, we're gonna put you up in the Borger Hotel. It's not much, but it's the best in town."

As we got in the car, J. F emptied the ash tray on the pavement. A gust of wind blew the ashes back onto the floor board. "What do you know about the history of Phillips Petroleum?"

I threw my coat into the backseat, then noticed the clutter of old newspapers and empty coffee cups. "Not much, but I do know it's a respected company."

"Tell you what I'll do, Jim. If you can tell me where Frank Phillips, the founder of the company, got his engineering degree, I'll buy you all the pork ribs you can eat at The Hawk's Nest tonight. If you don't get it right, you buy my supper."

I figured I was walking into a trap but played the game anyway. "The University of Oklahoma?"

"Nope." He took a drag on his cigarette and flipped the ashes out the window. "Frank Phillips wasn't an engineer. He was a banker. One more chance. Where was he born?"

"I don't know, but I'll guess Texas."

He looked at me, grinned, exposing brown stained front teeth. "Jim. You really don't know anything about this company. He was born in Nebraska. "

After setting me up twice, J. F. was ticking me off. Wasn't so sure I liked him now. "I told you I didn't know anything about the history of the company. Are you really going to make me buy supper because I didn't know the answer to your questions?"

"Of course. You should have known something about Phillips before coming here." He laughed so hard his shoulders heaved. "I'll fill you in. Frank and his brother moved to Bartlesville in 1903 when they heard about new oil fields. At the time, Bartlesville was Indian Territory. Oklahoma wasn't even a state. Frank took his savings and organized the Citizens Bank and Trust Company. He soon found the banking business extended into oil operations and began to acquire a few leases. His interest grew until 1917 when they incorporated Phillips Petroleum Company."

As we approached the town of Phillips, two miles from Borger, the stench from the refinery almost made me gag. "What's that odor? Rotten eggs?"

J. F. laughed as he pulled a pack of cigarettes from his shirt pocket and tossed it on the dash. "That, my friend, is the reason Phillips hired you. Natural gas is odorless. The additive used in the refining process gives it the rotten egg smell so its presence can be detected. The higher-ups in government say this is polluting the atmosphere."

"I don't know how anyone can live smelling that stuff every day."

"Like anything else . . . you get used to it. See the football field over there—Chesty Walker Stadium. When teams come in here to play, they accuse the coaches of having the refinery release those gasses on purpose to make their kids sick. Heck, it's that way every day. But that's the excuse they give when they lose. The community and school are bordered on three sides by the refinery. It's like living in the middle of a stink pit."

"You don't have to tell me that." I fanned the air in front of my nose. "What's the school mascot and who was Chesty Walker?

"They're the Blackhawks—Phillips Blackhawks. The name just sounds tough, doesn't it? Chesty Walker was one of the winningest coaches in Texas high school football. From mid-1930 through the 70's, the Blackhawks won eighty percent of their games. Now, I can't verify that, but I'd be close, close enough to bet on it."

I looked at him. "That's impressive. How'd they maintain a winning tradition?"

He took a drag, then dropped the cigarette out the window. "The community. Phillips is a small town, little over four thousand. Everybody knows everyone's kids. The students are expected to excel. It doesn't make any difference whether it's sports, band, or academics."

"Seems to be a special place."

"You bet it is. Look at the houses. What do you see?"

I glanced on both sides of the road. "They all look alike."

"Exactly. White asbestos siding with green composition roofs. An engineer with a Ph.D. may be living next door to a maintenance man. No class distinction. Just one big family that looks out for each other."

"The football teams interest me. Tell me more."

"Phillips is a blue-collar town that packs the stadium every Friday night. The people are tough. So are the kids. Shoot, the Blackhawks have to play schools twice their size just to fill out the non-district schedule. Most of the time they kick the living dog poop out of those big schools. The Hawks are bad, and everyone knows it. Hey, I talked about the boys' athletics, but the girls are known for winning state championships in volleyball. Their Coach, Freda Shuttles, a female Vince Lombardi. A top notch coach and a top notch lady."

J. F. pulled into the refinery parking lot. "I'll get you a pass at the guardhouse. It allows you access to the refinery engineering offices. I need to visit with the plant superintendent, Mr. McKenna. Go to the second hall, turn left. My office is the first one on the right. Make yourself at home until I get back."

As I entered Briscoli's office, I was shocked. Nothing but Texas Longhorn paraphernalia and Dallas Cowboy memorabilia. I laughed wondering if he knew I'd played ball in Oklahoma and Pittsburgh.

CHAPTER 48

A FRAMED BURNT ORANGE JERSEY SIGNED BY STEVE Worchester, an outstanding Texas running back of the early seventies, hung on Briscoli's wall. A football, inscribed by legendary coach Terrell Royal, rested on a shelf. A white helmet with a burnt orange Longhorn logo was the centerpiece of the room. This headgear, autographed by Tommy Novis, the greatest linebacker in UT history sat on a display stand in the corner.

Ol' Big Belly was going to blow a tire when he found out I'd played for Oklahoma.

The Dallas Cowboys were equally represented. Autographed photos of Roger Stahl and Coach Thomas hung on the wall. A wooden Cowboy star, nailed on the back of the door, highlighted the interior.

This guy was worse than a hyped-up mega-fan.

He'd caught me off guard with the questions about Phillips. Wondered how much he knew about my background. I'd make a bet with him when he came in.

The door slammed behind me. J. F. entered with a handful of blueprints. He pushed back his rolling chair, slamming it against the wall, before he sat.

"Man, you have a strong affection for football in Texas," I said with a forced smile, ready to nail him with my own questions.

"You betcha." He responded with a boastful grin and tapped his index finger on the desk. "The best football . . . high school, college, pros, is all right here in the Lone Star State."

Briscoli's ego started to wear on me. "Tell you what. Answer three questions about me, and I'll owe you a couple more bar-b-que dinners."

"You're on big fella." J. F. moved the blueprints to the corner of his metal desk. "Lay it on me."

"Where did I start high school?"

"Odessa, Texas. Permian High to be exact."

Darn. "Okay. Where did I graduate from high school?"

"Jim, you're gonna have to ask tougher questions. Belleville High School, Belleville, New Jersey." He grinned, locked his hands behind his head, and propped his feet on the desk.

You had to be kidding me. I'd get him with my last question. "I'll buy you lunch for a week if you can answer this one. Who was my high school coach in New Jersey?"

He put his feet back on the floor, slapped both hands, palms down, in the middle of his paper strewn desk. "Ronnie Mancuso." He propped his legs up again, reared back his head and laughed, a laugh that mocked me from the top of his head to his dirty, scuffed shoes.

Ticked off, I crossed my arms, slid down in the chair, and looked at J. F. My first paycheck would be spent paying off Briscoli, but he did know a lot about me. I'd give him that.

He leaned forward, resting his elbows on his desk, fingers interlocked. "Jim, I handpicked you for this job. There were ten other candidates more qualified, but I wanted you. You want to know why?"

My interest piqued, I said, "Yes."

"I know everything about you. Your life turned upside down when your dad died. Coach Mancuso said you were the best linebacker he ever had, and you took coaching extremely well."

How did he find Coach Mancuso? He retired and moved from Belleville five years ago.

"Coach Aderholt said you'd charge hell with a sling-shot. According to Coach Charles, you were the vocal leader of the Steelers. But you know what sold me? Tony Helmsly's mother, Glynna. She said your character, values, and integrity were off the charts, and she loved you as much as her own kids."

I swallowed, choking back emotions.

J. F. paused. "You're about as good a person as anyone could expect. Only two things against you. You played for the frigging Sooners and the doggone Pittsburgh Steelers. I'm gonna have to overlook those flaws, but think I can make it work."

Dad would've liked this guy. He was a straight shooter who knew what he wanted. Maybe I'd end up liking him after all.

CHAPTER 49

I'D BEEN ON THE JOB NINE MONTHS WHEN J. F. CALLED ME AT my Bartlesville office with an emergency. "Get on the company plane. I need you down here. Be prepared to work through the weekend."

"The Super Bowl's this weekend." And he wanted me to come to the refinery in Phillips. I closed my eyes and rubbed my temple. "What's the problem?"

"I found some safety issues on hydrocarbon units 22 and 23."

"Can you fill me in over the phone?" I was to the point of pleading. Pleading knowing it wouldn't work.

"No, it's more serious than I thought." Briscoli's voice was tense and direct.

I paused. "J. F., I've got a ticket to the Super Bowl in Pasadena. The Steelers are playing the Rams Sunday."

"I don't give a rat's rear. I need you now."

"Could you get Kuchera to help? He knows units 22 and 23 as well as I do?"

I heard a loud exhale. "If I'd wanted Kuchera, I'd be calling Kuchera. Now get down here." The receiver slammed in my ear.

Son-of-a—

I couldn't believe Briscoli was making me work that weekend. I dialed the Steelers quarterback, Terry Bradburn, at his hotel in Pasadena. "Hey, Terry. It's Jim."

"Pepperman, great to hear from you. I left your side-line pass at the will call window. I just talked to Tony Helmsly. You can stay in his room. Well, I guess you know that already."

"I can't make it this weekend, Terry. Something's come up at work. I'm bummed out, but there's nothing I can do about it."

"Dang, Jimbo. I hate that." He hesitated. "Gotta tell you something. I would never admit to my teammates, but I can't shake the thought we might lose this game. I'm tenser than a redneck singing at the opera."

I would've laughed at that little gem, but I knew he was serious. "Come on, Terry, you always have confidence in yourself and the team. You'll be fine."

"Not this time. It's gnawing on my backbone."

"You're nervous because the team has a chance to win Pittsburgh's fourth Super Bowl. It's just pre-game jitters, that's all."

"I hope you're right, but whatever you do, don't tell Helmsly. I gotta get this negative thinking out of my head. Do you want me to let Tony know you're not coming?"

"No, I'll give him a call tonight. One more thing. I'd better not see you choke or I'll be on your case. You know what I'm talking about."

"Yep, I've seen you in a foul mood. Don't want no part of you. Thanks for listening, buddy."

I never tired of hearing that slow Louisiana drawl. "We'll talk after the game. Give the guys my best."

I knew my Phillips job was important, but my heart was with my former teammates. They were my brothers. I couldn't explain it. Wouldn't even try. Soldiers in battle knew what I was talking about.

Hard to believe I'd miss the game.

But J. F. was irritable, more than usual, so whatever was going on must be serious.

CHAPTER 50

I'D SPENT THREE DAYS IN PHILLIPS WORKING AROUND THE CLOCK.
I thought the coffee pot would crash on me more than once.

It was Sunday morning, January 20, 1980, Super Bowl
Day. If I got to the Borger airport by 8:30 to meet the company plane, I'd get home in time to watch the game. But
first I had to swing by the refinery.

The Borger radio station reported it was snowing and
the temperature was twenty degrees with a wind chill of
seven. I hoped the weather wouldn't ground my flight.

J. F. asked me to leave the new drafting schematics
for hydrocarbon units 22 and 23 on his desk.

I checked out of the Borger Hotel and cleaned the
snow from the windshield of the company car. My hands
stung. My teeth clattered. Should've brought my gloves.
A thin sheet of ice caught the corner of the scraper, snapping the brittle plastic.

The frigid bite of the winter blast chapped my face.
I turned up the collar of my coat to protect my neck. I
forced the door open, started the car, and waited until
the heater warmed my frozen body.

I arrived at the refinery gate at 7:30 a.m.

One of the security guards motioned me through the
electronic door. "Hey, no need to show your pass. We

know who you are. Why are you here on Super Bowl Sunday? Briscoli punishing you for something?"

"Yeah. You know how he is, all work. Said he hasn't taken a vacation in years." Both guards laughed as they waved me through the unlocked door.

My hands were still numb from the cold and I rubbed them briskly. Sitting at J. F.'s desk, I wrote him a note explaining my changes on the new blueprints. I went to the file cabinet to put the old diagrams back in their folder. The wall clock showed 7:44. Not much time to catch my flight back to Bartlesville. I reached for the drawer handle, and —

"Kaboom."

A blast slammed me against the file cabinets. I slid to the floor and everything went black.

CHAPTER 51

Sounds rang in my ears. A shrill noise. A siren?

Where was I?

Everything around me shook. Like bumps on a road. Was I in a car?

"Up. Let me up." My words slurred, my tongue fat and rubbery.

"Don't move, Mr. Pepperman." The female voice was calm, but direct. "You've been in an accident. Please don't touch the oxygen mask. You're in an ambulance, and we're taking you to the hospital. We've strapped you down to keep you safe."

The ambulance doors swung open. The cold air made me shudder. Two men dressed in white moved me inside the building and transferred me to a gurney. The gurney bounced down a narrow, florescent lit hallway. The smell was not describable, but I knew it was a hospital.

"Dr. Marjo," an anxious voice shouted. "Where do we take him?"

"Trauma three." The woman who answered had a controlled voice that calmed me. "What are his vitals?"

"BP 120 over 80. Heart rate 124. Left pupil dilated."

A blurred vision of someone's face flickered in and out like a candle in a gust of wind.

"Did he regain consciousness on the way?" Her deep voice was clear and concise.

I was conscious now. Didn't they know?

"He said a few words responding to pain, and there's movement in his left hand and foot, but not the right." The lady's words were high-pitched and anxious, as though she was going down a checklist.

Who were these people?

"The cut on his forehead isn't serious." The woman with the strong, deep voice was apparently in charge. "I see no other lesions. Get him to x-ray. Stat."

I felt the gurney move again, then heard her say, "Get me Dr. Niva on the phone. He's at Northwest Texas Hospital in Amarillo."

My head was spinning like I'd been on an amusement park ride. People were talking about me as though I wasn't there. I was okay. I needed to go home.

"Dr. Niva, this is Dr. Marjo in Borger. We have a male patient, early thirties who sustained a head injury from a refinery explosion. We did a CT scan and can see an acute subdural hemorrhage. We've given him Manitol to reduce the swelling. Will you accept him?"

"Okay." The lady with the deep voice was Dr. Marjo. "You'll contact your emergency room and let them know he's coming? He'll be a direct admission. Are you in the Neurosurgical ICU now? Do you have an available bed? . . . Great. His injuries are on the left side of his head. Left pupil dilated. Speech slurred. He responds to pain and commands, but has pronounced weakness of the extremities on the right side."

I remembered the smells. Antiseptic, rubbing alcohol, sterilized gauze.

"A small laceration an inch above his left eye. . . . We know nothing about his medical history. His driver's license indicates he lives in Bartlesville, Oklahoma. We've tried to reach his family but unable to make contact."

My stomach rumbled and tightened like I was going to throw up.

"Yes, Dr. Niva, we're still hyperventilating the patient. . . . I don't think the helicopter is a viable option. They're telling me the wind gusts are between thirty and forty miles an hour, and the snow is picking up. He'll have to make the fifty-mile trip by ground transport."

"Mr. Pepperman, Mr. Pepperman, can you hear me?" The voice was male. Had a Texas twang.

"Yes." I sounded like a drunk. Felt a little drunk. But I wasn't.

"I'm Timothy Shorter, the emergency room doctor at Northwest Texas. I'm going to shine a light in each of your eyes."

The brightness was blurred, like a street lamp hidden in fog. Why were they making a fuss? Just send me home.

"We've looked at your CT scan. You need surgery."

What? Surgery? Why? I tried to ask him. Why wouldn't the words come out?

"I'll explain the procedure. Will you sign the permission form?"

"Yes," I whispered. Unable to hold a pen in my right hand, I scribbled my name with my left as a nurse steadied the clipboard.

When I woke up, the room was dark except for a dim light overhead. My face felt numb and my head throbbed. I knew I was in a hospital. My room must have been close to the nurse's station because I heard someone say, "Dr. Niva, this is Nancy Brumlee in the Neurosurgical ICU. Mr. Pepperman is responsive. . . . Okay . . . I'll see you soon."

"Mr. Pepperman, I'm Dr. Niva, the neurosurgeon who did the procedure. Can you see me?"

"Yes." What was wrong with my voice? I could hardly hear myself talk.

"Do you know where you are?"

"Hospital," I struggled to say. "People. . . talking about me. Am I going to die?"

Dr. Niva answered, "No, but you were in an explosion."

"An explosion?"

"The refinery at Phillips blew up and you were there. What's the last thing you remember?"

"Super Bowl. Got to get home."

"The game was played three days ago."

My heart pounded against my ribs, and my pulse increased. Three days. Three days. "Who won?"

"The Steelers 31-19." The doctor raised my left eyelid with his thumb and index finger. "You sustained a head injury known as a subdural hematoma. We had to drill a hole in your skull and remove a clot. The surgery was successful."

"My head hurts. Got anything to help?"

"Sure. There are some people here who've been waiting for you to wake up."

I turned my head slowly to see Mom, Blythe and Brook.

Mom walked to the head of my bed and squeezed my hand. "Good to hear your voice."

"I'm glad you finally woke up," Brook said. "I've got a crick in my neck from sleeping in that straight-back vinyl chair in the corner." I grinned. Brook being Brook.

"Mrs. Pepperman, could you all step into the hallway? I need to examine Jim."

Blythe stepped up to the bed. "I called Laura about the explosion. I knew you'd want her to know."

As they moved out of the room, I saw Blythe pat my right foot, but I didn't feel it. I knew she touched me, but I didn't feel it. I didn't feel it.

"Jim, take hold of my two fingers with your right hand and squeeze as hard as you can." Dr. Niva nodded. "That's good. You've regained some strength since your admittance. Now, pick up your left leg."

No problem. I did that.

"Try your right leg."

Concentrate. I could do it. Finally, a few inches. My knee felt like a sack of concrete was draped across it. Sweat rolled down my cheeks. My breathing increased and my body tensed. "Doc, am I going to be able to walk?"

"The part of your brain that controls the motor skills has been damaged. We'll start physical therapy on your leg in a few days. I'll know more about your condition then."

His words terrified me. It was as though my spirit had been yanked from my body. I wanted to give up.

Oh, God, please help me.

CHAPTER 52

I STARTED REHAB AT THE HOSPITAL IN AMARILLO. THE NURSES warned me my therapist had a reputation for being tough and demanding. They cautioned me about her no-nonsense approach. That was fine. I wanted my life back.

It seemed just when I had life under control, the explosion happened. I'd paid for Blythe's college and had money set aside for Brook. Mom had gone back to school and become a CPA, and I'd bought her a new house. All that because of my football career. Little did I know how pampered I'd been. Everything came easy to me because of my physical attributes.

My slow-motioned life in the hospital room gave me time to reflect. I'd fulfilled the promise I'd made to dad all those years ago.

But now, I was just another engineer. Worse, I was recovering from brain surgery. Briscoli said there were ten others more qualified for my job than me. Would Phillips let me go because I couldn't do my job?

Before the first physical therapy session, doubt clamped onto me like a steel trap. What if my motor skills were damaged beyond repair? What if my analytical skills were diminished? Could I adapt and prepare myself mentally for what might happen?

A sharp *tap, tap, tap* on the door of my room quickened my pulse.

A woman entered. "Mr. Pepperman, I'm Carolyn Mohr, your physical therapist. I'll be working with you twice a day. Here's the therapy schedule. Read over it. If you have any questions, I'll answer them this afternoon." Then, without so much as a smile, Miss Mohr marched out of my room and took her terrible bedside manner with her.

I looked forward to working with her as much as I'd look forward to someone breaking both my arms.

Mid-afternoon an orderly wheeled me to the therapy room for my first session.

"Mr. Pepperman, stand between the parallel bars, grab hold, and walk to the end. I need to make an initial evaluation." Miss Mohr barked orders like a constipated Russian general.

The orderly helped me out of the wheel chair. I steadied myself. Lightheaded from not walking in days, I began the challenge. Uncertainty hit like a blast from a jet engine.

I tried to break the ice with my female martinet. "What if I just run to the end and you time me?" No reaction. What was it with that lady? Or was she a lady? Maybe she was a robot.

I gripped the bars. So far so good. My upper body motor skills were fine. I tried to lift my right leg. It took all my strength to pick up my foot and move it six inches. I swear, every muscle fiber in my leg strained to move my three-hundred-pound foot. If my left leg was this difficult to move, I'd be toast. I was afraid to try.

"Mr. Pepperman, move your left leg." Her tone was more like a concentration camp guard than a trained professional. My gosh, where'd they find her?

I picked up my left leg. It was easy. Great. Now, my right leg again. It was harder than the first time. I glanced at Miss Mohr.

She looked me straight in the eye with zero emotion and slowly pulled her left hand toward her. "Come to me."

Okay. No positive response. No problem. I'd show this taskmaster what I was made of. She wouldn't break me.

It took five minutes to travel the ten-foot parallel bars. I'd never worked so hard in my life. Not even at the Steelers' summer workout. The back of my t-shirt was soaking wet. Every muscle in my upper back and shoulders burned.

I looked at Miss Mohr, expecting her to tell me nice job or something equally encouraging. But no. Not her.

She frowned and made a u-shaped motion with her hand. "Turn around."

I was exhausted and gave her a look that shouldn't be translated. The end of the bars seemed a mile away.

She folded her arms, then lifted her chin. "Walk back."

Okay, you maniacal witch. I'll show you.

I made it to where she stood at the end of the bars. I expected at least a conciliatory "that-a-boy," but all I got was, "We're going to the stationary bike."

This lady was not going to beat me. I'd die before I gave up.

And so it went for the next few days. After my third afternoon session with the Queen of Torture, I was totally fatigued when I made it back to my hospital bed.

There was a knock at the door and Briscoli entered.

His shoulders lurched forward. He looked at the floor and then glanced out the window. Then he looked me in the eye. "How are you, Jim?"

I fixed in on his stare. "I'm getting better."

"Jim, I have something to say. Will you listen?"

I nodded, sensing he put all the blame on himself for what happened. "Go ahead."

Briscoli pulled a chair close to my bed. He bit down on his lower lip as though he was measuring his words.

I waited. The man wasn't a coward. Facing me took guts.

"I feel terrible about what happened. I wanted your input. You're a bright guy with great analytical skills. You make my department look good, and I wanted credit for completing the safety project ahead of schedule. I should've . . ." He paused as he cupped his hand over his mouth as though ashamed at what he said. His eyes seemed to ache as he continued. "I wish I hadn't made you come. Can you forgive me?"

Dad taught me if a person took responsibility for his actions, he had character. He said I would be judged according to how I judged others.

"J. F., did you know the explosion was going to happen?"

His eyes narrowed, head slightly tilted. "Of course not."

I had to say something to take away his guilt. "Then don't blame yourself for my predicament. You had every right to tell me to come to Phillips. You're my boss. That's your job."

He swallowed before he continued. "Monday after the explosion I went to my office. A three-foot shard of glass was impaled in my chair. I shudder thinking about it. You could have been sitting there."

"But I wasn't."

If I hadn't gotten up to go to the file cabinet, I would be dead. Oh, Lord, thank you. Thank you.

Briscoli was a good guy. He shouldn't beat himself up over this. "J. F., we both can what-if ourselves to death. Let's take things as they are and go from here. It's not your fault. I don't know how all this is going to work out, but you can bet I'll do my best to walk again."

The tension in Briscoli's shoulders seemed to loosen. The muscles in his face softened and a smile slowly opened. "The spirit you're showing is the reason I hired you. No doubt in my mind. You'll walk."

Our eyes locked and we shook hands. Mutual respect.

CHAPTER 53

A FEW DAYS HAD PASSED SINCE MY SURGERY.

"I see you're still getting your name in the paper like you did in your heyday." Briscoli tossed a newspaper on my bed. "Thought you might want to read about the explosion."

"Believe me, I wish my name wasn't in the news when it relates to this." I clutched the paper with both hands and looked out the window before reading, not wanting to relive the experience.

AMARILLO DAILY NEWS—JANUARY 21, 1980
PHILLIPS REFINERY BLAST INJURES 30
Damage May Run into Millions

PHILLIPS—A series of explosions at the Phillips refinery yesterday injured 30 people and caused damages that could run into millions of dollars.

Most of the injured suffered superficial cuts from flying glass. Three Phillips Petroleum employees were hospitalized. Two were taken to North Plains Hospital in Borger and one to Northwest Texas Hospital in Amarillo.

A Phillips spokesman identified the individuals as Dru Sampson, Sam Perrine and Jim Pepperman. Samson and Perrine, both of Phillips, were reported in satisfactory condition. Pepperman, an engineer from Bartlesville, Oklahoma, received a serious head wound. Nothing has been released about his condition.

Witnesses said thick black smoke from the raging inferno billowed into the gray snowy skies. The blast moved houses on their foundations, collapsed ceilings, and blew doors off the hinges. Most of the damage was to homes near the explosion. However, some of the businesses in downtown Borger, two miles away, sustained broken plate glass windows.

"It looked like they dropped an atomic bomb," said a company official who made an inspection tour of the damages. "If this had happened on a Monday morning . . . God help us . . . hundreds of people would have been killed."

I placed the newspaper on the hospital table next to my bed. Hundreds of people could have been affected by this catastrophe, families torn apart by death.

I was even more thankful to be alive.

CHAPTER 54

A FEW WEEKS OF INTENSE PHYSICAL THERAPY GENERATED SOME progress. The Iron Maiden, Miss Mohr, was still busting my chops.

I waited in my room for our morning workout session and heard the familiar squeak of her tennis shoes marching across the linoleum floor. My taskmaster would be wearing white scrub pants with a matching shirt, a God-awful pink sweater, and have her hair pulled back in a ponytail. She'd be carrying a clipboard, and probably have on her black round-framed glasses that reminded me of Emperor Hirohito.

I crossed my arms and waited for Miss Congeniality. And there she was—exactly as I thought.

"Good morning and thank you for being predictable."

She laid her clipboard on the foot of my bed, adjusted her glasses with her middle finger. "And what does that mean, Mr. Pepperman?"

"It took me awhile, but I've got you figured out."

Miss Mohr sucked in air through her nose. "Oh, please enlighten me."

"I had a coach once who challenged me every day. When I screwed up, he made a point to tell me about it. When I did something right, he rarely gave me a pat on the back. He made me a better football player. Your tactics remind me of him, the way you motivate me."

The tip of her tongue circled her lips. "The coach you're talking about wouldn't be Ronnie Mancuso, would it?"

My jaw dropped. "How did you know?"

She smiled in a caring way I'd never witnessed. "I talked with Coach Mancuso. Every patient is different when it comes to recovery. I know more about what makes you tick than you think. Some people need positive reinforcement. Others, like you, respond to challenges."

I slapped my forehead. "Coach has called three times since the accident. He never said a word about you."

"I asked him not to. Now get out of bed. We've got work to do, Jim." She tucked the clipboard under her arm, stopped at the door and looked back.

I gave her a military salute.

She grinned and returned the respect.

My initial impression of Miss Mohr was that of a cold, heartless person. I was wrong. She was a professional who took her job seriously. Thank God for that.

CHAPTER 55

My treatment in Amarillo finished. Carolyn Mohr pushed me to a seventy-five percent recovery. The grueling workout sessions would continue in Bartlesville. I was grateful Michael Dean, my college trainer, had a rehab clinic a few miles from my home. He planned to work me just as hard as she did, but I was sick of physical therapy.

I drove by the granite markers of the local cemetery and thought of Dad. I was so frustrated. Why the accident? Why now, Dad?

An old teammate of mine from Oklahoma gave me a call.

"Hey, Jim. It's Mike Podzinsky."

I could hear people in the background. The chatter must be from his office.

His call came at a good point. I was a little less depressed today. "Pod, how are you, man?"

"Good. Thought I'd check in, see how things are going. Bad break about the explosion."

Shifting the phone, I supported my injured leg on the couch cushion. "I'm okay. Still trying to get my right foot to cooperate. Other than that, things are fine."

"Sorry for not driving down to see you. My business keeps me tied up like a calf at a rodeo."

I couldn't help but grin at his down-home analogy I'd heard a gazillion times. "Are you still living in Derby, Kansas?"

"Yep, just bought two more grain elevators. Trying to get someone to manage them. You need a job?"

"Heck, I don't know anything about grain. Why don't you call your old roommate Olendorf?"

"Shoot, that pretty boy wouldn't come up here. Not enough women for him."

I nodded and my face broke into an understanding smile, a smile of total agreement. "Yeah, I guess you're right. Is he still in med school?"

"Finished about six months ago. You'll never guess where he moved."

Pod hadn't changed. He'd ask a question you probably couldn't answer just so he could tell you. "And where would that be Pod?' Couldn't resist the sarcasm.

"Midland, Texas, of all places."

Now that got my attention. Midland was only fifteen miles from where I grew up in Odessa. "You're kidding?"

"Nope. Just opened his office. Said his first patient was an oil field worker who got his finger caught between a pipe and a chain. Cut the sucker right off."

I knew about those things. Happened a lot in the Permian Basin. I needed to talk about something besides accidents.

"Hey, Pod, I was coming back from therapy the other night and noticed those little amber reflectors lights on the side of the road. Remember when you and Olendorf knocked all of them down between Oak City and Norman. You got your pickup stuck on the last pole."

"Of course." He snorted a chuckle. "I also remember how ticked you were when we got you out of bed to help us."

"Yeah, I had my last final of the semester at nine that morning. You numbskulls. Changing the subject, have you heard from, J. Mo?"

"You're not gonna believe this. You know where he's living? Miami, Florida."

Good, he answered his own question.

"I went down last year. He's got a nightclub called Steelfingers. J. Mo's hair is long and braided. Looks like giant tarantula legs growing out of his head. It's the darnedest thing I've ever seen, but, I have to admit, it looks good on him. The band plays Jamaican music called ragu or something like that."

The ol' farm boy just butchered the English language again. "Wait a minute. The music the band plays, it's not ragu. That's spaghetti sauce. I think you mean reggae."

I could hear him blow air over his lips, making a flutter noise. "Whatever. How would I know? I'm from Kansas."

I heard someone interrupt his conversation. Pod tried to muffle the phone, but I could hear the almost cuss words. "Dad-gum-it."

"What's wrong, Mike?"

"One of my new drivers just backed into the side of the grain elevator. Gotta go."

"Okay, thanks for calling. I really appreciate it."

"No problem, Jim. Hang tough and let me hear from you."

"Will do."

I wasn't looking forward to talking when he called, too busy having a pity party, but bringing up old times was exactly what I needed. There were certain friends who would keep in touch, especially when you needed them the most. Podzinsky was one of those.

After a month with Michael Dean, the rehab of my leg reached a plateau, and I was able to work half-days at my job for Phillips Petroleum.

The cane, my wretched walking cane, was my cross to bear. The right foot still felt detached from the rest of my body, and the scraping sound my foot made across a floor made me self-conscious. I was paranoid thinking everyone watched me trudge the narrow hallways to and from my office.

When I was feeling sorry for myself, I was rude to my co-workers. I knew better than that. I was raised better than that.

Dad had always been there for me. Now I was too ashamed to talk to him.

Later on a gloomy March night, the temperature dropped and a storm had blown in. Thunder rocked the house and lightning flickered in the distance as I stared out the picture window in my living room.

The phone rang, breaking my trance.

I struggled to the phone without my cane. "Hello."

"Hey, Jim. It's Tony. How are you, man?"

I exhaled. People asked me the same question over and over. "Nothing's changed. I'm still crippled."

There was a long pause. "Wow, that's not the attitude of the Jim Pepperman I know. Can I do anything to help?"

"Not unless you're a miracle worker."

"I'm coming down this weekend."

"Don't bother. I'm not in the mood."

Tony's voice was sharp and to the point. "Hey, I said I was coming down, and I'm bringing Terry Bradburn with me."

"Fine. Do whatever you want." Depression still had a hook in me.

After hanging up, I felt bad talking to Tony with that condescending tone. He was one of my closest friends. He didn't deserve my anger. But I couldn't make myself call him back.

By the time the doorbell rang that weekend, I had mixed emotions about seeing Tony and Bradburn. On one hand, maybe they could help improve my attitude. On the other, I didn't want them to see me like this.

I struggled to walk from my chair to the door.

My buddies greeted me with hardy handshakes and good-natured slaps on my back.

"Come on in, guys. Congratulations on winning the Super Bowl. Have a seat," I said in a monotone voice, not showing much excitement.

"Jimbo, got a beer?" Bradburn tried to break the ice.

"In the fridge. You'll have to get it. My leg hurts."

"No problem. Tony, you want one?"

"Sure."

"Jim," Tony said. "I know you're hurting. What can I do to help?"

"I told you. There's nothing that can be done. It is what it is." The conversation continued, but the longer we visited the more rigid the tension became.

Tony turned to Terry. "We're out of beer. Why don't you go to the 7-11 and get some more?"

"Oh, no. Jim's got plenty." Bradburn pointed to the fridge. "Do you want another one?"

Tony gave Terry a look that would melt plastic.

The corners of Bradburn's mouth turned down and bobbed his head from side to side. He got the message. "You're right. I'll get a six pack. Do you want any pork rinds?"

Tony gave him another look that meant get the heck out of here.

"Fine, no pork rinds. I'll be back in a minute."

Tony pulled up a chair and glared at me, the kind of glare that would back down Big Foot. I'd never seen anger that intense in him.

I raised both hands, palms out. "Tony, I know what you're going to say. Tough it up, Pepperman."

His chin dropped, eyes raised. "Jim, I do have things to say. Don't interrupt me. Just listen. You got that?"

I nodded. I knew he was serious.

"First of all, I don't know how you feel. I do know it has to be difficult, but you're acting like a sniffling cry baby. You're feeling sorry for yourself because you can't get back total use of your leg. What about the guy in the wheelchair who can't walk? What about the mother with MS who can't get out of bed to care for her family? What about the soldier who came back from Vietnam with both legs blown off while protecting your right to play football on Sundays?"

I leaned forward, pointed my finger and started to speak.

"I'm not finished." Tony held up his hand. "Your family loves you. You're tearing them apart. And, Burl and Earl think of you as a big brother. They look up to you. Jim, you are my brother. I don't care if our skin color is different. I will not let you wallow in self-pity. Now get hold of yourself and start acting like a man. If you don't, I'll tell Big Mamma, and you know what she'll do."

I stared at Tony.

He stared back.

Neither of us blinked.

I looked away first and straightened my posture. "Heck of a speech. You're right about everything, but you know what scares me?"

Tony leaned back in his chair, arms relaxed by his side. "No, what?"

"Big Mamma Helmsly threatening to pepper my backside with your belt."

Both of us grinned, and then broke out laughing.

At that light moment, Bradburn returned from the 7-11. He set the beer on the counter, placed his hand on his chin. "You could've died in that explosion. You know, what doesn't kill you will make you stronger." He paused. Something pulled the proverbial light cord in his brain. "That would be a great song."

Tony looked at Bradburn. "Just don't try to record it yourself. Bring us a beer and a bag of pork rinds."

Bradburn's arms went straight over his head. "I didn't buy pork rinds. You let me know with that witch-eye stare you didn't want any."

"Okay," Tony chuckled. "Bring us a cold one."

My teammates' short visit was a turning point in my life. I realized I had given up. It wasn't going to be easy, but I challenged myself to overcome my problem.

The physical issues, I'd handle.

The depression. Well—I needed help.

Dad, I'm going to be okay. I'll fight just like you taught me.

CHAPTER 56

SEVEN YEARS HAD PASSED SINCE I FACED THE MOST CHALLENGING struggle of my life—the head injury suffered in the refinery explosion.

Now I looked forward to my twentieth high school reunion in New Jersey, Belleville Class of 1967. I'd kept in touch with a few of my classmates but had no idea about the others. I wondered what everyone was doing and what they would look like.

As I boarded the plane to Newark, a gray-haired man caught my attention. He could have been a twin brother of Mimphord, the old deckhand Dad met on the job in West Texas. What a character. He had befriended everyone in our family and become like an uncle to us kids. Dad thought a lot of him, and he often came for lunch on Sundays—if he hadn't been thrown in jail the night before.

After graduating from college, I kept in touch with the old deck hand. In our last phone conversation, he told me he was moving to New Zealand to retire.

Mom planned a family gathering to coincide with the class reunion. Blythe and Brook were coming in, and she invited Tony and his wife Tai Lynn.

I'd planned on waiting until Friday night to see Tony when they came to Belleville, but I wanted to see his

Grappling Club in Newark. I gave him a call to let him know I was coming.

The club was directly in the center of Newark. The old part of town was run down and dirty, but the Grappling Club was new, painted gold with black trim. Wonder where he came up with the color scheme?

Inside the workout complex, there were three wrestling mats. All occupied. At one end of the room, groups practiced techniques, and on the opposite end, others worked on strength and conditioning. About fifty kids were working out. The training was intense. I expected nothing less from Tony and his approach to winning.

He saw me standing in the doorway and gave a hand-up greeting. As he walked toward me, I thought of the first time we met—the stormy night at the diner when the electricity went off. He'd put his face up to the window looking for his mom. He was an imposing figure then as he was now.

We wrapped our arms around each other.

"Good to see you, brother." His deep voice exuded strength and love all tied into one.

"Back at you, my friend."

Tony looked up and pointed to his office. "Let's go up. It'll be a little quieter."

I moved a chair in front of his paper-laden desk. "How's that lovely wife of yours?"

"Tai's good, but she's on my case about losing a few pounds."

"You should listen to the lady."

He pointed with his index finger and lowered his head. "Hey, don't be on her side. She's more than enough to handle without you joining her."

I eased my hands behind my head. It was great to be around my ol' buddy. "Tony, when are you going to have some kids of your own?"

"We're still trying. I guess God's got other plans for right now. We'll see what happens."

When Tony moved his hand, the sunlight from the window behind him reflected off his Super Bowl ring.

"Tony, did you ever think we'd be fortunate enough to play pro ball and win three Super Bowls?"

He rubbed his chin, then shook his head. "Never in a million years."

I leaned forward, resting my elbow on the chair arms. "Remember Coach Charles telling us after we beat the Vikings in the championship game that there were two types of Super Bowl teams that people forget. One was the team that lost and two was the team that only won one."

"I do. I also remember he left no doubt that we'd better win more than one."

"Think about this Tony. Almost every player on our roster had been drafted by Coach Charles and developed under him. Very few players came to Pittsburgh from other teams."

"How could we have been so blessed?" Tony leaned back in his chair, interlocked his fingers and placed them in his lap.

I've had many friends, good friends, but none I respected more than Tony. He was doing remarkable things with the underprivileged kids of Newark. He took them off the streets and taught them discipline and principles—training them to win at life.

Eleven pictures hung in Tony's office of those who had received college wrestling scholarships in the last six years.

To help with the coaching, Tony hired a wrestling champion from the University of Iowa, his younger brother Burl. Considering how often Tony and I roughhoused Burl and his twin Earl, it's no wonder both excelled in the sport.

Earl had an interesting story himself. He was offered a wrestling scholarship to Penn State, but turned it down to join the Marines. He became an elite soldier of the Navy Seals.

I left Tony's for Nanny Brownlee's and a generous helping of homemade bread. I pulled into her driveway and smelled that wonderful aroma. But her door was locked, and the car wasn't in the garage. Where could she be? She'd called and said the bread was in the oven and get over there ASAP.

I heard a loud vroom and squealing tires. Nanny turned the corner driving the 1967 GTO she had given me when I graduated from high school. All I could see was her little head peering through the steering wheel and her tattered, crimson OU visor. I had to jump from the driveway onto the grass to keep her from pancaking my feet.

"Nanny . . . you're driving a little fast. You almost ran over me."

She slammed the car door and walked past me. "I had to go to the store and get butter. And don't tell me how to drive, Sonny Boy."

My head followed her as she strutted past me. I smiled at my sassy, diminutive grandma. It's cliché to say she was a corker, but there was no other way to describe her.

After gorging myself on hot rolls, I asked Nanny if I could take the GTO to drive around Belleville.

She pointed her crooked, arthritic finger at me. "Okay, but drive carefully and don't speed. I remember how reckless you were in high school."

Boy, was she one to be talking.

Cruising down Passaic Avenue brought back old memories. I remembered my first days in Belleville and all the uncertainties of being a teenager in a strange town. I noticed some new businesses on the street.

Terry Bensway had built a large State Farm Insurance office. He was a great running back in high school and will always be remembered for replacing Phil Anderson, the bully who tormented me. Terry tried to sell me life insurance every time I came home for Christmas. His persistency paid off, and I bought a big policy with an equally big premium.

I saw Jeff Langdon come out of the hardware store. He had on the oldest, slouchiest, drabbest clothes you could imagine. Déjà vu.

"Hey, you illiterate dirt-bag, get off the street," I yelled.

Jeff approached my car. "I'll remind you again, I'm not illiterate. Yale is an accredited university, unlike that hayseed Oklahoma college you attended. I'd also remind you I'm a federal judge and can have you arrested for being a dumb jock."

I smiled, shook my head, and pointed to the passenger seat. "Get in the car, Your Honor."

We drove to O'Reilly's Pub and sat at the table in the back, our usual spot. The place hadn't changed since our college days. The musty smell of stale tobacco and the flickering Budweiser light reminded me of old times. The memories, for the most part, were good. There was something about a neighborhood pub. Like it or not, they were a part of our culture.

"I was hoping you wouldn't come to the reunion," I said in a sarcastic tone.

He sniffed and wiped his runny nose. "Shut up, you knuckle-dragging Neanderthal."

I reached across the table and gave him a friendly slap on the top of his head. "How's Chief Langdon?"

"Good. Dad's going to retire next month." This time Jeff used a handkerchief instead of his sleeve.

"Jeff, your dad was a great mentor. He gave me good advice more than once. I appreciate how he looked out for me. Changing the subject, how's Susan? What's she up to these days?"

He took a deep breath, filling up both sides of his cheeks, then exhaled. "We got a divorce six months ago."

"What? You're still wearing a wedding band."

"I remarried." He gave me a don't-be-stupid look.

"Already?"

"Rachel, and she's a knock-out."

"Rachel. Is she a Belleville girl?"

"Nope." He belched and adjusted his worn fake-leather watchband.

"Where did you meet her?"

"Vegas." His sheepish expression piqued my attention.

"Vegas! What were you doing there?"

"We had a judge's convention."

"Is she a judge, too?"

Jeff slowly moved his head from side to side and began to laugh. "No."

From his reaction, I almost dreaded to ask my next question. "What does she do?"

Jeff paused, then shut his eyes. "She was a pole dancer."

I stared at him, mouth wide open. "You're kidding, right?"

"No, why would I be kidding?" He nervously circled the top of the beer mug with his index finger.

I hesitated, then broke out laughing so loud the bartender shouted, "Hey, you two. Quiet down back there." He smiled, shoved a cigar in his mouth, and resumed pulling a draft.

"Jeff, how many times have you been married?"

He stuck out his chin. "Only four."

I shook my head. Why should I ever be surprised by anything Jeff did?

"Jim, it wasn't my fault. The first three marriages . . . I was seduced."

"What about Rachel? Did she seduce you?"

"Yes, but this time I wasn't under the influence."

I rested my forearms on the table and bit down on both lips. I almost suffocated trying to muffle the laughter. My body shook and, I'm sure, my face turned red as the city fireplugs.

Jeff was one unique individual. Smarter than most, but his personal life? Questionable. Someone needed to write a book about him.

CHAPTER 57

AFTER JEFF AND I SWAPPED STORIES AT O'REILLY'S PUB, I drove to Gloria's Diner to see Big Mamma Helmsly. I saw a large sign truck and the crew removing the neon fixture. What was going on? Big Mamma's car was parked in front. She never parked there. I rushed into the diner. "Where's Glynna?"

The waitress, filling the ice bin behind the counter, pointed to the office. My mind cluttered with all sort of scenarios. None of them good. I pushed through the door. Big Mamma was at her desk scribbling on a note pad. She looked as though she'd been crying.

"What's wrong, Glynna?" My voice pitched with uncertainty.

Startled, she said, "Oh, Jim, you're not going to believe what just happened."

I reached across and placed my hands on hers. I anticipated the worst. "Tell me."

Glynna reached for a tissue and blotted her eyes. "Do you know Sharyn and Edwin Leitner?"

"Sure, they're the richest family in Belleville."

She cleared her throat, struggling to continue. "You know they own the diner?"

I nodded.

"Well, both of them were waiting on me when I got to work. I felt something was wrong."

"Go on, Big Mamma."

"Mr. Leitner said he sold the diner and the new owner was taking over today. I was no longer the manager."

Her words bored a hole in my heart. My eyes squeezed shut. How could he do that to her? She'd put her heart and soul into the diner.

I slammed my fist on the desk and stood. "Why would he do that? You've been the face of this diner for years. You made the restaurant what it is. I'm going to see that SOB right now."

"Jim, sit down. There's more." She wiped a tear with the back of her hand. "Mr. Leitner said, 'Glynna, do you remember the five dollars I loaned you when you started working here?' I said yes. He told me to pay it back right then, so I gave him the money." The sobs increased as she buried her face into her shaking hands.

"Then he said, 'Glynna, you just bought Gloria's Diner.' "

I sat back in my chair, stunned. "What did you say? I think I misunderstood."

"Mr. Leitner sold me the diner for five dollars."

Glynna and I looked at each other. It was as though someone pushed a pause button and time stopped. I leaned forward, resting my arms on the desk. "You own Gloria's diner, and you bought it for five dollars?"

She nodded and slid the deed in front of me.

"You deserve this, Glynna."

I pushed myself out of the chair and slowly moved around the desk to give her a hug.

She patted my cheeks and leaned back. "Do you remember Debra, the afternoon manager of the diner when you were in high school? She cooked you meals and told you to take the extra home to your family? You wanted to know who provided the meat, but no one would say."

"I knew it was you, Big Mamma. It didn't take me long to figure that out."

She smiled, her eyes shining in pods of tears as she shook her head. "No. It wasn't me."

I angled my head. "You didn't buy the steaks?"

She placed her hands on my shoulders. "I knew who did it, but promised not to tell. Your family was having a hard time making ends meet. He told me you needed good meals to get you through the football season. The meat was provided by Mr. Leitner. He did it."

I heard Glynna's words, but they didn't register. "I only met him once. Why would he do that? He didn't know me."

"He knew you, Jim. You didn't know him. He saw something extraordinary in you, and so did I. That's why I hired you."

Glynna reached for a tablet. "I've had some time to think since the Leitners left. You and Tony are my inspiration. Here's what I'm going to do. I'm changing the name of the diner to Big Mamma's. You were the first one to call me that. We'll offer two house specials — Tony's Pork Rib Platter and Jim's Mother Lode Meatloaf."

She looked up at me. "Hmmm . . . I'd better warn people. The specials will have in bold print — Beware . . . NFL Portions."

Some people gave up hope and lost heart. Glynna could have succumbed to life's challenges, but she didn't. She was faithful and God rewarded her.

CHAPTER 58

Blythe and Brook arrived Friday, the day before my high school reunion. Mom was happy to have all her kids home again.

Blythe had graduated from Texas Tech University with a degree in communications. She never considered another school. Memories of that cold football game in Lubbock made a lasting impression in her two-and-a-half year old mind. It puzzled me how she remembered the masked rider and the black stallion.

She was absorbed in writing an article on women and sports and had been typing all morning.

I wanted to talk about her job. "Sister, you know I was responsible for you getting hired by ESPN?"

She never looked up, kept right on banging those keys. "Oh, how's that?"

"You remember all the interviews I gave you after every high school game?"

She stopped long enough to give me a sour look. "Yeah, so what?"

I turned both palms up and gave her a pious grin. "Well, there you have it. Ol' big brother started it all. Thank you very much."

"Oh, good grief. I remember how you complained. The only reason you gave the interviews was because

Mom made you, and besides, you hid my tape recorder."

"No, no, no." I waved my index finger. "Brook did that."

"You big dope. You're accusing Brook because she's not here to defend herself." I had no comeback. Plus she was right.

Blythe was determined to become a sports analyst. I don't know how many television stations turned her down because of her gender. One station in Waco, Texas, gave her the break she needed. My sister had become the best known sportscaster in Central Texas and gained national attention when she covered the 1978 Cotton Bowl. She became the first female sideline reporter for ESPN.

Mom and Dad taught us to seek what we wanted and let nothing stand in our way. Dad often said, "Dreams are the fuel that ignites reality." Blythe proved his point.

She got the best of me in our sibling discussion, then I asked, "Where's Brook?"

Blythe pulled back a curtain in the living room. "She and Mom just pulled in the driveway."

With bags of groceries in her arms, Mom struggled to open the back door. I held it open and took her sacks. "Where have you guys been?" I pulled a banana out of a bag after setting them next to the stove.

"Ah, let me see. Oh yeah. We've been running a marathon. Where do you think we've been?"

I reached over and gave Brook a head noogie, the little wiseacre.

"Mom said you wanted me to bake some cherry kolaches."

"That's right, so get cracking."

Brook looked at me, lowering her chin to her chest. "Talk like that and you'll do without."

I clicked my heels together. "Nuff said."

Brook was a tomboy in grade school. She beat up so many boys I thought she would be the first female George Foreman. In junior high, she realized boys weren't as bad as she thought. By high school the tomboy had vanished.

My little sister graduated from Rutgers. It made Mom happy one of her kids went to a school close to home. Her degree was in Psychology. As it turned out, solving people's emotional problems was not for her

Brook wanted a job that made people happy so she went to culinary school and became a pastry chef. She hosted a cooking show on a major TV network in New York City. I was afraid to tell her no one wanted to watch other people cook, especially on the tube.

Mom. I was most proud of her. I'd often wondered how she managed to keep the family together and get an education on top of that. She went to night school, graduating with honors in accounting, and passed the CPA exam. She also had a head for business. She'd bought a rent house and planned to purchase more.

Her next project? Owning her own accounting firm.

CHAPTER 59

I ARRIVED EARLY AT THE BANQUET HALL. THE D. J. WAS SET-ting up his equipment for the reunion dance. I picked up a souvenir booklet and went to the back of the room to familiarize myself with my classmates. The homecoming committee did a nice job detailing everyone's life up to this point. The pages brought back old memories.

Just after I sat down, Delmar Boldin showed up. He and I were the only ones from our class to receive Division I college football scholarships. I motioned to him. "Delmar, back here."

He hadn't changed much since high school, less hair, but still a massive chunk of muscle. The last time we talked was two years ago. He'd just had his second neck operation. The first surgery ended his college foot-ball career. What a shame, he'd been a pro prospect, for sure.

The big lineman placed a friendly hand on my shoul-der. "Hey. How's the leg?"

"Fine. I get a little tired when I push myself too much, but other than that I'm as good as ever."

Boldin adjusted his chair and looked at me. "The wife of one of the coaches at Syracuse was in an auto accident and had a similar injury. He said her rehab was brutal."

I nodded. "Pure torture. You work for days and see no positive results, frustrating as heck knowing you may never improve." Talking about my ordeal stirred up bad vibes. I changed the subject. "Delmar, you've been at Syracuse a long time."

"Yeah, this will be my eleventh year as academic advisor for athletes. Hard to believe. Time does fly."

The conversation stalled as we both flipped through the reunion book. I stopped at the page with Ken Hunter's picture. He was the guy in my English class who always teased me about my poor spelling skills.

I tapped Delmar on the elbow with the back of my hand. "Did you know Hunter married his high school sweetheart Glenda Barbee?"

He nodded. "Yeah, I heard that."

I stretched out my legs and slumped in the chair. "You know he's a doctor, don't you?"

"Uh-huh. Smart guy, good looking. He had a lot going for him."

I cupped my hand over my chin and began to chuckle. "Just after he received his medical degree he moved to Austin, Texas. One night Ken called me. He was so ticked off he could barely talk. He'd bought a new Corvette. He parked behind his office in the most protected spot so no one could touch his prized sports car. Smart decision until an elderly patient ran into an aluminum light pole which fell on top of his car, crushing the top, knocking out the windshield, and smashing the steering wheel."

Boldin's head snapped toward me, giving me a disbelieving look. "You're kidding, right."

"Nope. You can't make up that stuff."

"Pepperman, come on. I know you're joking."

I turned in my chair. "I swear. It's true. Didn't make up one word."

Delmar slapped the table and belly laughed so hard his body shook.

After gaining control, Boldin saw a picture of Ray Robinsky in the directory. "Hey, it says Robinsky is a partner in a large investment firm. That doesn't surprise me. He was dang near a genius." Delmar's eyes lit up as he tapped me on the arm. "Do you remember the night he was kicked out of the basketball game?"

I grinned. "You know why, don't you?"

"Yeah, the ref said he traveled with the ball. Ray went bonkers and slammed the basketball down. It hit his foot and ricocheted right into the official's groin. I bet his business partners don't know about that little incident. Oh, oh, oh . . . look who just walked in, my old girlfriend, Deanna Flonders. I like you buddy, but we're done."

The way he light-stepped across the floor was impressive. A man on a mission.

I continued to leaf through the book. The picture of Louise Hillin reminded me of the episode with Jeff Langdon and the class favorite photo shoot at the Four Seasons Bowling Alley. Before the picture Louise made sure Jeff's shirt was perfect. When the yearbook came out, a spot the size of a quarter stood out like a red light on a bumper car. How in the blazes did the dirt monger Jeff manage to stain his shirt between the time Louise checked him and the time the photo was snapped?

Miss Hillin was not impressed. She was prim and proper. Jeff, a yokel. The old saying "opposites attract" conjured all sorts of images. What if Louise and Jeff had hooked up? No, would never happen. Louise married Mr. Chester's son Leo, who attended the Naval Academy. A much better match.

My light-hearted emotions changed when I saw Laura's picture. Still a good-looking woman. The bio read that she was married and had triplet boys. I closed the book and looked up.

Laura was standing at the registration table. My pulse accelerated.

She spotted me and walked toward the back of the room. I stood to greet her, and she gave me a gentle hug. We sat and I leaned in to whisper, "Do you remember the night you called to tell me you were getting married?"

"Of course."

Her tone questioned how I could even ask.

"Do you remember what you asked me?"

She raised her eyes. "Jim, women don't forget those things." Then she smiled, a smile that melted the buttons on my shirt.

"Well, tell me what you asked."

Laura angled her head and continued that magic warmness. "I said, 'Jim, I'm getting married and will you come to the wedding?' And . . . you said yes."

"What happened next?"

"I said, 'Jim, I'll break my engagement to Neal if you'll marry me.' Do you remember what you said?"

My lips were tight as I shook my head. "Don't have a clue."

She reached up with both hands and pinched my cheeks. "You're so funny. Oh, I called your mom, and our boys are fine."

"I hope they're acting better than the last time we left them with her."

I didn't know how I managed to land this beautiful woman.

Laura scanned the room. "I'm so excited. I saw Carolyn Peachly and Johnnie Morgano in the restroom."

Laura took my arm and turned me toward the door. "Is that Philip Johnstone? Quick, look in the book and tell me about him."

"He's married and living in Kansas. Says he's an agronomist, whatever that is."

"Oh, my gosh . . . there's Martha Kilpatrick and her husband Steve. Look, it's Carol Cockrell and Sandra Boscoe. I haven't seen them since we graduated." Laura ran screaming to see her old classmates.

I watched as she joined her friends.

Laura was such a people person. Just one of the reasons I was attracted to her. My mind flashed back to our wedding plans. We were to get married on February 14, 1980, but the Phillips explosion happened just weeks before the wedding. That changed everything. She wanted to get married while I was in the hospital, but not me. Physically and emotionally I was a mess. There were times I wanted to give up, but Laura never wavered in her resolve to help me recover.

About ten months into my recovery Laura said, "Jim, I broke off my engagement months ago. Do you think it was easy to tell Neal that I was going to marry you? He was angry with me, but furious at you. I'm ready to get married. I don't care if you use a cane to walk me out of the church. We've waited long enough."

A few weeks later, on Valentine's Day in 1981, we were married in Belleville. I'll always remember the cold, snowy Sunday afternoon when she became my wife.

There were so many things that reminded me of Laura. The first time I saw her at the diner a Frankie Valli song was playing. As fate would have it, tonight the first record at the reunion was "Walk Like a Man."

I joined my wife, took her by the hand, and led her to the dance floor. A special evening with a special lady.

Turn the page for a special excerpt from Book One of The Pepperman Mystery Series.

PERPLEXITY

SPECIAL EXCERPT FROM BOOK ONE OF THE PEPPERMAN MYSTERY SERIES

PERPLEXITY

BOOK ONE-THE PEPPERMAN MYSTERY SERIES

CHAPTER 1

JIM

CEMETERIES HAUNTED MY SOUL. ESPECIALLY THIS ONE.

I parked my rental, a brand new 1987 Lincoln, on a patch of gravel under a low-hanging red oak and tapped a nervous finger on the steering wheel. A steel band wrapped my chest, smothering me. Suffocating me.

I walked a thin line of love and hate with Holy Cross Cemetery outside Belleville. I loved this small corner of New Jersey. For the last twenty years this well-manicured mound of grass had been the only place I felt connected to Dad. I hated it for the same reason.

But I needed to talk to him. Had to tell someone. Had to tell him.

I closed my eyes, wishing we were at the old house working on my pickup under a shade tree. That's when we'd had our best conversations. Wisdom was his strength. When I was seven and having problems with a street bully named Gerald, he told me to learn to get along or stand up for myself, leaving me to solve my own problems. But I was a long way from seven.

I latched onto the steering wheel so hard my hands quivered. What would he tell me now? Would the proud way he'd always looked at me change once he knew what I'd done?

Shaking off the heavy memories, I reached for the door handle and paused, my fingers trembling over exposing my dark secret. I slowly lifted the handle. The door cracked open and air rushed over my face, providing a brief calmness. I pushed against the door and stepped out, each stride toward Dad's marker cumbersome.

My heavy feet kicked up bits of dirt and grass. Invisible hands squeezed my heart.

I touched the top of the tombstone. "Dad, I miss your leadership and guidance, but most of all I miss you."

A few months after I'd turned seventeen, he'd fallen from an oil rig in Odessa, Texas. Overnight I went from all-state linebacker for my high school team to a stand-in father for my two younger sisters. Working toward the playoffs was overshadowed by working to help support my family.

Because my parents were raised in New Jersey, Mom wanted Dad buried there. She pulled me aside after his graveside service and told me we were moving to Belleville to be closer to her family.

I'd been stunned. All I could think about was my senior year. Not only had I lost my dad, my best friend, and my security, but moving would almost surely ruin any chance of getting a football scholarship to the University of Texas. And I needed a scholarship if I wanted to go to college.

A blast of cold air brought me back to the cemetery. A chill crept over my neck and vanished. A chill in the middle of July? Maybe it was an omen not to share my secret with Dad. What if he could hear me? What if somewhere, somehow he'd kept up with my life and all the things I shared here?

"Hey, Dad." I knelt close to the granite stone and ran my fingers over the etched letters. *Patrick Pepperman.* "Laura and the triplets are at Mom's. I wish you could see those little guys. You'd be so proud, and I'm sure they'd love their granddad. You could spoil them with ice cream just as you did me. We'll be heading home to Oklahoma tomorrow. My high school reunion was yesterday. Hard to believe it's been twenty years for the Class of 1967. I didn't recognize half the people. I'm sure they said the same thing about me."

I was putting off the real reason I was here. But, first, I needed to let him know I'd kept my promise.

A cloud slid in front of the sun, providing a temporary shade. I took a deep breath. Kept going. "Blythe and Brook came in for the weekend. You'd love being around your daughters. They're outstanding, vibrant people. Just as I promised you, I paid for their college and looked after Mom. She's steady as a rock, always putting others before herself. Still the same lady you married. And guess what? She's also a CPA. Worked hard to make that happen."

I twisted my wedding ring, glad Laura hadn't come. Things were strained between us lately, and the words I needed to say to Dad were hard enough to say in private. "Laura says I mumble in my sleep. Sometimes I wake up in the middle of the night because of nightmares. She knows something's wrong. The hurt look on her face begs for answers, but I won't tell her. I can't tell her. She'd never look at me the same again."

I stared at his marker, hesitant to go on. "I don't even know if I can tell you. But I have to tell somebody." My past hung over me like a heavy shadow.

"No one knows what I'm about to tell you. I've buried it too deep." I closed my eyes and let out a deep breath. "A couple of weeks ago I went to a stag party for a co-worker. Hadn't been to a bar in years." I opened my eyes and stared at the letters that made up Dad's name. "My friend is a biker on weekends, and the type of bar he chose, well, let's just say, not a place to take your wife. It was about midnight when a big bruiser poured a drink on a little guy's head. Déjà vu. Instant recall of a similar night in Minnesota.

It seemed as if the lining of my stomach was being peeled away like an onion. "Something happened years ago. I blocked it out for so long, but now it's back. Most nights I wake up shaking in a puddle of sweat."

I struggled to keep my gut from ripping apart. Perspiration soaked my collar. "It happened after a game when I played for the Pittsburgh Steelers. We lost to the Vikings on their home turf. Our charter plane had engine trouble, and the team had to spend the night."

Once the story started to inch out of my subconscious, the need to release my secret pushed me to finish. "After dinner, I left the team and went to a bar three or four blocks from the hotel. And drank too much, too fast." I'd never done that before. It was stupid. Irresponsible.

"A loud-mouth jerk pestered a little guy at the end of the bar. Even spat into the man's drink." It reminded me of being tormented by that older boy when I was seven. "I told the guy to back off. Someone called him Weasel.

Appropriate, right? When he didn't back off, I slammed him against the wall, then the bartender got involved."

A single crow flew over Dad's headstone, screeching a hideous caw, bristling the hairs on my neck. Another cold blast of wind. An eerie stillness tingled across my skin.

I swallowed and licked my dry lips. "Weasel followed me out of the bar that night. Dad, he grabbed me from behind. And I lost it. I pulled him into the alley and beat him into a bloody mess. Wanted to stop." My voice cracked. "But I couldn't. I pounded and pounded until his nose exploded and blood gurgled from his lips. When he went slack on the wet asphalt, I ran."

My heart beat so hard I could hear it pounding in my ears. "The next morning the local news announced an unnamed man was found dead in an alley." I twisted away from Dad's tombstone. "I think it was him. I think I killed a man." Anguish mixed with relief flooded my chest.

A flock of black birds scattered from a grove of trees, squawking as though someone had forced their flight. A man dressed in jeans and a white t-shirt stood at the edge of the woods, legs spread, arms crossed.

My pulse quickened. I stood and our eyes locked.

He pointed at me, then turned and disappeared into the trees.

My gut screamed that something was wrong. Something pushed me, then a powerful shove as if someone had come up behind me. But there was no one. Just the urgency to move. Run. Get out of there.

I sprinted to the car. My fingers shook and the key missed the lock and dropped to the ground. I bent and grabbed it off the gravel road just as a bullet shattered the driver's side window, missing my shoulder by a few centimeters.

My heart sputtered, then beat faster and faster. What do I do? Where do I go?

"Son, the keys . . . move now," a voice whispered. Dad's voice. "Move to the other side of the car."

ABOUT THE AUTHOR

After Bill retired he told his wife he'd had an idea for years and wanted to turn it into a novel. He thought this would be a great story to share with the world. The result of that is *Pepperman's Promise*, the prequel to The Pepperman Mystery Series.

Read more about Bill at www.billbriscoe.com

CONNECT WITH ME ONLINE

www.billbriscoe.com
billbriscoe@billbriscoe.com
www.facebook.com/billdbriscoe

If you enjoyed *Pepperman's Promise*, I would appreciate it if you would help others enjoy it too. You can recommend it or review it. Reviews can be done at the retailer of your choice.

THE BILL BRISCOE NEWSLETTER

Sign up for my newsletter to receive up-to-date information of books, new releases, and events.

www.billbriscoe.com

ACKNOWLEDGEMENTS

I would like to thank the following people who helped bring this book to reality:

Editor: Lori Freeland

Cover and Video Artist: Fiona Jayde, Fiona Jayde Media

Formatting: Tamara Cribley, The Deliberate Page

Website and Computer Support: Michael Gaines

Critiques: Paula Taylor, Carolyn Rhea

Medical Expertise: Gloria Casale, M. D.

Oil Field Advisor: R. C. Bechtel

Proofreading Team: Barbara Lackey, Brenda Brownlee, Mike Pomper, Ora Mae Brownlee, Jeff Stenberg